STACY M. JONES

The Night Game

First edition

ISBN: 978-0-578-98681-4

This book was professionally typeset on Reedsy.
Find out more at reedsy.com

For Mandy

Acknowledgement

Special thanks to my family and friends who are always a source of support and encouragement. Thank you to my early readers whose feedback was invaluable. Special thanks to 17 Studio Book Design for bringing my stories to life with amazing covers. Thank you to Dj Hendrickson for your insightful editing and Liza Wood for proofreading and revisions.

CHAPTER 1

I woke and breathed in the quiet, knowing it wouldn't last long. It never did. I didn't want to speak my happiness aloud or even think about it for fear I might jinx it. I was officially a married woman. We'd arrived home from our honeymoon the night before and crashed.

My husband, Detective Lucas "Luke" Morgan, slept next to me with an arm thrown over my middle. I had slept soundly on my back. I'd always slept that way – like the dead, Luke called it. Over the last couple of years, I'd grown accustomed to Luke's arm around me or his hand resting on the top of my thigh.

We had no plans for the day except taking an easy Sunday and easing back into our lives. We had a good deal of unpacking to do but even that could wait if we wanted. We had married in Lake Placid, New York, north of my hometown of Troy. I had gone up before the wedding to spend time with my mother and sister and then Luke and our friends and his family had joined us.

I'd like to say that the time around our wedding went smoothly, but that wasn't the case. A missing girl from an all-girls school had taken my attention from wedding planning and then my father's reappearance into my life the day after my wedding threw us into chaos. The only saving grace was the day of our wedding had gone as planned. When we finally made it to the honeymoon Luke had

1

planned in Italy – it couldn't have gone better.

For a month, Luke and I did nothing but travel from town to town throughout the country and explore. We visited tourist hotspots but also found out-of-the-way hidden gems. We ate, drank, and made love with the leisure of two people without a care in the world. The only way that was accomplished was a solemn vow to each other that even if we found a dead body, we were backing out slowly and pretending we'd never seen it. We both kept our phones off the majority of the time and everyone that loved us left us alone, knowing how much we both needed a work break and time together.

Now we were back and I didn't want to resume life as normal.

"What time is it?" Luke stirred beside me and traced his fingers across my belly.

"It's too early to be awake. If we were in Italy right now all we'd be thinking about is breakfast and where we could get the best coffee." I rolled over and faced him, leaving a trail of kisses down his face.

Luke opened one eye. "Did you hear the sirens this morning?"

I gently put my hand over his open eye. "We are not back to work yet."

He playfully pushed my hand away. "I woke up when I heard them."

We weren't going to stop talking about this. I rolled onto my back and stared up at the ceiling. "I heard them, but I tried not to pay any attention. Your phone didn't ring so it couldn't be that important."

Luke's breathing was even but he didn't say a word. I grabbed for his hand and he interlaced his fingers with mine. I knew Luke well enough to know the energy shift in the room. He was holding back, which meant his partner, Det. Bill Tyler, had reached out to him from the Little Rock Police Department, where Luke was the lead detective in the violent crimes division.

"What did they say happened?" I asked with a sigh.

Luke didn't respond with words. He let go of my hand and pushed himself to an upright position against the headboard. The covers pooled around his naked waist. He eyed me until I sat up with him. This was the moment vacation officially ended and we were back to our normal lives. I turned my head to look at the clock to see the exact time of death – 8:21 a.m.

I pulled the sheet up to cover my naked chest and tucked it under my arms to hold it in place.

"Tell me all about it."

Luke knew how much it took for me to say those words. He pulled his phone from the bedside table and reread a text. "A woman was murdered inside a clothing boutique on Kavanaugh. When Det. Tyler texted, he said they had positive identification on the victim from the person who discovered her but were waiting for official word."

"How was she killed?"

"Blunt force trauma to the back of the head. She was struck several times with an unidentified object. There's been a series of burglaries and they think this one went bad." Luke put his hand on my arm. "Do you know any of the shop owners?"

"Not from any of the women's boutiques," I said absently. I tried to recall all the shops on Kavanaugh, which ran right through our Heights neighborhood. One of the things I liked most about where I lived was a row of shops and eateries built right into the neighborhood. It was all within walking distance and family-friendly. I couldn't walk the few blocks from my street to Kavanaugh without saying hello to at least a handful of neighbors. I didn't know all the women's boutiques because I rarely went into them. Being the higher end of size fourteen sized me out of most of those shops.

Luke got out of bed and grabbed a towel that he had thrown over a chair the night before. "Tyler said in addition to the murder most of the shops have been broken into. All the burglaries have happened in the evening soon after the shops close and no one has been hurt so

3

far."

"What's been stolen?" I watched as Luke moved around the room, pulling clothes from drawers and the closet. I knew without him telling me that he was heading to the crime scene.

Luke scrunched up his face the way he did when something didn't make sense. "That's the weird thing – nothing of any real value. A whole container of gummy worms was missing at the candy shop. There was a six-pack of beer stolen at the pizza shop. Most of the shops didn't have anything taken but things were moved around."

"It sounds like kids to me."

"You'd think that, but all the surveillance video was cut during the break-ins and now there's been a murder. That doesn't sound like kids to me." Luke threw a pair of jeans over his shoulder and headed for a shower.

I snuggled back down under the covers not ready to leave my bed. Luke was already in detective mode and nothing was going to snap him out of it. We wouldn't get our last day of peace, but I married a homicide detective. What did I expect?

I closed my eyes just as my cellphone chimed once, alerting me I had a text and then it chimed again telling me another had come through. I slapped at the nightstand until I palmed my phone and brought it into my line of sight. It was from Emma, my next-door neighbor and best friend. She had heard about the murder of Holly Bell. I guess it was official now. Emma said the whole neighborhood was buzzing with gossip. She wanted to meet for coffee and catch up with everything we had missed while we were gone.

I texted her back that I'd meet her at our favorite coffee shop in the Heights in forty-five minutes. I wasn't going anywhere without taming my wavy auburn hair. I dragged myself out of bed and wandered down the hall to the bathroom. I opened the bathroom door and was hit with a face full of steam. I crossed the bathroom and pulled open the

4

door to our walk-in shower.

"You missed me already," Luke teased and reached for my hand pulling me under the water with him. We redid the bathroom about a year ago. Our contractor removed the tub and added in a walk-in shower. It was a good size for the two of us, although this was a rare occasion. Normally, Luke was up and out of the house before I even opened my eyes.

I tipped my head back to let the hot water run over me. "Emma texted me. She said the victim is Holly Bell. Not sure how she knows that already though."

"You know gossip travels faster than the speed of light around here." Luke leaned in and put his finger under my chin to lift my lips to his. "How about we have a little fun before we start real life today?"

"That was all I wanted this morning."

Luke ran his hands over me. "You seemed a little grumpy. Let's change that."

Close to an hour later, I slow jogged my way to meet Emma at the coffee shop. I was late, which wasn't common for me. As soon as I pulled open the door and saw her sitting there, she laughed at my tardiness.

"Honeymoon phase," she said, smirking at me. She tucked her short dark hair behind her ears. "Enjoy it now. In a few years, you'll have kids and forget all about sex."

"Shush." I leaned over and pecked her on the cheek. She had two coffees sitting in front of her and slid mine over to me. "If there wasn't a murder this morning, Luke and I would still be in bed. I'm annoyed at a dead woman for ruining my day."

A woman with stiff white hair that looked like she had used an entire can of hairspray toyed with the cup in front of her. She spoke to her companion in a slow southern drawl as she chastised me with her eyes. My insensitivity wasn't appreciated.

"Holly Bell." I rolled the woman's name around in my mouth a few more times. "I can't say I know her. What shop did she own?"

"Bell & Bloom." Emma sipped her coffee. "I want to hear all about your honeymoon, but I want to know everything you know about the murder first."

"I don't know anything. Luke didn't even have the victim's name. Are you sure you got the right person?"

Emma pointed to the television in the corner of the shop. A local news reporter broadcasted live from two blocks away. "I got the information from the news. Let's hope they didn't broadcast before the police had a chance to tell her family."

That was one of the biggest challenges with death notifications. Information leaked so easily, especially with social media. I took a sip of coffee and let my eyes drift around the shop. I had figured more people would be there given the excitement down the street.

I turned my attention back to Emma. "Did you know Holly?"

"Not personally, but there was drama while you were gone." Emma slid her phone across the table and I lowered my head to look where she was pointing. She had the Bell & Bloom Facebook page pulled up. A post with angry emojis was front and center.

Before I could read it, Emma said, "I bet my monthly salary that it was a big girl who killed her."

"Big girl?" I asked with raised eyebrows. I knew that was Emma's nice way of saying overweight women. I much preferred 'fat' to any euphemism one could hurl at me, but given she was a size six on her worst day, she was more sensitive.

Emma nodded vigorously. "She was known to fat shame anyone who walked into her shop and then she posted negatively about other stores carrying plus-sized clothing. There was even a protest two weeks ago. If people didn't know her name before, they surely know her now."

CHAPTER 2

L uke felt himself smiling as he walked up to the crime scene. He had to force his thoughts away from Riley and the last few weeks they had spent together to get himself into the right frame of mind for work. Luke was sure if Riley had asked him to quit his job and move to Italy with her, he would have said yes. It was harder to be back than he had told her this morning. As much as he wanted to stay at home in bed with Riley, Captain Meadows and Det. Bill Tyler wanted his expertise on the case. He didn't feel like he had much choice but to come to the scene.

Luke flashed his badge to the young cop standing at the edge of the barricade and was given entry. The barricade had been set up so it cut off access to the row of shops on that block. Traffic had also been diverted down the side street. The crime scene techs were still doing their job and several Little Rock uniformed cops were standing around in the middle of the blocked-off road.

Because of the murder and heavy police presence, Luke assumed the streets would have been crowded with people milling around, but other than a few news crews, they were empty. Most of the shops on the street didn't open until later on Sunday mornings, if at all. The shops were along his normal jogging route, and it was normally quiet at this time of the morning.

Luke headed for the shop door, which had been propped open. He grabbed the booties for his shoes and snapped on gloves and then entered the shop. Det. Tyler stood near the register but Captain Meadows wasn't anywhere in sight. Luke looked around the clothing racks hoping to see the marked-off area where the body had been found but nothing so far.

He walked over to the counter and nudged Tyler. "You dragged me out of bed on a Sunday morning. You better make it worth my while."

"Look at you, married man. How was the honeymoon?" Tyler stepped back and appraised Luke, pointing to his middle. "Looks like you gained a few pounds."

Luke rubbed a hand down his flat belly. "Don't start with me, old man. You've got at least thirty pounds on me."

Tyler laughed. "It happens to the best of us. You get loved up right and the weight creeps on."

Luke made a mental note that he needed to get back to weightlifting and jogging off all the food he had consumed in Italy. "What are we looking at here?"

Tyler motioned for Luke to follow him through racks of brightly colored dresses and blouses to a doorway that separated the shop from the back work area. "Holly Bell, the victim, was the owner of the shop. She was found on the floor face down and had been struck from behind. The young woman who found Holly's body assumed she had been walking to the back office or stock room when it happened. The medical examiner said that there were several blows to the back of the head, but he'd know more later."

Luke looked around the area, which had been heavily marked with yellow tags indicating blood spatter. He didn't need the tags though. The blood marked the floor, walls, and clothing nearby. "I assume the attack took place right where she fell."

Tyler nodded once. "It looks like someone came up behind the victim and hit her. Then once she was on the ground, hit her several more times. That's the working theory at least."

Luke bent down in a low squat to assess the area. A large pool of blood marked where the victim's head had been. He followed the trail of blood with his eyes. "Either it was someone she trusted enough to turn her back on or she never saw it coming. Any idea about a murder weapon?"

"Nothing around here that we found. Of course, we won't have any idea about the weapon used and the marks it made on her skull until the autopsy is complete. Purvis wouldn't venture a guess while he was here."

Ed Purvis had been the Pulaski County Medical Examiner for as long as Luke had worked for the police. If there was evidence to be found, he'd find it. Luke stood and turned toward the shop door. "I know there was some mention that this might have been a burglary gone wrong, but the position of her body doesn't indicate that to me."

"I thought the same. It was the first cop on the scene who mentioned burglary. I texted that to you before I got in here and looked around."

"What about surveillance video?" Luke asked, angling his head around looking for cameras.

"It wasn't on." Tyler hitched his head to the side for Luke to follow.

They stepped around the blood spatter spots where the body had been found and went into the back. There were two large rooms directly across from each other in the back of the shop. The doorways faced each other and both were open. One room was used for extra stock. There were boxes of clothing and racks where they were hung and pressed. The other room looked like an office.

Tyler pointed to the office. "The surveillance system is set up in there. She has an app on her laptop that controls the surveillance system. You can see past videos on there, too. Looks like they are backed up for thirty days. Looks to me like it was shut off a few days ago and hasn't been turned on since."

That didn't make much sense to Luke. Clothing boutiques like Bell & Bloom were notorious for having high rates of shoplifting. Luke walked over to the computer and clicked the pad on the laptop to move the mouse. Tyler had the surveillance video app open. He navigated through a few sections and confirmed what Tyler had told him.

Luke raised his head. "We have any reason why surveillance has been shut off?"

"None. We haven't had a chance to speak with anyone yet other than the young woman who found Holly's body. She said she was coming in to help Holly with a few things and found her. I didn't question her about much else at the time. She didn't have blood on her and no weapons. She made the 911 call. The medical examiner only removed Holly's body about an hour ago. Captain Meadows is making the death notification to Holly's husband right now."

In all the time he'd worked for the Little Rock PD, he'd never known Captain Meadows to make a death notification. The man normally remained hands-off and let the detectives do their job. "Is this high profile?"

Tyler nodded slowly. "Holly Bell is the wife of Prophet Chance Bell or whatever he calls himself these days."

Luke cocked his head to the side. That was a name he hadn't heard in a long time and had hoped to never hear again. He rocked back on the balls of his feet. "When did the good prophet get out of prison?"

"About six months ago for good behavior."

Prophet Chance Bell had run a compound on the outskirts of Little Rock. No one could ever quite figure out Chance's religious bent or even if it was religious at all. He made predictions that never seemed to come true and he had far too many young women and girls around for what he was doing to be on the up and up.

His followers were often seen protesting at random places around the city or offering peace and love hippie style on sidewalks and street corners. His whole schtick was shrouded in mystery and none of it made a lot of sense, except that Chance was angry with the world. It all came crashing down when Chance's right-hand man had been rushed to the emergency room for a snake bite from something that they were doing out in the woods. No one outside the compound ever got a satisfactory answer what they were doing, but the mystery of it all was enough that it set the gossip mill buzzing. While Chance and the guy were in the hospital, a nurse overheard a conversation about a shipment of guns coming into the compound. Another conversation mentioned a good deal of LSD. Guns, drugs, snakes, and young girls – a deadly combination. The last thing the Little Rock police wanted was another Waco or worse still another Charles Manson.

Luke and a team, including DEA agents, served a warrant to Prophet Chance Bell and found enough evidence to charge him and bring him in. They also found more snakes than Luke cared to remember. He shivered now just thinking about it.

When Luke had interviewed Chance back at the police station, the man refused to speak to him. He said very little to Luke and wouldn't even look him in the eyes. They brought in other detectives to have a crack at him, but Chance asked for an attorney. No one could speak to him after that. They had more than enough evidence to make their case though.

Chance's influence had been so insidious that his followers needed serious psychological care after his conviction. There were stories of physical and sexual abuse that came out after the man's arrest and incarceration. Chance had been given a five-to-ten-year sentence, and if Luke's math was correct, he had served about seven years. Holly Bell had not been the man's wife at the time.

Luke shook his head trying to shake the memory of Prophet Chance Bell free from his mind. He locked eyes with Tyler. "When did he marry Holly?"

"About three years ago. She was a prison bride." Tyler gave a half-hearted shrug.

Luke never understood women who married men in prison or took up with men who had been convicted of serious crimes, especially Chance. It wasn't just the guns and the drugs. While Chance had never been charged or convicted of the physical and sexual abuse, the allegations had made the news.

At the time of his arrest, his followers denied anything like that was happening. It was only later, after many received counseling, that a few had given interviews for the local news station and newspaper but none had been willing to make a police report. Without a victim willing to come forward, there wasn't much that could be done.

Luke leaned back and folded his arms over his chest. "Let me guess. This is why Captain Meadows wanted you to call me in?"

The corners of Tyler's mouth turned up in a smirk. "As I said, it's not a simple burglary."

Luke chuckled. "No, just one of the most annoying cases of my career coming back to haunt me. I'm not dealing with any snakes this time."

Tyler threw his hands up and grinned. "Where do you want to start?"

Luke moved past him out of the office and back toward the main part of the shop. "The only place to start – who is Holly Bell and why did someone want her dead?"

CHAPTER 3

Cooper Deagnan tried to catch his breath on his back in his bed. He was certain his fiancée was trying to kill him. After having sex twice, instead of curling lovingly into his side and taking a nap, which was all he wanted to do, Adele had shot out of bed claiming she was famished and the only cure was French toast. Even though he was exhausted from more cardio than he'd managed on a gym floor in a long while, Cooper couldn't be happier. He had proposed to Adele in New York right after Luke and Riley's wedding and had come back to Little Rock ready to start a new life with the woman he loved.

Adele's criminal law practice had been growing by leaps and bounds and his private investigation firm wasn't doing too badly either. They had spent the time and money to make some improvements to Cooper's downtown loft to make it less a bachelor pad and more a love nest for the pair of them.

Cooper's eyes drifted closed and he relaxed into his bed, pulling the soft cotton sheet up to his waist. "Save me some French toast," he called, even though he had no intention of moving anytime soon.

"I didn't even start it yet. The news is covering a murder that happened this morning in the Heights." Adele's voice drifted from the kitchen down the hall to the bedroom and finally roused Cooper from his bed.

He sat up and rubbed the sleep from his eyes. "Who was murdered?" A murder in the Heights wasn't common so it was news no matter who had been killed.

"Her name is Holly Bell. She's the owner of a boutique shop in the Heights."

The name didn't mean anything to Cooper. He got out of bed, pulled pajama bottoms from the floor, and pulled them up, snapping the elastic waistband against his taut belly. His stomach grumbled.

"I'll make that French toast if you can't be bothered to feed your man," he teased as he left the bedroom and walked the short hallway to the kitchen.

The bread, eggs, and cinnamon were arranged on the counter ready to go. Adele sat on the couch in the living room with her eyes glued to the television. Cooper didn't think she'd be making them breakfast anytime soon, so he got down to work.

The small kitchen island bridged the living room and the kitchen. He pulled the ingredients over to the island so he could watch television as he worked. "What happened?"

Adele spoke over her shoulder. "Holly Bell was murdered in her shop this morning. It was blunt force trauma to the back of the head. Luke gave a brief statement to the media. There are no suspects at this time, but they are early in the investigation."

"I'm sure Riley's not happy he's back to work." Cooper turned the burner on and put the bread in the pan.

"Real life had to come soon enough." Adele pushed herself off the couch and made her way to the kitchen. She came up behind Cooper and wrapped her arms around him, resting her head against his back. "I'm tired now."

Cooper laughed as he flipped the bread. "You should have napped when I told you to."

Adele traced her finger down his back. "I was too hungry to nap

14

then. I figured we'd..." She never finished her thought because her cellphone rang from the bedroom. Adele left Cooper in search of her phone while he finished making breakfast.

Adele was still on the phone when Cooper arranged food on two plates on the center island. He poured them both orange juice and made himself coffee. Adele preferred tea and fixed it herself. Cooper never made it right. He sat down to breakfast as Adele finished her call.

When Cooper heard Adele end the call, he asked, "Who was that?"

"Dr. Henry Wright. His son, Isiah, has been arrested for the break-ins happening in the Heights."

"Who made the arrest?" Cooper asked, taking a sip of his coffee. He knew it wasn't Luke because he wasn't part of the burglary division. He only handled homicides.

"I don't know, but I'm going to need to eat this quickly and go meet Dr. Wright." Adele sat down on the stool next to Cooper and dug into her breakfast. In between bites, she said, "You should come with me. I might need an investigator on this case. Might as well hear the information firsthand so you won't have to interview him again."

"Is the son in jail right now?"

Adele nodded. "They won't be able to have a bail hearing until morning."

"I'll come if you think the dad won't mind me being there." Cooper gave her a sideways glance. Adele had been hiring him to work on some of her cases. So far, it had worked out well. Many of Cooper's clients were criminal defense and family law attorneys. It made sense they'd work together, but Cooper didn't know how well the professional would merge with the personal long term. At least, they were on the same side, which wasn't always the case for Riley and Luke.

Adele finished off the rest of her breakfast. "Like most fathers whose kids have been arrested, he tells me Isiah is innocent. He's willing to do anything possible to prove that."

An hour later, Adele and Cooper walked the four blocks from the loft to Adele's office in a brick four-story building in downtown Little Rock. Adele had made a comfortable office space for herself and her assistant on the second floor. Adele unlocked the door and flipped on the lights as she entered. It wasn't a large space but it was good enough to suit her purposes.

The main lobby had chairs, a comfortable couch, and a television. Adele's assistant had a small office off the lobby while Adele took the bigger office with a large window overlooking a city street. At the end of the hall was a small conference room and library that Adele filled with all the scholarly books on law and investigations that she needed to best serve her clients.

Cooper waited in the lobby while Adele went to her office to grab paperwork Dr. Wright said he had emailed to her. She came out of her office shaking the printed pages in her hand.

"Dr. Wright said that the cops are now trying to accuse Isiah of murdering Holly Bell. I'm going to need to get over to that jail and make my presence known."

"Did he tell his son not to make any statements?"

"Yeah, but you know how kids are." Adele looked down at the printed email. "Isiah is eighteen and a senior in high school so technically an adult." Adele didn't want to leave him there to meet Dr. Wright alone but she didn't have a choice.

Cooper stood with his hands in his pockets. "Just go to the jail now. It won't take you more than thirty minutes. I'll meet Dr. Wright when he gets here."

Adele turned to him. "Are you sure? I'll call and tell him what I'm doing and that I left my investigator here to meet with him."

Cooper waved her off. "It's fine. Better to make sure Isiah invokes his right to counsel before it gets more out of hand than it needs to be."

Adele handed him the emailed pages. "Read this while I'm gone. It should get you up to speed about Isiah. He goes by Izzy so if you see that name, it's the same person."

Adele rushed down the hall to her office and emerged a moment later with her purse. She waved goodbye to Cooper and headed out of the office. Cooper slumped down on the couch and started reading the father's email about his son.

Izzy was a senior at Central High School and was straight-A grade student. Cooper flipped through the secondary pages of Izzy's school transcripts. The kid had never even had a B before. He excelled in basketball and baseball and planned to attend either Stanford or MIT, wherever he got more scholarships. Izzy was the youngest of three children and his parents were still together. It looked from the records like they had recently moved to a home in the Heights on N. Filmore Street.

"I'm guessing you aren't Adele Baker," a man said from the doorway. "I'm Dr. Henry Wright."

Cooper raised his head and dropped the pages on the couch next to him. He stood and introduced himself to the tall, broad black man who took up most of the doorway. Cooper was no slouch himself at six-foot, but Dr. Wright was at least six-four.

"Adele will be back soon. She wanted to get over to the jail to make sure that they knew Isiah had counsel."

Dr. Wright nodded once. "My son has never been in trouble before. He's never even had a suspension at school. Now, he's being accused of burglary and they asked him about a murder. I don't understand."

Cooper walked over and shook the man's hand. "Adele should be right back and then we can discuss everything. I'm sure we can get this sorted out."

Together they walked back into the lobby and sat down. Dr. Wright sat in one of the chairs and stretched his long legs in front of him. He ran a hand over his bald head and down his graying stubbled face. "I've heard that Adele is fierce in the courtroom. That's what my son needs right now."

"Let's hope it doesn't get to that," Cooper said, picking up the papers he had been reading. "Adele gave me the email you sent. It's hard to believe that Isiah would break into shops."

"That's what I said when they came this morning and arrested him." Dr. Wright blew out a frustrated breath. "I don't even understand how it got this far. I didn't even know my son was a suspect. To tell you the truth, I had heard there were some local burglaries, but I didn't pay much attention to it. I'm an emergency room doctor at St. Vincent's Hospital and work keeps me fairly busy. Izzy is always at school or with his friends."

"I saw that Izzy attends Central High School. I would have assumed living in the Heights, he would have gone to Hall High School."

Dr. Wright smiled. "If it were up to me, he'd be in private school. We moved to the Heights a few months ago and Izzy didn't want to transfer. I don't think he's made that many friends in his new neighborhood. Most of his friends go to his high school. Izzy isn't home much because of how busy he is with sports and studies."

"What about your wife, Izzy's mom?"

"Allison travels for work and isn't home much. That's part of the issue with Izzy's alibi. My son is home by himself many evenings while I'm at the hospital." Dr. Wright looked down at the floor and shook his head. "There's no one to provide him an alibi even though he told me he was home."

Cooper knew in his line of work that parents were often the last to know what their kids were doing. Not that he had any reason to suspect Izzy but the police must have. Cooper inched forward on the couch and rested his arms on his knees. "Dr. Wright, there must be something that has raised the cops' suspicions about your son. Not having an alibi is one thing, but how did they connect him to the burglaries in the first place?"

With regret in his voice, Dr. Wright admitted, "I don't know, but I assume it's the crowd of boys he's gone to school with since grade school. A few of them have been up to no good, but I thought Izzy had stopped spending time with them."

Cooper wasn't sure he understood. "You think it was this group of friends that got Izzy involved with the burglaries? I thought you said you knew he was innocent?"

Dr. Wright rubbed his forehead. "I don't know what I'm saying anymore." He stayed quiet for a few moments seeming lost in thought. Then he locked eyes with Cooper. "I don't believe that my son could have committed these burglaries. If he's being tied to them, it's because of a group of friends he had from school."

"You've got part of that correct," Adele said breathlessly from the doorway.

CHAPTER 4

I cradled the coffee cup in my hand as I watched Emma's face light up. She loved good gossip, and, if there was anyone in the Heights who had it, it was Emma. As a mother to two young children – Sophie and Joe Jr. – Emma was part of the inner mommies' circle in the Heights. The kind of women I'd never be friends with, not for lack of trying, but rather, a lack of ever being accepted. They were the kind of women who wore Lululemon to mommies' brunches and pushed their designer strollers past my house looking at me with a mix of pity and concern. Emma fit in though – she was one of them.

I took a sip of my coffee and smiled over at her. "Tell me what you know."

Emma's voice was no louder than a whisper. "A few weeks ago, Holly wrote on her business Facebook page that she was angry that a women's athletic shop in West Little Rock now had fat mannequins. She said, and I quote, 'it's teaching the fatties that it's okay to wear cute exercise clothes and stay fat.'" Emma blushed even having to tell me that much.

"What am I supposed to wear when I exercise – a garbage bag?" I tried not to laugh because Emma's expression was as serious as it got. It was obvious how horrified she was by the comment and having to repeat it. It was a stupid comment to have been made, especially on a business Facebook page, but I wasn't sure how it was that big of a deal. People said stupid things on social media all the time.

Emma reached her hand over and rested it on my arm. "She got so much hate, she had to shut her Facebook page down and close the shop for several days. There was even a protest of bigger women in their exercise clothes marching up and down in front of her shop. They were lifting weights on the sidewalk and one woman even skipped rope."

I patted Emma's hand. "I'm not sure how this is relevant. Do you think one of the women protesting killed her?"

"You don't understand, Riley," Emma said her eyes getting round. "Everyone was up in arms about it. The whole city is outraged. It made the news. After Holly opened back up again, old men went into her shop just to yell at her. She only has a few supporters left."

"Your friends in the mommies' group?" I asked but already knew the answer.

Emma nodded. "They agreed with her, but of course, they are too polite to come out and say it publicly. One of the women told me that Holly got death threats and that a woman in the neighborhood stops in the doorway of her shop and flips her off – every morning!"

I covered my mouth with my hand, but the laughter came out anyway. Emma swatted at me and scolded me. "I'm sorry," I said, trying to get control of myself. "I'm not laughing because she was murdered. I'm laughing because the whole thing sounds so ridiculous. I know people get sensitive about fat-shaming and it's cruel, but the response seems a bit over the top for one terrible and stupid comment on social media."

"No, Riley, you don't understand." Emma looked around to see if there was anyone paying attention to us and then she leaned into the table, pulling my arm so I'd lean in too. Once her mouth was close to my ear, she said, "It was more than that. Several women have come forward to say that Holly told them they were too fat to come to her shop. A few other women posted how Holly had made them feel bad while trying on clothes in her store. A few women even left crying. She would get out the tape measure once a week and force her employees to share their measurements. One girl was told she needed to go on a diet, and she was barely a size six. Holly was a bully and downright awful to people, and I think she paid for it with her life."

That was indeed more serious. "Do you have a suspect in mind?"

"Jordan Collins," she said with a knowing look.

"Is that name supposed to mean something to me?"

Emma sighed, clearly frustrated by my lack of knowledge. "You don't keep up with anything, do you? Jordan Collins is a fat activist blogger and podcaster. She came out of the body positivity movement. I figured you'd know about her."

"Because I'm a chunky monkey?" I smiled and watched Emma's face fall. *A fat activist.* I didn't realize there was such a thing. "I don't know who she is. You know me, I don't read women's magazines or follow fashion or women's issues..." My voice trailed off. The truth was I didn't follow much of anything outside of work. My life was filled with murder.

"You're hopeless." Emma sat back and apprised me. "What do you think? Do you think someone like Jordan could have killed Holly?"

"I don't know anything about her."

Emma clicked the screen on her phone a few times then handed it to me. "Read this. It should tell you everything you need to know."

I tipped my head down to read the article from a well-known women's magazine. Jordan Collins was apparently as famous as Emma had said. Not only did she write a scathing article about Holly, but some could have taken it as a threat. *But would the woman make a real threat so publicly?*

Jordan had been a plus-sized model for several years and was now working as an influencer – a category of celebrity I thought silly and overblown. The article accused Holly of being misogynistic and a bully. In the end, Jordan said that women, and society as a whole, would be better off without women like Holly. She didn't detail how she'd rid the world of her though.

I handed the phone back to Emma. "It says that Jordan lives in New York City."

"Lives, right. Not vacations," Emma said clicking her tongue. She snagged her phone back from the table, pushed her finger around the screen some more, and then showed me a close-up photo of Jordan dated last night. The woman smiled into the camera with her face completely made-up, her blond hair perfectly blown out, and a hand perched on an ample hip. I had no idea how she walked in the bright red heels she was wearing.

I looked from the photo back up to Emma. "What am I looking at here?"

Emma jabbed her finger into the phone. "Look at the restaurant she's standing in front of!"

I glanced down at the photo again and focused on the surroundings. Through the window behind her, the lights were turned low and couples sat at wooden farm tables that had small white votives in candle holders. I'd know them anywhere. "Main Street Taproom. Jordan Collins was in Little Rock last night?"

"Exactly! What was she doing here?"

Emma had a point. It's not like Little Rock was a big tourist destination, and given the article, her appearance in the city right before Holly's death couldn't have been a coincidence. There couldn't be that many reasons for Jordan to be in the city.

Emma snapped her fingers to get my attention. "Do you think you should tell Luke?"

"I can mention it to him. I'm sure he'll know more once he's back from the scene." I said that but thought better of it. He didn't always

23

love when I nosed around in his cases, and I was sure Cooper had more than enough work to keep me busy. "I'll tell Luke gently. He's not always receptive when I get involved in his cases."

Emma eyed me. "I thought after the last few cases, he was over it. You've helped so much I don't see how he wouldn't be happy."

"You'd think that, but we haven't talked about it since we got back." I took another sip of my coffee. "We haven't even been back a full day yet. Let us ease into life again."

"A murder like this isn't going to simmer on the back burner, Riley," Emma said with a tone of annoyance. "Plus, if Jordan Collins is here now, I'm sure Luke will want to interview her. It's going to be much more difficult for him to do if she goes back to New York City."

That was true even though I wasn't sure Emma was on the right track. It was suspicious that Jordan was in Little Rock, but for all I knew, she was here writing a follow-up story. It's possible her editor wanted the local flavor. Emma seemed more geared up and interested in a murder case than she normally was. I found it a bit odd. I found Emma's whole demeanor a bit odd.

"How are you doing with two kids at home?" I asked her, changing the subject.

Emma shifted her eyes away from mine. "I'm fine. My mother takes the kids now and then. She has them right now."

"I can tell you're not fine so spill it. The whole time I've been listening to you something about you has seemed different and I couldn't quite place it."

"Yeah, what's that?" Emma asked noncommittally like she wasn't sure she wanted the answer.

"You're bored." I said the words I knew she wouldn't dare say herself. Emma never gets excited like she was right now. She never wants to figure out who the killer is. She loves a bit of gossip for sure, but when it comes to solving a homicide, she's the one who lectures me to stay

24

out of danger. Emma didn't respond to what I said.

I touched her arm. "Emma, it's me. You can admit to being bored at home with two small children. Before your babies, you had a career and a life outside the house. It's only natural that staying home now full-time is going to be a transition."

Emma sunk low in her chair. "I feel terrible admitting it, but you know I was planning to go back to work right before I found out I was pregnant with Joe Jr. He's a sweet baby, but I want to be able to work. I talked to Joe about hiring a nanny."

"What did he say?"

"You know Joe. He never says much. He wants me to be happy and said if we can swing it financially then that's all that matters. We can swing it. His construction company is booming." Emma looked away.

"Then what's the problem?" The words were barely out of my mouth when it occurred to me. "The mommy brigade? Let me guess, they'll look down on you if you choose to go back to work."

Emma's shoulders slumped. "Oh Riley, you have no idea. I brought up going back to work and their immediate reaction was to feel bad for me that we were going broke. I said I want to work and they asked me if I hated my kids."

"Do you honestly care what they think?"

Emma shrugged. "Besides you, I don't have many friends and most of them have kids Sophie's age so we will be seeing them all through her school years."

I rolled my eyes and sighed. I didn't understand allowing anyone to make me feel bad about anything – especially the women in our neighborhood. "If you want to go back to work, go. Happy moms make better moms."

"Let's find Holly's killer first and then I'll think about it," Emma said with too much excitement in her voice. She was going to get me in trouble on this case.

25

CHAPTER 5

C ooper stood as Adele walked into the lobby of her office. She had the look of excitement on her face that she wore when she was sure she could win a case, which boded well for Izzy Wright.

"What did you find?" Cooper asked.

Adele shook Dr. Wright's hand and formally introduced herself. "I'm so glad we were able to meet today. I needed to go to the jail. I told Izzy not to make any statements to the police and he assured me he wouldn't. He believes he knows how the burglaries were tied to him."

Adele sat down on the couch where Cooper had been sitting and he sat down next to her. Cooper and Dr. Wright had their eyes focused on Adele.

"Izzy had some friends—" Adele started to say.

"I knew it." Dr. Wright cursed. "I knew those stupid kids he went to high school with would get him on the wrong path."

"No, Dr. Wright. No, you don't understand." Adele spoke with an authority in her voice that made him sit up straighter in the chair and listen. "It wasn't kids Izzy went to school with. Izzy said it was boys from the new neighborhood. He saw them one night leaving one of the shops."

Dr. Wright furrowed his brow. "I don't understand why Izzy didn't tell the cops this when he was arrested." He stood up abruptly and gestured toward the door. "Who are they? Let's bring them to the cops."

Adele shook her head and waited for him to sit back down. "It's not that easy. It seems Izzy was with a young lady that night after curfew. They had met up in a parking lot in her car and...well, he was discreet and didn't tell me what they were doing but you can imagine. Anyway, it was as Izzy left her to walk home that he heard voices and he walked out to Kavanaugh from the parking lot and saw the boys leaving a shop. Izzy saw four boys and he thinks he can identify one of them."

Dr. Wright let the information digest for a moment and Adele gave him time. When he was ready, he said, "I still don't understand. Izzy is eighteen years old. I'm certainly not happy he was creeping around in a parking lot with a girl, but it's not the end of the world. At least, now he has an alibi. Who is this boy?"

Adele hedged and locked eyes with Cooper before turning back. "That's the thing. Izzy won't tell me who it is and he won't tell me why he won't tell me. He won't tell me the girl's name either."

Dr. Wright pounded his fist down on the arm of the chair. "Then we'll make him tell you!"

"It's never that easy," Cooper said, hoping to calm him down. "We'll get the truth out of him, but it could take some time."

"We don't have time," Dr. Wright said, regretfully. He blew out a frustrated breath. "What happens now?"

"There will be a bail hearing tomorrow morning and given the charges, he will be given bail. Then he'll be released and await trial." Adele hesitated and Cooper knew she had more to say. "We have one hiccup," she finally said.

"Just one?" Dr. Wright said sarcastically. "Sounds like we have several."

"Your son's watch was found at one of the crime scenes. It's the only burglary that they can tie him to. The cops assume that if he was at one, then he was at all of them. Many of the charges are weak."

Dr. Wright leaned forward. "That's how they caught him then. I gave my son that watch for his sixteenth birthday. His name was engraved on the back with a special message. He's never without it." He grew quiet and rubbed his hand down his face. "If the cops have the watch, then Izzy has been without it without me realizing. I'm starting to feel like I don't know my son."

Adele checked the paper she had in her hand. "It was found in the shop of the most recent burglary. Izzy can't remember when he lost the watch or if it was stolen. Initially, Izzy thought he put it in his locker before basketball practice like he normally does. But he can't remember what happened after that practice. Now, he's not sure if that's when he lost it. He's been trying to remember. The only thing he knows is the watch has been gone for about two weeks."

"Why didn't he tell me?"

"He assumed you'd be angry with him. Izzy has been hoping that it would turn up. He wondered if one of his friends was playing a prank on him knowing how much the watch meant to him. They all denied it and he believes them."

"He would," Dr. Wright said with his voice tight. "Izzy is an eternal optimist. He believes in the good in people. Even if he had thought someone had stolen it, he'd probably say that they needed it more than he did. He'd never falsely accuse anyone."

"Dr. Wright," Adele said softly. "I don't believe your son committed any crime. This is early in the investigation and there's time to uncover the truth. Once he's out on bail, we'll be able to find who committed the burglaries and your son will go free."

Dr. Wright had his mouth set in a firm line. "Where was my son's watch found?"

Adele hesitated to share that information. "You can't visit the shop or speak to the owner."

"I wouldn't do anything to jeopardize my son's chances in court. I'm merely curious."

Adele lowered her head to the police report and read off the name. "Hattie's Cauldron: Potions & Pastries."

"That strange psychic shop?" Dr. Wright asked, his distaste for the place apparent. "My son would never go in there. He's a man of science and reason."

"They have really good pastries," Adele said, offering a smile. "I've met the owner, Hattie Beauregard-Ryan. She lives in your neighborhood. She's a lovely woman and kind-hearted. It's possible we could convince her to drop the charges, but even at that, the police might insist."

"Whatever you can do. The detective that arrested Izzy said something about him being a suspect in the murder that just happened. Did they say anything about that?"

"Nothing. I think it was a threat to scare him," Adele explained, sitting back on the couch. "Holly Bell's shop is near Hattie's shop, so if they believe it was a burglary gone bad, then your son may be tied to it. That's why it's important he doesn't speak to the detective alone. They can twist what he says. There is no evidence linking him to the murder that I'm aware of right now."

"Does Izzy have an alibi for last night into this morning?" Cooper asked. He wasn't sure what time the murder had been committed.

"He had friends at the house last night until midnight and then I was home after my shift. I got in the door at seven-thirty this morning. Izzy was arrested shortly after. How long ago was that psychic woman's shop broken into?"

"Friday night. It took them a day to track down who owned the watch and then brought Izzy in." Adele paused for a moment and read

29

over Izzy's statement. "Were you there when they questioned him initially?"

Dr. Wright rubbed his eyes. "Izzy is legally an adult. They wouldn't let me be present while they questioned him. I didn't even get a chance to tell him to ask for a lawyer."

"He asked," Adele assured him. "They don't have much of a statement at all, except that he's never been in Hattie's shop and that his watch was stolen two weeks ago."

"That's hardly enough to make an arrest," Cooper said, not understanding the detective on the case at all. "Seems like a huge rush to judgment."

Adele nodded. "That's what I thought. We'll get it sorted, Dr. Wright. We have a good working relationship with law enforcement."

"I'll speak to your son," Cooper added. "My partner, Riley Sullivan, is good at interviewing people your son's age. We'll find out the truth. I promise you that."

Dr. Wright looked at Cooper and then at Adele. "Money isn't a problem. Take whatever time you need to get the job done." He stood and pulled his wallet from his back pocket. He opened it and pulled out a check. "I've made this out to you and signed it, just tell me the amount of the deposit to get you started."

Adele stood and took the check from him. "Come into my office and we can square away the details."

While Cooper waited for Adele and Dr. Wright to finalize the details, Cooper grabbed the police report that she had left on the couch for him. Izzy had been charged with eight counts of burglary. Each charge was a class C felony punishable by three to ten years in prison and a fine of up to $10,000. Izzy could be looking at some serious time in state prison.

Cooper glanced down at the arresting detective's name. Det. Lou Sawyer. It wasn't someone Cooper was familiar with and he knew most of the detectives on the force. He had worked for the Little Rock PD long before he branched out on his own. That wasn't a name he knew or had even heard before. It was too fast of an arrest though and Cooper wondered what Captain Meadows would think about it, especially given Izzy's background. The man was more than fair.

Adele finished with Dr. Wright and then he left with a simple nod of goodbye to Cooper. Adele came over and slumped down on the couch next to him. "What do you think?" she asked, resting her head on his shoulder.

Cooper shook the police report. "I think the arrest was made too quickly. I understand Izzy's watch was found at the scene. Unless this Hattie woman knows something we don't, I can't see how they would have made an arrest that quickly. Did she give any statement at all?"

"I didn't see one. I don't know that she's aware an arrest has been made. You'll need to interview her for me."

Cooper cocked one eyebrow. "That's better suited for Riley."

Adele sat forward and looked at him. "Why? Hattie is a nice woman."

"I don't buy into that whole psychic thing. She's scamming people, so she can't be that nice."

Adele playfully smacked his chest. "You don't even know her. I think you'll like her if you give her a chance. Besides, it's an interview. I didn't say you had to be her best friend. Riley can do the interview, but Hattie might be charmed by you."

"Or she might put a curse on me."

Adele shook her head. "One minute you say she's a fraud and the next she's putting curses on you. Pick a direction."

Cooper laughed and pulled Adele close to him, dropping a kiss on her forehead. "I'll talk to her. Riley and I will get started on this case in the morning. We have a few things to wrap up and then this will take priority."

"I'll pay my usual rate...plus expenses." Adele offered him a

31

suggestive look. "We haven't christened my office yet."

Cooper grinned as a warmth grew beneath his belt. He was sure she was trying to kill him. "If you hand me a check right after, I'm going to feel weird."

Adele stood and offered her hand, pulling him up from the couch. "I'll pay you your retainer tomorrow if that makes you feel better."

Cooper laughed and let himself be led to her office, not even bothering to try to hide the smile on his face.

CHAPTER 6

Luke made it home in time for Sunday dinner. Riley had texted him mid-day to tell him that she had gone grocery shopping and had some steaks she was going to grill along with baked potatoes and a salad. It would be the first dinner in their house as husband and wife.

When he arrived home, Luke made a beeline for the fridge and grabbed a cold beer, and then found Riley in the backyard at the grill. "Aren't you chilly?" he asked, taking a sip and then leaning over to kiss her. The air had long ago chilled with daytime temperatures falling into the fifties.

"I'm a New Yorker, this is summer for us," she laughed and flipped the steaks. "I love this time of year down here. How did it go today?"

Luke offered to help her and when Riley declined, he relaxed into one of the chairs they had on the patio. "It's going to be a tough case. I ruled out burglary fairly quickly. I don't think that's the motive at all. I'll need more information about the burglaries that happened. I heard they arrested a suspect. I'll need to rule him out. I need more information on the victim. Tyler and I interviewed her employees today and all of them had solid alibis. They weren't able to provide much information otherwise."

Luke took another swig of beer and looked up at Riley. A few strands of hair had escaped from her ponytail and she had already washed her face so she was free of makeup. She didn't look anywhere close to her thirty-seven years. He and Cooper would be forty soon and he was dreading the aches and pains it would bring. She had thrown on black yoga pants and one of his old tee-shirts. She never looked more beautiful to him.

"Why are you staring at me like that?" Riley asked without losing her focus on the steaks.

"How'd you know I was staring? Eyes in the back of your head?"

"Something like that. Quit checking out my backside and tell me about the case."

Luke chuckled. "Mrs. Morgan, how could you accuse me of something so awful?"

Riley swiveled her head with eyebrows raised. "Mrs. Morgan? I'm not your mother," she said with a wave of the metal tongs.

"Not changing your name?" Luke knew he shouldn't even go down this road. Riley had never promised to change her name, and at the time, he hadn't pressed the issue. Now though, he wanted her to have his name. It mattered to him in a way it hadn't before.

Riley turned back to the grill. "We can discuss my name later. Tell me more about the case."

"I have a personal connection to it. I arrested Holly's husband several years ago."

Riley pulled the steaks and foiled baked potatoes off the grill and put them on a plate. She nodded her head toward the back sliding door so Luke got up and opened it. "Let's eat and you can tell me about it."

She carried the plate to the round kitchen table that she had already set for dinner and then grabbed the salad bowl from the fridge, setting it down in the center of the table. She went back to the fridge to get something to drink while Luke fixed their plates.

When Riley came back and sat down, she asked, "Who is Holly's husband?"

Luke told her about Prophet Chance Bell and all the details of his crime and arrest. He took generous bites of food as he explained. Riley ate with her eyes focused on Luke, enthralled with the story. When Luke was done, he admitted, "I had hoped this was a guy I was never going to have to see again. I've arrested and interrogated a lot of people during my career, this guy was something else. It was too much for me."

"Why?" Riley asked, confusion on her face like she was missing something.

Luke knew he wasn't explaining well. He had never told anyone not even Tyler or Captain Meadows. "He creeped me out so much and he was also able to trigger me right into a rage. I felt like I was coming face to face with someone who hated me to my core. He created such hysteria with his followers. I constantly had my back up and was on edge."

"Did you have to make the death notification?"

"Captain Meadows did that for us." For that, Luke was eternally grateful. The more time he could stall having to speak to Chance the better. It wasn't going to last long though. "Tyler and I are going tomorrow morning to speak with him. We were going to try tonight but Chance refused. Captain Meadows said he wanted his lawyer present."

Riley finished the last bite of her steak and then seemed to mull something over before speaking. "What was Chance's following like?"

"Lost," Luke said and then paused. He hadn't met many of them and didn't want to speak badly of people that had gotten themselves caught up in something that scarred them for life. "They were people searching for something, Riley. They didn't seem like they knew themselves too well and were open to suggestion. I think some of them were good people who genuinely put their faith in the wrong person. Others, I think Chance tapped into some deep-rooted hatred they had. They took it as permission to feel the way they had been feeling."

Riley put her fork down. "Who did they hate?"

"Everyone," Luke said, his tone as serious as could be. "There wasn't a group they didn't hate. They protested against everyone one day and then were out preaching love the next. It was a bit like living inside his head – not sure which way to turn. I don't recall one group of people they didn't rail against."

"What about fat people?"

Luke caught the look in Riley's eyes. She knew something and was taking the long way to tell him. He leaned back in the chair and folded his hands across his middle. "What do you know?"

"I'm not sure that I know anything," Riley admitted, setting down her fork. "I met Emma while you went to the crime scene. Holly had gotten herself into some trouble over the last few weeks. She had written something stupid on Facebook about a store carrying athletic wear for plus-sized women. More stories about her fat-shaming people in her store came out after that. There was even an activist who wrote a column in a national magazine. The woman, Jordan Collins, had some harsh words for Holly. Now, she's here and Holly's dead."

"Don't people say stupid things on Facebook all the time? It's pretty much why I stay off it."

Riley tilted her head to the side and looked at him. "Stupid things, yes. But not things that cause a whole community to get angry and protest in front of your store."

Luke raised his eyebrows. "There was a protest?"

"It was a big deal, Luke. I brushed it off when Emma told me, but when I got back home, I spent some time looking online. You need to look at Holly's Facebook page for Bell & Bloom. The comments left for her weren't just negative – there was some serious language used in the comments and threats. I'm wondering if part of the reaction was that Holly is married to Chance Bell and people remember him and the arrest. I didn't know all that until you just told me. I'm sure you're not the only one who doesn't want a repeat of that in the community."

Luke let Riley's words sink in. He'd had no idea that Holly had a bit of scandal before the murder. It certainly put a new spin on the case. "This activist – Jordan Collins – what do you know about her?"

Riley delayed responding by clearing the dishes off the table. Luke stood and helped her, letting her marinate the question before she was ready to answer. He had learned a long time ago that it was best not to push Riley for a response to anything. It was only once she stood at the sink with her hands in the sudsy water washing the plates that she responded.

"Jordan seems like her heart might be in the right place. Of course, no one should be judged based on how they look or their size. No one should be judged for how much they weigh. I've faced it a time or two myself."

"When?" Luke said. He had to temper the anger that rose in him that anyone would be hurtful to Riley.

She laughed. "Calm down. It was a long time ago. I went to a yoga class and the instructor asked me if I'd be more comfortable in the back. I didn't move and then she asked me a few times if I needed to modify a pose. She didn't ask anyone else that. I've been doing yoga for years and was perfectly capable of following along. After class, she told me that she'd prefer it if I went to a different class. When I asked her why she said she didn't cater to women my size."

"How did you handle it?"

"I told her off and left." Riley dried her hands on a dishtowel and leaned against the counter. "No one knows what to do with a fat woman with confidence. It throws them off their game. You can't fat shame someone who doesn't feel shame for who they are. I know who I am."

That was precisely why Luke fell in love with her. Riley did know who she was and her confidence was rarely shaken. "You think Jordan is different than you?"

Riley hung the dishtowel on the hook. "She's angry like she has something to prove. Truly confident people don't have anything to prove to anyone. I read some of Jordan's other articles and none of them had the same tone as the Holly article. Jordan is an activist and she's passionate about the subject. The article about Holly though was on a different level. It was personal."

"Is she local to Little Rock?"

Riley shook her head. "She's from New York City or at least that's where she lives now." She went to the kitchen table and grabbed her phone and handed it to Luke. "Open Instagram and look at her profile. Check out the last photo she posted."

Luke never used Instagram, which made him feel like he was seventy years old. He didn't use social media much at all. He couldn't take the constant updates in people's lives. He didn't care what other people did, wore, or ate. Sometimes he had to use it for a case, and he always ended up feeling like a bumbling idiot – like he wanted to go out and find a twelve-year-old to help him on his case.

Finally, after much scrolling and clicking, he found the photo Riley mentioned and he stared down at it, knowing the background looked familiar. "Is that the Main Street Taproom?"

"Look at the date."

It was posted last night around eight in the evening. "Couldn't this have been taken a while ago and then she made the post last night?"

"She could have, but she didn't." Riley reached her hand out to take her phone back. She clicked around and then turned the phone to face Luke. "I checked Facebook, too. Jordan checked in at the restaurant last night. She's here in Little Rock, Luke, and she's staying at the Capital Hotel with the guy seen in these other photos. I called and asked to be patched through to her room. I hung up when she answered. She's there now."

"Any idea what she's doing in Little Rock?"

The look on Riley's face said it all. "Jordan posted earlier this week that she was heading down south to confront a bully."

Luke ran a hand down his face. "I better get down to the Capital Hotel then and have a conversation with Jordan Collins before she skips town."

"Sounds like a plan." They finished cleaning up from dinner and then Riley kissed him goodbye. He left without calling Tyler to join him.

CHAPTER 7

A t nine the next morning, I drove to downtown Little Rock to meet Cooper at his loft. Luke never had a chance to speak to Jordan the evening before. She hadn't been at the hotel and a search of the area hadn't turned up anything. Luke said they'd try again today.

I parked in a two-hour parking spot a block away from Cooper's condo and walked to his building. As I pulled open the front lobby door, I walked right into Adele. She juggled her bags and a to-go coffee cup from the shop on the first floor of the building. We air-kissed hello and I promised that I'd be in touch soon.

"Both of you need to come to my office when you're done catching up," Adele said over her shoulder as she headed down the street to her office. She didn't explain more.

Cooper had told me Adele needed help on a new case, but he hadn't told me anything about it. He said I'd need to clear my schedule, which was fine by me because I didn't have anything pending anyway.

By the time I made it into the building and up the elevator to his floor, Cooper had already texted me twice to see when I'd be there. I didn't bother responding. I got off the elevator and walked down the hallway and found his door slightly ajar. I knocked once and pushed it open, calling to him.

"You seem like you're in a hurry," I said, sitting on the couch.

"We have a lot to do." Cooper finished what he was doing at the kitchen sink and then joined me in the living room. "You know those burglaries that have been happening in the Heights?" he asked, sitting down on the couch with me.

"I've heard mention of them. I don't know much about them though. Luke told me about the homicide case."

Cooper held his hand up to stop me. "We'll get to that. The burglaries may be connected."

I shook my head. "Luke doesn't think so."

"Are you sure?" Cooper asked with a trace of skepticism on his face. He raked a hand through his hair and gave me a curious look.

I reiterated my point and then added, "Unless you know something I don't. Luke didn't seem to think it was connected. He's running down leads today on the homicide case. None of them have anything to do with the burglaries that I know of anyway."

"That's good if it's true."

"I'm not lying to you." I wasn't sure what he was getting at, but it was clear he knew far more than he was telling me. "Why don't you tell me what's going on and we can take it from there. I feel like we are having two different conversations."

Cooper propped his ankle on the opposite knee and leaned back into the couch. "Det. Lou Sawyer made an arrest on the burglary cases. Adele is representing the kid. Well," Cooper paused and corrected himself, "Isiah Wright isn't technically a kid. He's eighteen, a senior in high school, and lives in the Heights with his parents. I saw the arrest report and spoke to Isiah's father, Dr. Henry Wright. He's an emergency room doctor. There's possible evidence Isiah was at one crime scene but nothing on the others. Plus, he has an alibi."

I could tell by the tone in Cooper's voice he believed Isiah was innocent. I zeroed in on him. "I heard a *but* in there."

"I don't think the kid did it."

It was usually me that made excuses for people. Cooper rarely gave anyone the benefit of the doubt, which in our line of work made sense. "He's only tied to one burglary and he's got an alibi for it?"

"Not exactly," Cooper corrected. "Isiah was with a girl in the parking lot of a bank when one of the burglaries happened so he has an alibi for that night. His watch was found at the scene on another night. He's only tied by physical evidence to the last burglary, but he's being charged for all of them. As far as I'm concerned, if he can alibi himself for one, he's not guilty of any of them."

I knew Cooper had to have more evidence to back up what he was saying because he never made sweeping generalizations. "Explain to me your thinking on this. I'm not sure I follow."

Cooper expelled a frustrated breath. "Izzy, that's what he goes by, wouldn't tell Adele the name of the girl who could give him an alibi. That night, when he was walking home, he saw four boys leaving a store that had been broken into. Isiah thought he recognized one of the boys. I'm not sure how positive he is on the identification but he mentioned to Adele he probably knew the boy. The only problem is he wouldn't give her the boy's name."

"Is there a reason he won't offer it up?" It didn't sound like a true story to me, but rather an excuse for a kid who had gotten caught.

"He wouldn't say. That's one of the things we need to find out."

"Is that all?" I asked with a laugh.

Cooper's jaw tightened. "Riley, I can see that you don't believe me. Maybe you will once you read the police report." He shoved himself off the couch and disappeared down the hall. When Cooper returned a moment later, he had papers in his hand. He offered them to me. "I'm not saying that Isiah is completely innocent, although I'm leaning in that direction. But it was a rush to judgment on the detective's part. We need to speak to him and find the other guys."

I lowered my head to read the police report and scanned through the information, getting a sense of what Cooper had told me. There didn't seem to be a whole lot of evidence. A watch at a crime scene in a shop open to the public didn't seem to mean a whole lot. I was sure that I had lost earrings and even a necklace once. Had it turned up at a crime scene, I could have been in Izzy's position. The lack of evidence and Izzy's background and good grades coupled with the fact that he had never once been in trouble with the law swayed me in the direction of innocent. I wasn't fully convinced but swayed.

When I was done absorbing the information, I handed the papers back to Cooper. "I understand your concern. It seems there are a few places to start. First, with the detective, but in all likelihood, he won't speak to us. We can speak to the shop owner where the watch was found, but we need to speak to Izzy first. Is that where Adele was rushing off to this morning?"

Cooper's facial features relaxed. "Izzy's preliminary hearing was set for nine-thirty. She was heading over to the courthouse. She said she'd text me when they are done. We can interview Izzy and see what that gets us and go from there."

"We'll wait for her text then." I reached for Cooper's hand and squeezed it. "I can't believe you're engaged," I squealed, barely able to contain my excitement. There wasn't much time between Cooper proposing and Luke and I leaving for our honeymoon to celebrate with Cooper and Adele or even ask him any questions.

Cooper looped his fingers through mine. "I figured I'd be a bachelor the rest of my life – a third wheel tagging along with you and Luke."

"Never a third wheel. Did you set a wedding date yet?"

"Not yet." Cooper's eyes got a little misty. "We are going to keep it small. I don't have any family other than you and Luke, and Adele's parents aren't too sure about our connection."

That surprised me. I couldn't imagine anyone not liking Cooper. "They aren't happy for you both?"

His smile tightened. "They are happy she is happy, but the way we met didn't exactly spell romance. They are worried that Adele got swept up emotionally. They also don't like that she moved and gave up her law practice in Atlanta. They said I could have more easily moved there."

"Adele made that decision though," I said, concern creeping into my voice. "You would have moved but Adele wanted to do it."

Cooper nodded. "I offered to move to Atlanta and she said no. She wanted a fresh start."

That's what I thought had happened. Adele was one of the most practical and rational women I had ever met. It was why we got along so well. Adele and Cooper had met through unfortunate circumstances during the murder investigation of Luke's sister, Lily. Her case had been tied to a series of murders. Adele's sister had been among the victims. Cooper went to Atlanta to investigate and met Adele. They fell for each other almost immediately and hadn't wavered since. The way Cooper told the story, he knew right when he met her that the relationship would evolve. It took everything he had to be appropriate and sensitive to Adele during the investigation. Once the case was solved, Cooper finally admitted his feelings and found they were mutual. Adele moved to Little Rock shortly after.

I squeezed Cooper's hand. "Adele's parents will come around. They probably need more time around you and Adele together to see it's real. Since meeting, you haven't spent too much time with them."

"I hope you're right." Cooper relaxed back into the couch and angled his head toward me. "How are you and Luke? Marital bliss all you thought it would be?"

I didn't get a chance to answer him because Cooper's cellphone rang. He reached for it on the couch next to him and answered the call. It was Adele asking us to come to her office as quickly as we could. Izzy and his father were arguing and Adele wasn't sure that she could handle it on her own. Their booming voices had rattled her assistant and driven away another waiting client.

I could hear how rattled she sounded. Cooper hung up and jogged to his bedroom to grab his wallet and keys. Then we were off and made the walk from their condo to Adele's office in less than ten minutes. As we took the stairs to her office the voices grew considerably louder. Dr. Henry Wright wasn't going to accept that his son refused to tell him the name of the guy he saw leaving the shop.

We walked into the office and down a short hallway to find them in Adele's small conference room. Izzy sat at the table with his back ramrod straight in the chair. His head was bowed and his hands were folded on the table in front of him.

Dr. Wright towered over his son and had one large hand planted on the table and the other on the back of Izzy's chair. He bore down on the boy like an angry giant ready to kill his prey. Izzy held steadfast though and didn't break his silence. He didn't even look up when we entered the room.

Adele, who stood on the far side of the room watching the scene unfold, stepped toward us. "Cooper. Riley. I'm so glad you're here. Dr. Wright, this is Riley Sullivan, Cooper's investigative partner."

Dr. Wright stood upright and it was only then that the sheer size of the man was revealed. I walked toward him with my hand out to introduce myself. His hand engulfed mine and he gave me a curt nod.

"Maybe you can do something with my foolish son because I can't make any headway. His whole future is at stake and he's not saying a word to save himself." Dr. Wright threw his hands in the air and shoved past me, his frustration and anger on full display.

Cooper locked eyes with me, and I could tell by his expression he wasn't sure what to say. I looked toward Adele. "Why don't you take Dr. Wright for some coffee and leave us here to speak with Izzy. A break might do some good."

Dr. Wright left without even looking back. He muttered to himself about how stupid his son was being. Adele followed him out.

I reached into my pocket and pulled out a few dollar bills. "Cooper, maybe you can get us a few sodas. I'm sure Izzy would like something to drink."

The young man finally looked over in my direction and offered a stiff smile. He thanked me and Cooper took the cash and left. As soon as he was gone, I pulled out a chair across from Izzy, who may have been eighteen but looked younger. He had kind eyes and a handsome face with high cheekbones and a squared jaw. His hair had been trimmed nearly down to his scalp.

I gave Izzy a little bit of my background and tried to make him feel more comfortable. The energy between us was light. He relaxed his posture as he spoke to me.

"I'll accept that you can't tell me who this other guy is, but answer one question for me. Why can't you tell us?" As far as I was concerned, the *why* was more important now than the *who*.

Izzy lowered his head and stared at the table as if it was the most fascinating object in the room. After far too long in silence, he swallowed hard and met my gaze. "The guy I think I saw is a detective's kid. The girl I was with that night is his sister."

CHAPTER 8

"Did Captain Meadows tell you how the death notification went yesterday?" Luke asked Tyler as they made their way into the Capital Hotel. Jordan Collins had not called Luke back but he had put an officer on the hotel in the wee hours of the morning to make sure she didn't leave without them knowing. He had no cause to detain her, but at least Luke could keep track of her. He hoped she was asleep in her room.

"Captain Meadows said that Prophet Chance, as he wanted to be called, didn't seem to be the least bit upset. When Captain Meadows asked why he was calm at the news of his wife's murder, he simply said it was a sign of the end times." Tyler shook his head and laughed. "I was looking at some videos of him online last night. He's called for the end times at least five times and so far, nothing. Don't people start to call fraud after maybe the second or third prediction doesn't happen?"

"People will convince themselves of anything." Luke wasn't surprised by people anymore. He had done the job for so long that he'd seen the best and worst of human nature.

Luke walked through the lobby of the hotel and right up to the counter. He needed to confirm Jordan's room number. He worried the person at the desk the night before might not have given him accurate information because she had been hesitant to provide it. The last thing he needed was more stonewalling. He could go to the room and check again, but he wanted confirmation first.

He flashed his badge. "I need the room number for Jordan Collins."

The woman behind the counter stared at him. "Do you have a warrant?"

"I don't need a warrant to speak to someone. I went through this last night." Luke mentioned the number he had been given, but she refused to confirm it.

Instead, she reached for her phone. "I think it's better if I call her and ask her to come downstairs."

Luke reached his hand over the counter and put his hand on hers and lowered the phone back into the holder. "Let me speak to your supervisor or we are going to have your lobby crawling with cops. We know that won't be good for business."

The woman, who Luke guessed to be in her mid-forties, although the deep lines in her forehead and around her eyes could have indicated older, didn't budge. "We have a protocol here."

Luke tempered the berating thoughts that raced through his mind and he reached for his phone. He held up his cellphone and shook it. "If I have to make this call, trust me you're not going to be happy and neither is your boss."

The woman stood there silently watching him, which only served to infuriate Luke more. Before he could make the call, a young man popped his head out of the doorway behind the counter. "Can I help you?"

Luke introduced himself and flashed his badge again. "We need to speak with one of your guests. To not cause a scene, we need her room number. This woman has refused, so either I can cause a bigger scene than needed and get a whole lot of cops down here or you can give me what I need and I'll be on my way."

The young man went to the computer, nudging the woman out

of the way. He asked the guest's name and then typed it into the computer. He raised his head to Luke and told him 422. "Just walk straight through the lobby and there is an elevator on the left."

Luke thanked him and walked with Tyler in the direction of the elevators. "What was that about?"

Tyler looked back over his shoulder. "I don't know but she doesn't look happy. One of us should take the stairs while the other grabs the elevator."

Luke had already given that consideration. "I have a feeling she's going to tell Jordan we are on our way no matter what I said to her."

Luke walked to the elevator with Tyler and, when the woman at the front desk wasn't looking, he doubled back toward the wide center staircase and jogged up the first flight before he was spotted.

Luke jogged up to the fourth floor and pulled open the door and came face to face with Jordan Collins. She was dressed in yoga pants and a long sweater. Her face was free of the makeup she wore in her social media photos so he nearly didn't know it was her, but her eyes were a rare shade of light blue that he instantly recognized.

"Going someplace?" Luke asked, using his body to block the door to the stairs. He leaned back against the door and folded his arms while he stared at her. She was taller than he had figured by at least a few inches. At six-foot, she had to have been at least five-nine or ten.

Jordan pointed toward her sneakered feet. "Just taking my morning walk. Excuse me," she said, trying to nudge him aside. She blew out a frustrated breath. "Since you won't get out of the way – do you want something?"

Luke flashed his badge and pointed down the hall. "Let's head back to your room and chat. We have some questions about a case."

Jordan stepped back but held steady. "I don't want to speak to you. You should have gotten the hint when I didn't call you back. I'm not interested in speaking to you." When Luke didn't move out of the way, she turned angrily and marched down the hallway with him in hot pursuit.

Jordan didn't make it far because the elevator doors opened and Tyler blocked her path. He flashed his badge and introduced himself. "Jordan is refusing to speak to us, Det. Tyler. I guess we are going to have to take her down to the police station for formal questioning." Luke stood in the middle of the hall with his arms at his sides. "Funny that she hasn't even asked why we want to speak to her. Guess she already knows, which doesn't bode well for her."

Tyler looked around Jordan. "Do you think her social media followers will enjoy that she's being brought in as a homicide suspect?"

"Wait," Jordan said, her resolve melting. She spun around to Luke. "I'm a homicide suspect? Who died?"

"Holly Bell." Luke searched her face and he almost believed for a second that she didn't know.

Jordan reached her hand out to the wall for support. "I don't understand. Who killed her?"

"That's what we're here to find out."

"You can't possibly think that I have something to do with it?" she yelled, her voice becoming high-pitched and screechy.

Luke bristled at the sound of it. "Calm down and stop yelling. There are other guests in the hotel." He put his hand on her shoulder and spun her toward Tyler. "Let's go to your room where we can speak in private."

"Do I need my lawyer?" Jordan mumbled. "I feel like I need a lawyer. Are you going to arrest me?" She fired off questions as she led the way to her room and Luke and Tyler followed behind her.

Jordan slipped the key into the lock and pushed the door open. She headed right for the small round table at the far corner of the room and sat down. She looked up at them through tear-streaked eyes. "I've never been in trouble in my life. I didn't kill Holly Bell."

Tyler sat across from her, but Luke remained standing. He leaned against the dresser. "You were in Little Rock to see Holly Bell, correct?" Jordan gave a slight nod of her head and Tyler asked her the question again. This time she spoke in the affirmative. Jordan wiped the tears from her eyes and pulled in her stomach, sitting up a little straighter. "I'm sure you heard what Holly wrote on her Facebook page. It was hateful and I wanted to speak to her about it for my blog."

Luke knew there was a level of sensitivity he'd have to take. "Tell me about your blog."

Jordan looked up at him as if gauging if he was serious or not. When Luke didn't say anything else, she shrugged. "I chronicle things like this from both sides. I'm what they call a fat activist. I try to educate people about fat stigma and how to prevent bullying."

"What did you hope to gain by speaking to Holly?" Tyler asked, leaning back in the chair.

"I wanted an explanation on why she said what she said. I figured I might be able to educate her."

Luke knew she had left out part of the story. "I'm guessing by your expression it didn't go that way."

"Well, no..." Jordan hesitated, and Luke gestured with his hand for her to continue. "I went to Bell & Bloom to speak with her, and you wouldn't believe the look she gave me for walking through the door. Right off the bat, she told me she didn't have any clothes to fit me. I told her that wasn't why I was there. I explained who I was and she laughed in my face."

Jordan lowered her head and stared at her lap. Her voice remained low and her embarrassment evident. "Holly called me all sorts of names. She told me I was disgusting and that she was embarrassed to have me in her shop. She said women like me didn't deserve nice clothing or anything else. She said that if she had my body, she'd have killed herself."

Luke had to fight the instinct to reach out and comfort her, but Tyler crossed the boundary for them. He put his hand on her arm. "No one deserves to be spoken to like that. I've been married more years than I can count. My wife and I both saw what Holly said and we were both disgusted by it. I can understand why you wanted to confront her. It's brave that you did. How did you feel when she said those things to you?"

Jordan's head snapped up and gone was the vulnerable woman she first presented. Rage burned hot in her eyes. "How do you think I felt?"

Tyler noticed the change, too. He let go of her arm and slid back in his chair. "I assumed you'd be upset about it. Did you have words with Holly?"

"It was more than words, and she deserved it." Jordan tipped her head back and laughed, a maniacal movie laugh that made Luke roll his eyes.

He wasn't sure if this was meant to shock him, performance art, or if the woman had mental health issues. "Are you admitting you killed Holly Bell?"

Jordan pushed herself from her chair. "I didn't kill her, but I'm glad she's dead! Do you think I'd go to prison for that waste of space? We argued and I told her exactly what I thought of her. When Holly dared to put her hands on me and tried to shove me from the shop, I hit her right in the face." She balled up her hand into a fist and shook it toward Luke.

"You assaulted her?" Luke asked.

Jordan brushed him off. "I defended myself. She was alive when I left the shop."

"When did this happen?"

"The night before she was murdered." Jordan put her hands on her hips and stared at Luke, seeming unaware of the mistake she made.

Luke stood tall and bore down on her. "I thought you said you didn't know Holly was dead. What were the dramatics in the hallway for if you already knew?"

There was a moment of recognition on Jordan's face. Then she quickly recovered. "I knew, but I assumed it would look better if I acted like I didn't know." She pointed toward the television. "It's been all over the news. How could I miss it? You should tell your news stations that Holly is getting more airtime than she deserves. She was a horrible human being."

Tyler stood and shoved the chair back to the table. "She didn't deserve to die."

"I wouldn't expect a man to say any different."

Tyler's face grew red. "I told you I wasn't okay with what Holly said, but you had no right to hit her."

Luke held his hand out to stop Tyler. They didn't need to get off track. "Jordan, where were you from the time you left Holly's shop on Saturday to Sunday at eight in the morning?"

Jordan narrowed her eyes and looked on the verge of saying something she'd regret, but as Luke stepped toward her, she stepped back. She walked over to the side of the bed and yanked her phone from the table. She stood there huffing and scrolled through her phone.

A moment later, she stood in front of Luke, thrusting the phone toward him. "I chronicle everything."

Luke took the phone and lowered his head to see what she had pulled up. It seemed the woman took a photo of everywhere she went, every outfit she wore, and anything she ate. Luke had never seen such mundane content in his life. "These don't have time or date stamps."

"Are you ninety? Look at my social media. I post in real time." She snatched the phone from his hands and pulled up Instagram. "Here, look through that."

Luke scrolled through the content and sure enough, she posted every thirty minutes. There were no posts though for the wee hours of Sunday morning when Holly was murdered. "Where were you Sunday morning?"

Jordan opened her arms wide and spun around in a circle. "You're looking at it. I had a late night Saturday and I needed my sleep."

"Is there anyone who can corroborate that?" he asked with eyebrows raised.

Jordan smirked. "You'd think not, wouldn't you? But I came home with a man from the bar." She jotted down the man's name and phone number. "He left around ten on Sunday."

"I'll follow up, but in the meantime, don't leave town." Luke and Tyler left while Jordan hurled a string of curses at their backs.

Once they were down the hall and stepping into the elevator, Tyler turned to Luke. "That one is a real piece of work. She might want to stop to consider that if people don't like her, it's got nothing to do with her size but rather the terrible attitude."

Luke chuckled. "Not a fight you're going to win. We need surveillance video from the hotel. I'm calling to get a warrant."

CHAPTER 9

"What do you mean the guy you saw is a detective's son?" I asked, not sure I heard Izzy right the first time. Izzy's mouth set in a firm line. "I told you that you wouldn't believe me. That's why I didn't bother telling Miss Adele. She wouldn't believe that it's a cop's son committing those crimes."

I understood why he wouldn't tell, but if he was being serious then he didn't have a choice. "You're going to need to tell me the whole story including the young man's name." Izzy balked and I wasn't having it. "I believe you, Izzy. Otherwise, I wouldn't be sitting here wasting my time. I need to know what you saw and then Cooper and I can make a plan to help you."

Izzy slumped in the chair. "I'm beyond help."

"No one is beyond help." There was something more he wasn't saying. I could see it in the way his features tightened. "Is there something you aren't telling me?"

"You're not going to understand."

"Try me."

Izzy kept his focus on me for several moments. I wasn't sure if he'd tell me or not. He didn't trust me yet. Finally, I relaxed my posture and unclenched my jaw that had tightened while I was speaking to him.

"Izzy, listen," I said softly. "My only reason for being here is to help you. You have a story to tell, and I want to hear it. I assume that wasn't the case with the detective who arrested you. I know he suggested you might have been involved in the murder of Holly Bell, but I don't believe that for a second. I can help you, but you have to trust me."

Izzy turned his head away and wouldn't meet my eyes. His voice was soft and low. "I don't want to make this a black and white thing. That's what they always accuse us of doing."

I let the words wash over me and read in between the lines. "Are you saying that the guys you saw that night were white and that you're afraid if you accuse a bunch of white guys from the Heights of committing those crimes that no one will believe you because you're black?"

Izzy shifted his eyes toward me but still didn't look directly at me. "Something like that. I'm new to the neighborhood and everybody has been nice to me and my family except for a few people – mostly guys my age who go to the other high school. These burglaries happened after we moved to the neighborhood. I guess it's easy to blame the new black kid."

"Your watch was found at a crime scene," I reminded him. I wasn't going to discount what he was saying, but I needed him to understand that it was more than the color of his skin.

Izzy turned now to face me completely. "How do you think it got there?" he asked, his voice cool as ice.

"You tell me." I pulled back and didn't give him an inch. "That's why I'm sitting here, trying to get the story out of you. You've assumed Adele, Cooper and I won't believe you and yet here we are trying to help you. You're going to have to trust one of us. What about your father?"

Izzy let out an angry chuckle. "You think my father is going to believe me when I accuse a bunch of white kids? He assumed already that it was kids I'm friends with at school. I don't think it even occurred to him that it could be white kids – and my father is black." It felt a bit like walking a tightrope. I knew one false move and trust would never be established. I let my guard down. "Izzy, I can't account for your father's views. I'm not going to sit here and tell you how you should be feeling. All I'm going to do is tell you that I know you didn't murder anyone, and I don't believe you had anything to do with those burglaries. I can't help you though if you don't want to help me."

I scooted my chair back from the table and stood. "You're going to have to trust someone – it might as well be me. You let me know when you're ready to talk." I headed for the door, but he called me back.

"You're different," he said evenly.

I stopped at the door but didn't turn around. I let the silence be my answer.

"What I mean is that you're not like most people. You aren't making assumptions and telling me how I should feel. Adults do that all the time."

I smiled even though he couldn't see it. "It might surprise you that I don't feel like an adult much of the time." I turned around and went back to the table and sat down. "I'd like to think that I'm not so old that I don't remember what it was like being your age. Now, we haven't had the same experiences. We are also from different places. I grew up in New York."

Izzy smiled at me for the first time and showed off a row of perfectly straight white teeth that I assumed were the result of braces. "I didn't think you were from here. No accent. Where are you from?"

"I grew up in upstate New York."

Izzy had a look of admiration on his face. "New York is cool. I went with my dad a few times."

I assumed he meant New York City, which is usually what people in the south meant when they said New York. I was going with it though.

If it scored me cool points, all it could do was help. "It can be fun. What was your favorite part?"

"Central Park and so much to see and do. Not like here."

We talked a little bit more about New York and Izzy seemed to relax the more I got him talking. Cooper dropped off our sodas and then disappeared again. He seemed to sense the rapport I had built and probably didn't want to mess with the vibe. After we ran out of New York things to talk about, I locked eyes with him.

"Are you ready to tell me about that night?"

Izzy took a sip of his soda and then set it down. "I've been seeing Amelia long before I moved to the neighborhood. I play basketball and she's a cheerleader for another school. We met at a football game. Her father and her brother do not approve of her dating a black guy so we've been quiet about it. That's why we met up that night in the parking lot. I know my dad thinks it was some random hook-up, but it's not like that. We were talking that's all. I respect her too much to screw around in a car like that."

He stopped and assessed my expression and when he realized I wasn't judging, Izzy kept going. "Amelia said she was going to a friend's house and I walked to meet her. I know you are probably thinking that if we are sneaking around, we should have gone farther away from home. I don't know why. I guess if either one of us needed to get back quickly, it was easier there."

I didn't care where they were sneaking around. That wasn't for me to judge. "Did Amelia see them too?"

"No. Amelia had to go back home so she left before me. After she left, I started walking and because it was so nice out, I took the long way back and crossed onto Kavanaugh. That's when I heard them. They were loud and laughing and saying they couldn't believe they had gotten away with it again."

"The burglaries?" I asked.

Izzy tipped his head to the side. "The way they were talking about it, it was like a game – some mission like in a video game."

"Did they see you?"

Izzy shook his head slowly. "I ducked around the corner, but I saw them coming out of a shop. Three of them were in the shadow of the building, but the one guy's voice sounded familiar and then the light from the streetlight allowed me to see his face. I thought it was Amelia's brother."

"You think or you know? It's two different things."

Izzy remained quiet for a few moments then looked at me. "I know."

Even though he said the words, there was doubt in his voice. Even without a name, I'd be able to track him down. He had told me Amelia's name and I knew she and her brother were children of a detective who lived in the Heights. I had enough to go on even if Izzy didn't tell me.

"Did you hear them talking about anything else?"

Izzy sat back and thought for a moment. He was more animated now and spoke with his hands. "One of them said something like they'd have to check that shop off their list. Another said, 'On to the next,' or something like that. They sounded excited, amped up, like my teammates and me after we win a basketball game."

"How did your watch end up at one of the stores?"

Izzy tapped at his wrist where his watch would have been. "I rarely take it off except to play basketball. At first, I thought it was stolen from my locker at school. I take it off when I have practice, but earlier today I remembered the last time I saw it. I was playing basketball in a park in my neighborhood. I had thrown a water bottle, my keys, and my watch down in the grass by the side of the court. There were other guys out there with me and one of them was Amelia's brother. At first, I couldn't remember if I had my watch with me or not, but now, I'm certain I did. It makes sense, too, if he's the one breaking into the stores and now my watch is in one of them."

"Do you know the other guys who were out there with you both that day?"

"I could make you a list."

"Good. That's a start." I watched his face and his features had softened the longer he spoke to me. "I need the name of Amelia's brother. I know you don't want to tell me, but you've given me enough that I could easily track him down. Save me the time and just tell me his name." I put on my best pleading face and hoped for the best.

"I'll tell you," Izzy said, giving in. "First, you need to understand how he treats me. He has gone out of his way to try to start fights with me. He'll come by the house when my parents aren't home and throw things at the windows. He's smashed my car window. My dad doesn't know who did it, but I do. He's seen me out with my friends, and he calls me names and has told me a handful of times that I don't belong in the neighborhood. I try to ignore it as best as I can."

"Doesn't it make you angry?"

"Yeah, sure, but I'm trying to get a college scholarship. I can't have a stupid fight with him ruin everything." Izzy said the words and then recognition of the trouble he was in came crashing back down on him. He closed his eyes and rubbed his temples.

"Does anyone else know he broke your car window?"

Izzy opened his eyes and nodded. "My neighbor. He's the one who told me who it was."

"What's his name?"

"Jackson Morris. He was something high up in the Army. I think he's retired now." Izzy knocked on the table. "He lives right across the street from the woman whose shop my watch was found in. I know her and I've helped her carry in her groceries a few times when her niece isn't around. She's a nice lady. I'd never break into her shop."

"I think it's time, Izzy. Who is this guy?"

Izzy gulped down a breath. "Scott Sawyer."

The last name sounded familiar, but I couldn't quite place it. Izzy watched me until recognition took hold. When it did, my stomach dropped to the floor. My eyes locked with Izzy's. "The son of the detective who arrested you?"

"Yes, ma'am."

CHAPTER 10

L uke leaned back in his desk chair and kicked his feet up on the open drawer. He linked his fingers across his midsection and closed his eyes. Anyone looking at him would have thought he was taking a nap or flaking off work. He wasn't doing that. Luke was mentally going through the evidence he had to date about the murder of Holly Bell. None of it made sense to him yet.

They were still waiting to see if they could get surveillance video from the Capital Hotel because the manager had refused to give it to him. It angered Luke at the time but he understood. It was a violation of privacy for every guest of the hotel and they needed a darn good reason to do it.

A judge would sign off after it was reviewed and they'd be good to go. There was no reason in the world that a judge would refuse to let Luke see surveillance video that could rule in or out a homicide suspect – even though *suspect* might be too strong of a word for Jordan Collins.

He brought a picture of Jordan into his mind's eye. She had an edge about her, anger he didn't understand. Luke could rationalize and say that what she was doing as an activist might be doing the world a service or at least helping people feel better about themselves. He was all for confidence and self-esteem. The way she went about it though didn't quite work for him. He didn't understand how anyone would be open to education and thinking differently if they were screamed at to do so.

Luke slumped forward in his seat and dropped his feet to the floor with a thud. He pulled a manila file folder from his desk. Luke undid the latch at the top and pulled out the glossy crime scene photos that he had asked the lab to enlarge for him. The rest of the photos were on his laptop but a few of the body shots he had wanted bigger so he could examine them better.

He studied the back of Holly's head. Her skull had taken a blow from the back toward the right side of her head, giving Luke the impression that the killer was right-handed. The blood spatter indicated she fell to the ground and then the killer struck her several more times. Luke checked his phone to see if Purvis had called from the medical examiner's office yet. Nothing.

Luke dropped the photos on a pile and leaned back. Jordan was tall enough and probably strong enough to overpower Holly and strike her in the back of the head. Once the woman was on the ground, Jordan could easily finish her off. Luke wasn't sure if Holly would have turned her back on Jordan. After running through several scenarios in his mind, he settled on one simple thought. Holly probably underestimated Jordan and never thought the woman would hurt her.

Holly probably laughed at the idea that Jordan had traveled from New York City to confront her. Jordan also said that she had punched Holly the night before or so she claimed. For all Luke knew, it was that Sunday morning.

Luke needed a better handle on the murder weapon. That would tell him what they were working with. Luke reached for his phone to call Purvis but never got a chance to pick it up. Captain Meadows stuck his head out of his office and called Luke and Tyler over.

"Maybe he's finally going to tell us about his meeting with Prophet Chance," Tyler said, pushing his chair back from his desk and standing.

"I've been waiting all day so I hope so." Luke followed Tyler through the detectives' bullpen with desks scattered throughout. There was no clear path because they hadn't been laid out on a grid. They might have been at one time or another, but detectives moved their desks around to get more comfortable in the space.

As Luke passed by a desk, fingers gripped his wrist. He shook his hand free and looked down to see who touched him. It was Det. Lou Sawyer.

The man angled his head to look up. "The stupid judge gave that dumb kid bail." He called the kid a derogatory name and waited to see if Luke would respond. When he didn't, Sawyer added, "You need to interview him. I'm telling you right now he's good for that murder."

Sawyer had been in the department for close to twenty years. He had worked his way up from beat cop to detective. It took him longer than average, but if you asked Sawyer, he was the best detective in the place. He claimed he'd been passed over for politics and a string of nonsensical reasons. Luke didn't know the man personally, but his detective work was sloppy and he often rushed to judgment. Sawyer had asked Captain Meadows more than once to be transferred from burglaries to homicide only to be turned down time after time. Sawyer never quite got the message.

"He's on a long list of many. Put the file on my desk and I'll give it a read."

"That uppity new defense attorney took the case." Sawyer cursed again, calling Adele a vulgar name and then he shrugged. "I guess you guys stick together."

Luke balled his fists. "Who sticks together?" he asked with an edge in his voice.

The detective seemed to think better about what he was going to say because he didn't respond to Luke's question. Sawyer grunted and pulled a file from his desk. "Just do your job and interview that punk."

"In here now!" Captain Meadows called from his doorway after witnessing the scene and the growing anger on Luke's face. When he didn't move, his boss called him again. "Det. Morgan, not everything needs a response. Get in here now!" Luke stepped toward the man's desk and then turned sharply on his heel and went into Captain Meadows' office. His boss slapped him on his back as he walked through the doorway. "You know he says things just to get you going."

Luke raised his eyebrows. "Sawyer says what he says because that's what he thinks."

Captain Meadows nodded but waved Luke off. "True enough but battling it out isn't going to solve anything. You don't need to rise to every occasion. Besides," he said sitting down at his desk, "we've got bigger fish to fry. Pull up a chair."

Luke let his anger go and sat down. "I assume you want to tell us about the meeting with Chance Bell."

Captain Meadows tossed a paper to Luke across the desk. "The search warrant came through about an hour ago. Chance is combative, didn't seem to care that his wife was murdered, and already lawyered up. He offered no alibi and told me that we'd be speaking to him over his cold dead body."

"Same as he ever was," Luke said dryly.

Tyler glanced over at the search warrant in Luke's hands. "Who is his lawyer?"

Captain Meadows clicked his tongue. "He didn't say or rather he wouldn't tell me. Just said he'd be in touch."

"So that's it?" Tyler asked, turning his head.

"Not by a long shot. You and Luke are going out there today to oversee the search. While you're there, you're going to see what you can find out."

Luke tossed the search warrant back on the desk. "You know I have a history with him. He's not going to speak to me. Chance blames me for breaking up his following and putting him in prison."

Captain Meadows leaned back in his chair and smiled like a Cheshire cat. "That's exactly why you're going. Chance needs to be riled up. Right now, he thinks he's got the upper hand and he's pulling a power play. You need to knock him down a peg. Put some fear of prison right back into him."

Luke could happily do that. He didn't think it was going to make that much of a difference though. "Do you think Chance killed his wife?"

"I don't know," Captain Meadows said. "It's frequently the husband or partner. With Chance's record, he's even more suspicious. I would think he might have chosen a better way to kill her than in her shop."

Luke speculated, "He could have read about the burglaries and decided that it might take the focus off him. Nothing was stolen though that we know of right now."

"Not that we know of." Captain Meadows pointed toward the door. "What was Sawyer talking about related to the burglaries?"

Luke inched forward in his chair. "He arrested some kid in the Heights who he's sure killed Holly Bell. I don't think so. She turned her back on her killer. I can't see any woman doing that with a random burglary."

Captain Meadows gestured for Tyler to get up and close the door. When it was secured tight, he leaned forward on his desk and pointed toward the detective's bullpen. "I have issues with the arrest. Sawyer didn't run it by me before he acted and the case is weak. Plus, I don't think it's one person who is breaking into those shops. There's too much at play – cutting the surveillance, case the place ahead of time, and what has been stolen? Not much of anything. This wasn't one kid."

Luke took some satisfaction in that the case had been handled poorly.

He hated that he felt that way since a poor solve rate impacted all of them. Riley had texted him a while ago and told him Adele had the case and that she and Cooper were investigating. He told Captain Meadows. "Adele, Cooper's fiancée, is the kid's defense attorney if you want to reach out to her."

Captain Meadows made a note of her name on a legal pad in front of him. He asked Luke for her office phone number and he jotted that down, too. "That's good. We might need to play some clean-up on that case, but you need to do me a favor after you speak to Chance."

Luke nodded. "Anything."

"Go interview that kid for me and rule him out of the homicide case. See what you can get out of him for the burglaries, too."

"I don't know that Adele will let us anywhere near him."

"Just try," Captain Meadows said dismissively.

Luke and Tyler shared a look. "We'll do our best. Anything we need to know before going out to see Chance?"

"The only thing he mentioned when I made the death notification was that he wondered if one of her employees killed her. I guess there had been some drama." Captain Meadows' expression tightened. "He didn't tell me what the drama at the shop was, though. I know Tyler didn't get any info from the employees and they all have an alibi. That's all Chance seemed to know."

Luke asked a few more questions and gathered what he needed. Before they got up to leave, Captain Meadows asked, "What happened with that interview at the Capital Hotel this morning? Anything promising?"

Luke gave him the rundown on Jordan Collins, including needing to get a search warrant for the surveillance video from the Capital Hotel. Captain Meadows assured him that he'd have the video in hand by the end of the day.

"I don't know if I believe Jordan killed her or not," Luke said. "She's on the suspect list though. She admitted to punching the victim shortly before her death. We are going to need to see if anyone can corroborate Jordan's story. There's a guy she said she was with all night into the morning and we need to run down that lead, too."

"Check in before the end of the day and let me know how it's going. If I hear anything on the autopsy report, I'll call you right away." Captain Meadows waved them off and asked them to close the door when they left.

Tyler and Luke walked to their respective desks and grabbed their belongings for a long day in the field. Luke noticed that Sawyer clocked their every move from the moment they walked out of Captain Meadows' office until they were out of his line of sight as they walked down the stairs.

"What's with him?" Tyler asked when they got to the bottom.

"I'm not sure. But he's got a real bug up his backside about the kid he arrested." Luke shoved open the door and sunlight hit him in the face.

CHAPTER 11

After Riley got the name of the kid who had been burglarizing the store from Izzy, she let Cooper come in the room with them and she explained the story again. Izzy confirmed everything that Riley said. Cooper wasn't sure why he couldn't have been there to hear it, but Izzy seemed to trust Riley and that was all he needed to know.

Izzy made them both swear not to tell Dr. Wright anything until they were able to find evidence. Izzy seemed afraid his father wouldn't believe him even after Riley and Cooper assured him that they were fully on his side.

Once Dr. Wright took Izzy home, they updated Adele who seemed relieved that someone had gotten the full story from him. She had a defense now and that was all she cared about. Although, she hoped they'd find evidence long before anything had to go to trial. Cooper promised they'd do their best on this case for her and Izzy.

Riley headed to the high school to talk to some of the guys Izzy mentioned were at the basketball court when his watch was stolen while Cooper went to Hattie's Cauldron: Potions & Pastries. A knot formed in his stomach that he couldn't shake. The thought of meeting someone who claimed they were psychic set his teeth on edge. He didn't believe in all that and had investigated several cases where people had been swindled out of their hard-earned money by a psychic who had promised to cure them of all of life's problems.

His hands tensed on the steering wheel and he bit his lower lip harder than he meant. He had to force himself to relax his hands as they began to cramp. Cooper would rather be doing anything other than having to go speak to a psychic.

He reached the shop and pulled over in an open space on Kavanaugh Boulevard. Cooper cut the engine and sat there staring across the street at Hattie's Cauldron: Potions & Pastries. He'd been in many of the shops along this stretch of Kavanaugh but never this one. He was a little embarrassed by the idea of anyone seeing him go in there. Cooper took a deep breath, looked quickly in the mirror above his visor and gave himself a pep talk. *Don't be ridiculous. Just go in and ask the questions like every other investigation.*

Cooper slapped the visor up and got out of the car. He jogged across the street and when he reached the shop door, he didn't allow himself to hesitate. He pulled it open and stepped inside. Cooper's eyes darted around the place. He was at once overcome by his own foolishness for having worked himself up and wrapped with a sense of calm. There were tables and chairs for reading and enjoying treats and some metaphysical items for sale. Several older ladies sat in the middle of the shop at a long table. They were laughing and enjoying themselves.

A woman standing behind the counter seemed harmless enough. She reminded him a little of Adele the way she wore her hair braided in a twist at the top of her head. She smiled and waved him over. "I'm Sarah. Can I help you today?"

Cooper walked over to the counter, introduced himself, and explained why he was there. "I was hoping to speak to Hattie. I know she wasn't here when the burglary happened, but I have some routine questions. She might be familiar with the young man who was arrested."

"Sure," Sarah said. "First, let me get you something to drink and a snack on the house."

"No, thank you. I'm fine."

Sarah laughed. "Hattie isn't going to let you get away with that. You're working hard and she's going to mother you. I can already tell. It's what she does."

Cooper had assumed he'd have his guard up during the meeting, but Sarah put him at such ease he almost didn't trust her. He found himself smiling and agreeing even though he wasn't sure he wanted to. "Coffee is fine, thank you."

"Try the chocolate croissant," yelled one of the older women at the middle table. "You'll never want to eat anything else ever again."

Cooper belly laughed in a way he hadn't in a long time. There was something about this place he couldn't quite put his finger on, but his defenses were down and a warmth of happiness spread through him. "I guess I better have the chocolate croissant, too."

He chatted with Sarah while she fixed his order. He asked about the kinds of customers who came to the shop and how long they had been in business. Sarah told him Hattie's history and how long she had lived in the Heights and a few funny stories about people's first impression of the shop and then how they felt when they left.

"It's not what most people think," Sarah assured him. "Even when I first came here, I was hesitant because of stories I've heard about psychics swindling people out of money. Sometimes I don't know how Hattie stays in business with the number of people she turns down or what she gives away for free."

"She sounds generous."

Sarah handed Cooper his coffee cup and a plate with the chocolate croissant. "It's more than that. Hattie has a way of making people feel like they are at home. My brother moved here not knowing anyone. Her niece, Harper, retreated here after a bad divorce. Hattie has a way of taking people in and making them her family."

"Are you talking me up again?" asked a woman standing next to Cooper.

Cooper turned his head toward the person speaking. Hattie stood about five-four and had short silver hair. She reminded him of an actress that he couldn't quite place. Cooper tipped his head to the side and filed through recent movies he'd seen until he landed on a *James Bond* movie he'd rewatched recently. Judi Dench. That's who Hattie reminded him of. They had the same face shape and haircut and infectious smile.

Sarah made the introductions and Hattie nodded in approval at Cooper's chocolate croissant.

"I don't want to say they are life-changing, but you're never going to want to live without them," Hattie teased. She praised her wonderful baker and then asked, "Would you rather talk in the back or one of the tables out here?"

The place wasn't busy at all so Cooper pointed toward a table. "I don't want to take up too much of your time."

"Nonsense," Hattie said sitting. "I have a feeling we are going to be fast friends."

Cooper was surprised not by what she said, but the confidence in her voice. "Have you ever worked with a private investigator before?"

Hattie pursed her lips. "You don't strike me as someone who believes in ghosts."

Cooper opened his eyes wide and set down his cup. "I don't. Although, I try not to completely discount what I don't know. I wouldn't be a good investigator if I assumed I knew everything."

"Good way of being. To answer your question then, we have a private investigator from the 1940s who likes to hang around the shop and help out from time to time."

For some reason, her answer didn't shock Cooper. He wasn't sure how much he believed her but at the same time, he knew she wasn't lying to him. It was a dichotomy in his head he couldn't quite make sense of. "That would have been a great time to have been a private investigator."

"As long as you don't sleep with your clients."

Cooper coughed. "I don't think there's ever a good time for that." He took another sip of his coffee. "Can you tell me about the burglary?"

Hattie took a breath and sat back with her hands folded on the table. "Normally, it's Sarah or another girl I have working for me who come in first thing in the morning, but this time I opened the shop. The front door glass was broken. I know I shouldn't have walked inside but I did. Nothing seemed to be disturbed though. I had heard about the burglaries. My niece, Harper, had been bugging me about getting a security system and surveillance video, but I couldn't be bothered."

Hattie gestured around her shop. "What do I have here to steal? I'll show you the back area. I have a reading room, office, and kitchen. I never keep money here. I bring it home each evening and go to the bank in the morning. There are some metaphysical supplies, but I can't see anyone stealing them."

It sounded much like the other break-ins. Cooper glanced around the shop. "Was anything disturbed?"

Hattie pointed to the counter. "There was a watch sitting dead center on the counter where people order. At first, I thought one of the girls had found it when they were cleaning the night before, but when I asked, both said no. We turned it over to the detective who came to the shop."

"Det. Lou Sawyer?"

Hattie nodded. "Sarah is dating Det. Tyson Granger and we expected it to be him. That's who we know and are comfortable with, but he told us it wasn't his case." Hattie's tone and demeanor changed slightly when she spoke about Det. Lou Sawyer.

"Did you like the detective who took your statement?"

"I don't like speaking poorly of anyone." Hattie sat back and watched Cooper for a few moments. Then she leaned in. "He was rude to me from the moment he entered the shop. It wasn't so much what he said but how he said it. He acted like I didn't know anything about my shop. He kept insisting that something was stolen, which it wasn't. Then he asked me if anything was left behind. I told him about the small purple marble and the watch."

Cooper furrowed his brow. "I didn't read anything in the police report about a purple marble."

"That's because he didn't take it." Hattie blew out a frustrated breath. "After the cops came, Det. Sawyer walked in the back with me. I didn't go back there until the cops came. Sitting right in the middle of my desk was a purple marble. It wasn't mine and it's not something I carry in the store. I had left my desk at four in the afternoon the day before. The girls closed up at six. They didn't know anything about it."

"What was Det. Sawyer's response when you told him?"

"He snickered at me and told me that a thief wasn't leaving me a purple marble and that I must be mistaken. He insinuated that at my age it's easy to forget things." Hattie pounded her fist down on the table loud enough that Sarah looked over and the other customers turned around. "I may be up in years, but I'm not so out of it I forget what's on my desk!"

"I believe you," Cooper assured her. "I believe the detective made a rush to judgment on this case."

Hattie raised her eyes to him. "Arresting Isiah Wright, you mean?"

Cooper confirmed. "I met the young man's father yesterday and met Izzy this morning. I don't believe that he broke into your shop."

"Well then, that's one thing you and I have in common." Hattie stood and grabbed Cooper's empty coffee cup. "Let me get you a refill and then we can talk about my relationship with Izzy. He'd never break into my store and we need to make sure he doesn't go to prison for something he didn't do."

CHAPTER 12

The tenacity in Hattie's voice and strength of conviction impressed Cooper. He watched as Hattie walked away, surprised at how he felt about the woman. He'd only spoken to her for a few minutes, but she was nothing like what he assumed when he first heard about her. She came back with two cups of coffee – his cup and one for herself.

She set the cup down in front of him and then sat down across the table. "I probably shouldn't have gotten so fired up, but I don't like injustice. Det. Granger warned me not to get involved."

Cooper smiled at her. "Do you get involved in criminal matters?"

Hattie looked away but the smile that tugged at her lips told Cooper all he needed to know. "I make a nuisance of myself with Det. Granger, but he likes it. We've helped him solve a few homicides."

"We?"

"My niece, Harper, and her boyfriend, Jackson. Sarah has helped, too. They kind of fall in our lap and we get involved. I have a few special gifts as does Harper and Sarah that help us out from time to time."

Cooper angled his head down and locked eyes with her. "Your ability has helped solve murders?"

"It's helped here or there. Harper has a knack for crime solving so it's her curiosity and her gifts combined." Hattie waved him off. "The bottom line is that if you're not going to help Izzy then I will. That young man didn't do anything wrong."

Cooper reached for his coffee cup and lifted it to his lips, never taking his eyes off Hattie. She was determined and he believed she'd do what she said. "You're sure Izzy is innocent. Tell me your impression of him. How did you meet? His father didn't seem to think he'd know you."

Hattie relaxed back into the chair. "I met him soon after he and his parents moved to the neighborhood. Dr. Wright came over and said hello one day while I was out in the yard. Another day I spoke to his wife. That was before they knew about me. Since then, there's been a few times I've been outside raking and Izzy has offered to help. There was once or twice I was carrying groceries in and he helped me."

"How did he interact with you?"

"He's a kind young man." Hattie took a sip of her coffee and then paused. She set her cup down slowly. "Izzy seemed like a fish out of water. He's young and a new neighborhood can be a challenge. I don't think he fits in too well with the neighborhood boys. Of course, some of them are all brawn and no brains. Izzy is thoughtful and intelligent. He's also an athlete, but I suspect he'll get much further in life with his brain."

Hattie's assessment of the young man wasn't that far off from Cooper's. "You mentioned some of the other young men in the neighborhood. My understanding is that Izzy doesn't get along too well with them."

"That's correct," Hattie confirmed. "It goes beyond normal teasing. Scott Sawyer seems to be the ringleader. He's got a group of guys he hangs around with who hang on his every word. I caught them smoking pot at the corner of my street a few times."

"Did you tell his father?"

"I'm not a narc." Hattie laughed. "It's none of my business what he does. I only brought it up because it shows he's not the perfect son his father makes him out to be. Scott is a troublemaker. He's one of those guys that goes out of his way to seem appropriate and helpful, but you can tell by the smirk on his face that it's all fake. Oh sure, he thinks he's fooling everyone but he's not. He had it in for Izzy the moment he moved to the neighborhood."

"Do you have any idea why?" Cooper didn't want to put words in her mouth or speculate.

Hattie raised her shoulders in a shrug but didn't lower them. Her body remained tensed as she spoke, conveying the weight of her message. "I wondered if it was because there aren't many black kids in the neighborhood their age. I thought that was Scott's issue and it might be, but it's more than that. The more I watched them, it seems to me that Scott doesn't like anyone he can't control. He certainly can't control Izzy, who didn't fall all over Scott at the first meeting. I think that's what sparked off the whole thing. Izzy wasn't going to be a follower and Scott felt threatened. Izzy had his school, friends, and interests that didn't include hero-worship of Scott. Izzy wasn't with him so he was automatically against him."

"It sounds to me like Scott has been waging a war Izzy didn't ask for and doesn't participate in."

Hattie pointed at him. "You're exactly right. Izzy has been going about his business, but every opportunity he has, Scott tries to knock him down a peg. Izzy doesn't even interact with him or act as if it bothers him so that makes it worse. It would almost be better if Izzy flipped out on him and made a show of being angry. That doesn't seem to be Izzy's style."

"You seem to know a lot about this. Has Izzy confided in you?"

Hattie tipped her head to the side and smiled. "A few times. But I approached him about it. He didn't come to me, and even when I asked, he was hesitant to tell me. Izzy's mother travels for work all the time and his father works in the evenings. His siblings have grown and moved out so he's alone in the house. His father expects a lot of him."

Cooper took another sip of his coffee. "Izzy said that he had carried your groceries a few times and that your other neighbor witnessed a broken car window. I don't mean any offense, but I didn't get the sense you were that close."

Hattie offered him a teasing smile. "If you were an eighteen-year-old boy sharing your feelings with an old lady who happened to be the neighborhood psychic, would you tell anyone?"

Cooper absorbed her words and then chuckled. "I guess not. Did you witness Scott's behavior toward Izzy?"

"I didn't see him break the car window if that's what you're asking," Hattie started, taking another sip of coffee. "I've heard him call Izzy names and taunt him, trying to goad him into a fight. I've never seen Izzy stoop to that level though."

Cooper searched her face. "There is no way you believe that Izzy could be responsible for the break-ins?"

"Not of my shop," Hattie said adamantly. "I can't imagine him breaking into anyone's shop. He's too busy to be in that kind of trouble. I also don't think it's in his personality to do something like that."

Cooper agreed with her. "Do you know if Izzy is dating anyone?"

Hattie pursed her lips together. "Are you talking about him and Amelia sneaking around together?"

Cooper wasn't sure why but he was surprised she knew. "You know about that?"

Hattie nodded. "The poor kids aren't any good at hiding it. I've never seen her go to his house, but he leaves and walks down to the corner and she will pick him up occasionally. I know Amelia and she's nothing like her brother or her father. She's a sweet young lady."

"Do you think Scott knows Izzy is dating his sister?"

"No," Hattie said with force, making Cooper lean back. "If Scott knew that, there'd be a price to pay and it would certainly be more than what's happened to date."

Cooper locked eyes on her. "Like framing him for burglaries he didn't commit?"

Hattie started to speak but then closed her mouth and thought about what Cooper said. She raised her eyebrows. "That could certainly be a possibility. That would mean that Scott is the one committing the burglaries."

Cooper recounted the story that Izzy told them. He watched as Hattie's face contorted in concern and then in fear. "You can see our dilemma," Cooper said in closing. "We believe that not only did Det. Sawyer arrest the wrong guy, but his son might be the one responsible. Det. Sawyer is also accusing Izzy of killing Holly Bell."

Hattie's hand flew to her mouth and she shook her head. "That can't be. He'd never do something like that." She glanced around the shop, seeming unsure of what to say. Finally, she locked eyes with Cooper. "You need to speak to my niece, Harper, about Holly Bell. She had gone for a morning run and saw a woman outside of her shop the morning she was killed. She called Det. Sawyer to ask if he was handling that case but he told her that the cops already found the guy responsible. He wouldn't even listen to what she had to say. I had no idea he meant Izzy."

Cooper held his hand up. "The detective who is in charge of the homicide investigation is a friend. He's my investigative partner's husband. Det. Sawyer may keep pushing the idea that it's Izzy, but Luke will not take it seriously unless there is evidence and I can't imagine there will be."

"I would hope not." The store had started to fill up with people and Hattie glanced toward the counter. "I don't want to rush you, but I should help Sarah soon."

"It's fine. I have everything I need and will follow up with your other neighbor and with your niece. Can I have their contact information?" Hattie told Cooper how to reach Harper Ryan and Jackson Morris. "Please speak to them and come back if you need anything." Hattie stood and smiled down at him. "Stop in anytime you want to chat or have a snack. You're more than welcome. You have a kind face and good energy."

Cooper thanked her and stood. He wasn't sure why but he felt drawn to Hattie. He reached out and took her hand in his. "I appreciate you speaking to me today."

Hattie tipped her head back to look him in the eyes. "If you don't mind me saying, you may not have a traditional family, but you're supported and very loved – on this side and the other. You mean a lot to people that are close to you." With that she left him and walked away, leaving Cooper to stand there a bit stunned.

He swallowed emotion that seemed to creep up on him unexpectedly and he struggled to focus his eyes. It had come out of nowhere and hit him like a punch to the heart. There was no way for Hattie to know he had no traditional family left but the message had resonated and meant more to him than she could know. He sucked in a breath and threw his shoulders back, tempering the breakdown that could come if he let himself think about it too much.

Cooper propelled himself toward the door, turning slightly to wave goodbye to her and Sarah. He didn't know why but he knew he'd be back.

CHAPTER 13

A fter gathering as much information as I could from Izzy, I left with a plan to stop by the high school to speak to some of the young men Izzy had mentioned. I got stonewalled by the administration before I even got started. I was told that there was no way I was going to interview anyone at the school, even those who might have already turned eighteen. If I wanted information, I could speak to them at their houses with their parents' permission.

I had expected as much but had taken a shot in the dark that maybe I could worm my way into meeting with one or two of them. I searched for each of them on social media and downloaded a few of their photos. I hoped at the very least I'd see them but had no luck with that either.

I sat in my car at the curb near the school and texted Cooper to tell him that I had taken a swing and a miss at the school. He updated me all about his meeting with Hattie, including that she had found a strange marble on her desk. Cooper asked me if I'd be willing to speak to her niece, Harper, at her office. She had information about the murder investigation, but he didn't have time to speak to her. He told me when she'd be available and would be expecting me that afternoon. So much for getting to say no.

I asked him why we wouldn't send it to Luke. Cooper's response made my stomach rumble.

I don't know what she's going to say and want to rule out it's not going to implicate Izzy first.

Fair enough. I didn't think Izzy was even a possibility, but I understood Cooper's reasoning.

I checked the time and had two hours before Harper was expecting me. I let Cooper know I was going to do a quick canvass of some of the other shop owners to see if they had anything interesting to say.

I drove back to my neighborhood, parked in my driveway, and walked the few blocks to the section of Kavanagh that had all the shops. The first two places I stopped – a hair salon and the pizza shop – didn't have anyone knowledgeable enough about the break-ins who could speak to me. I left my card and asked for them to call me back.

The third shop I went into – one that sold kitchen and household items – the manager, Lisa, was at the register. After I introduced myself and told her why I was there, she escorted me back to her office so we wouldn't disturb the customers.

"I thought this was a done deal," she said over her shoulder as she went behind her desk and told me to pull up a chair. "I was told there was an arrest."

"There has been an arrest, but I don't believe the police have the right person."

Lisa furrowed her brow. "Who do you work for again?"

I mentioned Adele's name. "She's the criminal defense attorney representing Isiah Wright."

"You're hoping to undo the hard work that the police did?" She had a tone to her voice I didn't like.

I tried to temper my defensiveness. "I'm here to make sure Isiah Wright gets a fair defense. He has a right to defend himself. I believe there was a rush to judgment and I'm making sure that all the evidence comes to light."

Lisa studied me for several moments. "You live in the neighborhood, don't you? I think I've seen you around."

"I do and have for a while."

Lisa squinted her eyes at me. "You're with that detective. Luke Morgan."

"I'm his wife if that's what you're asking." *Wife* didn't roll off my tongue naturally. I seemed to stumble over the word. It would take some time.

"What does he think about you messing up the investigation?"

I blew out a breath. "I'm not messing up anything and he's supportive of my work. My investigation partner and I have worked with the local cops on various investigations. We've helped solve a few homicides, too."

That didn't seem to sway her.

I relaxed hoping she would as well. "Think of it this way. If I find evidence that Isiah is guilty, then I give it to Adele and she works on helping him plead guilty, saving the city money on a trial. If I find he's innocent, then we can help the cops bring the real culprit to justice. Otherwise, your shop is liable to be robbed again."

Lisa shifted her eyes away from me and stayed quiet. I wasn't sure if she was considering what I said or was going to come back with another question. Worse yet, she could decide to kick me out of her office.

"It wasn't much of a burglary," Lisa said suddenly with force, causing me to sit up straighter. "Nothing was taken. The back door to the storeroom was opened. The cops think the lock was picked and the surveillance system was shut off. A wire was cut in the hallway disabling it. Then he came in and did whatever he did and left. I still can't find anything that was taken."

"No cash or items stolen?"

"No cash. If he stole something small like a whisk or a refrigerator magnet then I wouldn't notice, but who would steal something like that? It's like he broke in just to get in."

I had considered that already based on what Izzy had told me. Shop owners were having to replace locks and fix broken windowpanes so damage had been done. "Was it expensive to fix your video surveillance?"

"A few hundred dollars but my insurance company covered it. They were surprised nothing else had been stolen, so I think they were happy that's all it cost."

"This might seem like an odd question. Was anything left behind?"

Lisa squinted seeming unsure of what I meant. "You mean did the person who broke in leave evidence behind? The cops would know that."

"No, that isn't what I meant." I tried to find the words without leading her. "I've heard an item was left behind at another crime scene and was wondering if it happened to you, too."

Lisa bit her lip and turned her head to the side in thought. "I don't know if this is anything important. That morning when I got to the shop, I found a pink marble near the cash register. I didn't think anything of it but it was out of place. We don't have kids in the shop and it's not something we carry. I was the one who had closed the night before and definitely did not put it there or even see it there. But it was sitting right next to the cash register on the counter."

"What did you do with it?"

Lisa reached for a side drawer of her desk and slid it out. She fished her hand around inside until she got a smile on her face and then placed her hand palm up on the desk. Right in the center of her palm was a pink marble. "Is this important?"

"I don't know to be honest with you." I fixated my stare on the marble, wondering if they could have gotten prints from it. "I don't know its significance, but it's possible the person who broke in left it." I raised my eyes to hers. "Is there a reason you kept it?"

Lisa left the marble sitting on her desk. She leaned back in her chair.

85

"One of the women who worked for me noticed it while the cops were here. She thought it was odd and that was before I told her I didn't know anything about it. She slipped it into my desk after the cops left and I forgot it was there until you just mentioned it."

I looked down at the marble and back up at her. "Do you think I can take it with me?"

Lisa hitched her jaw forward. "I don't see why not. My employee mentioned it to the detective that was here and he didn't seem to care about it. Take it." As I stood to reach for it, I noticed a flyer on her desk. From what I could see reading upside down there was a community meeting scheduled for later this evening to discuss crime in the area.

Lisa caught me looking at it. "It's for business owners. You can't attend."

I remained standing as I sensed she was done speaking to me. I didn't want to press my luck in case I needed to ask her anything else later. "I think it's a good idea you meet to discuss crime in the area. Not only with the burglary that happened but other crimes that could occur. We need to ensure we live in a safe community."

Lisa raised her eyes to me and smirked. "Then maybe you shouldn't be working so hard to see the criminal go free."

"Lisa," I said my tone already getting away from me. "Do you know Isiah Wright?"

"No," she responded curtly.

"Has he ever been to your shop?" I was met with no response. "Have you heard of him before you were told he was arrested?" The same cold stare but no words were spoken. I put my hands on my hips. "Then I don't understand the animosity to someone accused of breaking in and doing no more than leaving a marble near your cash register. To my knowledge, Isiah Wright has never been seen on video. There are no fingerprints. He's never been found with stolen merchandise and he has an alibi for at least one of the burglaries."

I huffed loudly and turned for the door. I couldn't let it go though. I angled my body back to her. "I hope for your sake you're never accused of something you didn't do and the people around you rush to decide you're guilty with no evidence."

"He's a kid who doesn't belong around here," she said simply like I'd let it drop.

I leveled a look at her. "What are you, about fifty?" I said sarcastically, knowing from the report she was in her early forties. "You've had a chance to lead your life. Isiah is a kid, just barely turned eighteen. Something like this could ruin his entire life. The very least we can do is make sure he's guilty."

I turned on my heels and walked out of her office without looking back. She didn't call out to me either. I walked to the front part of the shop, smiled at the woman behind the counter and left the way I had come in. My heart raced and my hands were sweating, making it hard to hold onto the tiny marble. I had no idea why she had gotten me so keyed up, but I wasn't in the mood for any nonsense and all Lisa offered was nonsense.

I marched myself back to my house still annoyed at the exchange. As I walked up the driveway, Emma called from her house next door. She held her daughter Sophie by the hand and had her son propped on her narrow hip. We waved and she yelled from the front door asking if I had any gossip, which was code word for any updates on the case. I shook my head but promised I'd tell her when I learned anything. She promised the same.

Sophie held out her tiny arms and wanted to come over to my house to play. I hated telling her no so I promised that I'd bring her back a surprise. Her little face lit up and she bounced up and down while Emma frowned.

"Nothing that makes noise," she instructed and then shot me a look that told me I'd be dead if I even thought about it. She jostled the baby on her hip and then pulled Sophie back inside. I'd have to write myself a note to remember to pick Sophie up a little something. Otherwise, I'd forget and a four-year-old can be unforgiving.

I dropped the marble on my desk in my home office, fixed my hair, and swiped some gloss across my lips. I had twenty minutes before I had to be in Harper Ryan's office. That was enough time to drive downtown and park.

I pulled up the website for *Rock City Life*, where Harper worked, and scrolled to the masthead. This interview wouldn't be so bad after all. Staring back at me was my old boss – Dan Barnes. He had been the editor of the Little Rock newspaper when I first worked the crime beat. We were like oil and water and I missed him desperately. He was one of those people I lost track of after I moved from Little Rock and then returned.

Dan was one of the grumpiest people I'd ever worked with. He had threatened a few times to quit and go work for a publication that was far less stressful and more enjoyable. It looked like he carried through with the threat after I left. It would be great to see him. I hoped he could say the same.

CHAPTER 14

L uke drove while Tyler pulled up any information that he could find on the internet about Chance Bell. He had scoured social media for any nugget of information they could find. Since getting out of prison, Chance hadn't had any interaction with law enforcement until now. He had been a model community member, at least on the surface and in the public eye.

"He's got an Instagram page of photos from what looks like his property. There are a few sunsets, a vegetable garden, and some inspirational quotes. Not much else. He doesn't have a Facebook account that I can find, but I did stumble on what I think is his Twitter account. He's not going by his first name. He is listed as Prophet Bell."

"Sounds like him," Luke said as he took the turn off the main road to a side dirt road. There was no sign or name of the road. There was also nothing but tall fields of grass on each side. If a car was coming in the other direction one of them would have to pull to the side into the grass to let the other pass.

It had been a long time since Luke had come down this road. Memories of the day they had arrested Chance flashed in his mind. That day, Luke was far from alone. They had the FBI and DEA with them and had planned for an all-out firefight. Thankfully, the agents who stood back from the house and hid off in the high grass weren't needed. Chance had come peacefully, even if he had threatened them all with damnation. Luke had assured him at the time that he'd take his chances.

"Luke," Tyler said, drawing him out of the past. "It would seem Prophet Chance is back to his old tricks again at least on social media. He's preaching here about end times and has a website linked to Twitter where he's accepting donations and has several videos available with his content."

"Play one of them for me."

A few moments later, Prophet Chance's booming voice echoed throughout the car. He claimed to have a direct connection to spirits who were instructing him on what to do and say. He informed his listeners that the non-believers might shut him down and the government was out to get him to hide the truth. He went on to preach all sorts of things Luke had never heard in church or from Sunday school. It was the same thing Prophet Chance had preached before. Last time, there were guns and drugs and followers living with him on his compound. Now, he had an online platform and a broader reach.

Luke exhaled a breath and wished he were back in Italy with Riley. He angled his head to look at Tyler. "I've heard enough."

"Me, too." Tyler clicked the button on his phone and Chance's voice ceased. "He's a sick guy. I don't understand how he can have such a following."

"People want something to believe in, especially people who are going through a hard time themselves. Last time, Chance had several young women who didn't have family or friends. They floated from one place to the next kind of untethered. They were looking for something to believe in. They were looking for a new family. It's not dissimilar to the women who had taken up with Charles Manson. Some of them were from solidly middle-class backgrounds, but they had been kicked out of their homes or were dissatisfied with life in some way. There was no one watching out for them and they were vulnerable."

Luke pulled the car over to the side of the road in the weeds and put the car into park. He turned to Tyler and explained more. "Chance is a good-looking guy and he's charming. I'm not surprised someone like Holly Bell would have been attracted to him or married him even while in prison. On the surface, he seems normal. It's once you start pulling back the layers you start to see the red flags and by then it's too late. He's narcissistic and highly manipulative."

Tyler nodded in understanding. "What angle do you want to take today?"

"The crime scene unit should be along shortly and then we are going to have to get him to clear out. I'm hoping once he's out of the house, he'll be willing to speak to us. I don't even know what we are searching for inside the home. It's not like he's going to have a bloody blunt object laying around with Holly's DNA on it. Chance is smarter than that."

Luke heard the rumble of vehicles behind him and he turned his head to see the crime scene unit vans advancing. "I'll take the lead with Chance, just back me up."

Luke pulled his car back out in front of the line of vehicles and drove the rest of the way, playing over in his head the last interview he had done with Chance. He had been shut down before he had even gotten started, and they couldn't have a repeat of that now.

The large house came up quickly on the left side of the road. It looked like the same ramshackle Victorian that Luke had been in before. Not much had changed – it still needed a paint job or a power wash, the driveway had never been paved, and the car kicked up rocks as they drove over it. The large front tree had a tire swing attached to a rope that had long ago started to fray. The grass needed to be mowed, probably with something stronger than a push mower.

Luke's pulse quickened when the front door opened and Chance Bell stepped out into the sunshine before he even pulled the car to a stop. Chance had the same mop of brown curly hair and scruff on his face. Prison had only helped his physique. It looked to Luke like the man had gained about twenty pounds of muscle.

Tyler had noticed the same and whistled. "The dear prophet doesn't look like someone I'd want to go up against. He looks like he could hold his own in a fight."

Luke didn't respond because there was nothing to say. He put the car in park and cut the engine. He patted his gun on his hip and zipped up his bulletproof vest. He tapped his chest once. "Let's do this."

Luke got out of the car and met Tyler in the front. He flipped the clasp on his holster and put his hand on the top of his gun, not yet drawing it from its case. "Chance Bell," he said, his voice strong and even. "We have a warrant to search your home and your property."

A slow smile spread across the man's face as he lazily took one step after another down his porch. He opened his hands wide. "I assumed you'd be here sooner or later. Have a look around, Detectives. You'll see all is in order."

Chance hadn't recognized Luke yet or if he had he wasn't acknowledging it. Luke gave him more instructions and asked him to step away from the property. "Is there anyone else inside?"

"It's only me for now. Others will be here this afternoon for a lesson."

"Lesson?" Luke asked but feared the answer.

"I'm a prophet, Detective. I bring messages to the people. It's my life's destiny."

Luke bit his tongue. He nodded once and advanced toward the house, shouting instructions to the rest of the team. It was only when Luke got right up next to Chance that the man stepped back and appraised him.

When recognition took hold, Chance's jaw tightened. "You were the one who arrested me. I didn't think you'd still be working. I had foretold that the error of your ways would catch up to you. You're lucky that hasn't happened yet."

"Got a promotion, actually." Luke slapped the man on the back. "I guess not all your predictions come true. What are you – about zero for a hundred at this point? If I were you, I'd consider another line of work."

Tyler shifted his eyes to Luke and smirked, and then turned back to Chance. "This warrant covers all property here as well as electronics. Where can I find your computer? You've been doing some interesting online videos lately so we know you have a set-up for it."

Chance turned away from them, folding his arms over his chest. He walked out to the far corner of the driveway and sat on a tree stump.

"Guess he's not going to be helpful," Tyler said, looking at the man and back to Luke.

"I didn't expect him to be." Luke looked around at the crime scene investigators ready to search. He waved them in. "If you go through the place with them, I'll try to see if he'll talk to me."

Tyler wished Luke the best and then headed up the front porch stairs into the house. Luke took a deep breath and made his way over to Chance. He stopped a few feet from him and angled his head down to look at him.

"I'd like to speak to you while the search is going on." Luke waited for Chance to respond but he didn't say a word. He sat there with his legs folded under him and his hands splayed across his legs like he was some kind of Yogi mid-meditation. Chance's eyes were open, but he didn't seem to be focused on anything.

Luke wasn't put off. "I'm sorry about the loss of your wife. As you know, she was murdered Sunday in the early morning hours. Did she always go into work that early?"

Chance didn't move. He stayed in the same position, staring off into the distance. "Her shop isn't open on Sundays."

"Right," Luke said slowly. "But she was in the shop. What made her go into the shop so early?"

"Why would I know that?"

"You're her husband or at least that's what I was told."

"You know everything your wife does, Det. Morgan?"

It was the first time he had addressed Luke by name. "No, I don't know everything my wife does, but I'd certainly know if she left our bed on a Sunday morning headed to work on her day off. There'd be some kind of explanation."

"I never forced Holly to give me her schedule."

Luke took a frustrated breath. "Let's back up then. Did you know that Holly was going into work that morning?"

"Yes." Chance broke a smile and wagged his finger at Luke. "You're catching on."

It took everything Luke had not to reach down to the tree stump and lift him by his shirt and slam his fist into Chance's face. "Do you know why Holly went into work that morning?"

"No." Chance shrugged. "She might have said something about going through inventory."

"Where were you during this time?"

Chance opened his arms wide. "Here at home. I'm not interested in fashion."

"Can anyone corroborate that?" Luke wanted to outright ask him if he killed his wife, but he didn't want to shut down the conversation or antagonize him – just yet anyway.

Chance chuckled and raised his eyes to Luke. "You mean besides the dog and the cow?"

Luke nodded his head once and his fingers curled into a fist. His fingernails dug into his palms.

"Around eight I spoke to a few people online. My office was in the background. I'm sure if you spoke to them, they'd tell you."

Luke got their names and made a note in his phone. "What was your marriage like with Holly?"

Before Chance could answer, Luke's cellphone rang and he checked to see who was calling. He had hoped it was the medical examiner and he wasn't disappointed.

"I need to take this," Luke said to Chance before stepping away.

"I'm here," Luke said answering quickly.

"I've got the autopsy report ready for you." Ed Purvis paused for a moment and then explained, "I'm ruling it a homicide, which you knew. Blunt force trauma to the back of the head. It looks like it was a hammer and the clawed end of it at that. The approximate time of death is six-thirty. This was a personal attack and someone who had a good deal of rage for the victim."

The information didn't narrow Luke's suspect list in the slightest, but at least now they had the time of death and the murder weapon.

CHAPTER 15

I made it to downtown Little Rock in record time. I hit every green light along the way and didn't have to slow down for much of anything. I even found a spot to park with relative ease. I was lost in thought as I walked the few blocks to the *Rock City Life* magazine's office. I had zoned out and was lost in a myriad of thoughts when I heard my name from a familiar voice.

I stopped in my tracks and turned my head around until I spotted a familiar face. Dan Barnes stood in front of the office where I was heading. He hadn't changed a bit other than the smile that spread across his face when he waved. He never smiled at me before. Typically, his voice had been raised and there were threats of firing and banishment from the newspaper. It was good to see him happy. It made him look younger, too.

"Are you back in Little Rock causing trouble?" Dan asked, reaching to draw me into a hug.

I pulled back from the hug and flashed my ring finger at him. "I live here full time now."

Dan reached for my hand and checked out my engagement and wedding rings. "Oil tycoon?" he laughed. "No, let me guess. That detective you were dating who'd never give you an exclusive?"

"That's the one. He gave us exclusives all the time," I reminded him.

"You were too impatient. Luke needed to be drawn out slowly."

"I thought you left. Did he hunt you down in New York and drag you back kicking and screaming?"

"Nothing like that. I'm a private investigator now and a case brought me back. Luke and I reconnected after that."

Dan narrowed his eyes. "Are you the person Harper's meeting this afternoon?"

"My business partner, Cooper, said he scheduled it. I hope I'm not diverting you from work."

Dan waved me off. "I came downstairs to get us coffee from the deli. Do you want anything? I'll grab it and then we can catch up when you're done with Harper." I declined anything from the deli, and he held the door open for me while giving me directions to Harper's office.

Before I got to the top of the stairs, a woman who fit Harper's description appeared. She had long honey blonde hair, a trim figure, and a heart-shaped face. Her eyes were the most striking feature other than the pleasant smile. She waved me up with enthusiasm.

"I assume you're Riley," she said when I got to the landing. I confirmed and she led me through the open loft space to her office. She pointed to a chair that sat across from her desk. "Sit down. Get comfy. I'm not sure how I can help, but I'm happy to tell you anything I know."

I was struck by the quiet in the office. "I can't imagine Dan Barnes working here. He was my editor with the newspaper and he spent his day in chaos shouting at everyone. He threatened to fire me every day."

Harper sat down in the chair behind her desk. "He's threatened to fire me too, but that's usually because I bring trouble to the office."

Harper did not look like the kind of woman who brought trouble anywhere. When she spoke, I picked up the faint New York City accent. I assumed by how she carried herself she was from the upper east side. I asked her where she was from and Harper confirmed my suspicions.

"I'm from upstate. Troy," I explained.

"I know that area! I drove through frequently on my way into Vermont," Harper said. "Troy has also shown up in several movies." Harper was right. Troy's downtown streets were often used when filming movies set from the 1880s. The brownstones were authentic from that era. After a brief discussion about the movies filmed there, Harper got right down to business.

"Hattie mentioned to your investigative partner that I saw a woman outside of Bell & Bloom, but it's more than that. I heard Holly fighting with someone the morning she was killed," Harper said, and then she paused and relaxed back in her chair. "I try to run every morning and I was up early on Sunday. I couldn't sleep so I thought I'd clear my head. It was a little after six when I ran by her shop and heard raised voices. As I approached, I wasn't sure where it was coming from at first, but then as I passed by Bell & Bloom it was coming from inside."

"Did you stop and see what was going on?"

Harper shook her head. "In retrospect, I should have. I feel a bit guilty because maybe I could have prevented her murder. I didn't stop though because," Harper drew out the word and scrunched up her face, "I didn't care."

I didn't hide my surprise. "I heard Holly had some trouble in the neighborhood recently."

"It was more than trouble. She insulted every woman who wasn't a size six or below. Many of them are our readers. Dan and I discussed it and decided to drop her advertising in our magazine. We let her know about a week ago and she flipped out on us. She was down here screaming and yelling that we had no right to drop her and that she'd ruin *Rock City Life* if it was the last thing she did."

Knowing Dan, that didn't go over well. If anything, it would make him dig in deeper. "I'm assuming that didn't get Dan to change his mind."

Harper laughed. "You do know him. It didn't endear her to him at all." She watched me for a moment, I think trying to decide how much she could trust me or maybe how to phrase what she was going to say. Finally, Harper relaxed her posture and leaned her arms on her desk. "You were a reporter, so you get it. We had invited Holly here to talk about her post right after it first happened. We run an online edition of the magazine, too. Since her post caused such an uproar, we thought we'd write about it. I had hoped it was a misunderstanding that people took too far."

"Was it?"

"No," Harper said ruefully. "Holly meant every word and then some. Then she doubled-down. She asked us to stop running ads for stores that carried plus-sized clothing. She even went so far as to ask us to stop posting event photos that featured larger women. She specified women too, not men. As she put it, if women are fat, then they shouldn't have the luxury of wearing nice clothes or being featured in a magazine. Holly insisted we needed to change our content and turn down those advertising dollars because we were contributing to the problem."

I couldn't hide the shock on my face. Luke and I had been in a few photos once when the magazine covered an arts charity ball we had attended. I was probably one of the women that Holly referenced. "She went all in then."

Harper motioned like she was throwing a ball. "She went all in and way out to left field."

"What did Dan do?"

"He tried reasoning with her at first. That was more than I was willing to do," Harper admitted. "I was ready to kick her out, but I think Dan wanted to understand her perspective. When he couldn't get anywhere, Dan told her that she needed to leave and that we wouldn't be running a story about her, changing our advertising, or who we featured in the magazine."

I could tell by Harper's stern expression that it hadn't ended well, but I needed to know the details. "How'd Holly take it?"

"Even worse than I would have thought. She screamed all kinds of obscenities, said we were part of the problem, and then she even tried to take a swing at Dan."

My eyes got wide. "She tried to hit Dan? What did he do?"

Harper chuckled. "I shouldn't be laughing, but Holly missed and fell to the ground quite dramatically. She made a real show of it. After that, Dan and I walked into my office and closed the door. We let her tantrum herself out and then she left. I hadn't seen or heard from her again."

"Until Sunday morning."

"Right. Until that morning." Harper frowned and a worry line creased her forehead. "That's why when I heard her arguing with someone, I couldn't be bothered. As I said, I wasn't sure where the voices were coming from at first. When I figured out it was Holly's shop, I didn't even venture to look in the windows. I figured she had been hateful with the wrong person or she was still facing backlash from what she had done."

Harper certainly fit the mold of the thin attractive woman that Holly would have catered to. "Have you ever been in Bell & Bloom?"

"Twice before," Harper said. "They have some nice clothing, but the two times I was in there, it wasn't a comfortable experience. The first time, Holly screamed at her employee in front of a shop full of people. Really humiliated the young girl. The next time, I heard her telling a lovely woman that her hips were too big for a dress she had tried on and that she looked *hideous*." Harper stressed the word in a way I assumed Holly had.

"How did she stay in business?"

"I don't know." Harper threw her hands up for emphasis. "The woman Holly called hideous barely had hips at all. I don't know what Holly's issue was, but she attacked everyone for any tiny thing she perceived as a flaw. She was an equal opportunity hater."

"When did you see the woman in front of her shop?"

"The first time around all I heard were the angry voices. I'm fairly certain it was a woman. When I crossed Kavanaugh towards home on the way back from my run about thirty minutes later, I looked to make sure no cars were coming and that's when I saw a woman standing on the sidewalk. I can't be sure if she was in front of Holly's shop or down a little near Hattie's, but she was in the vicinity. I was about two short blocks away."

"Can you remember what the woman was wearing or what she looked like?"

Harper shook her head. "I'd probably know her if I saw her, but even at that, I was exhausted after my run and I only saw her for a few seconds. I barely even registered her standing there. I saw her and noted there was no traffic coming and took off running again."

"It may not even be connected," I said aloud but more to myself.

"Right," Harper agreed. "I had no idea at the time it would be important."

I asked Harper a few questions about Isiah Wright and she confirmed she hadn't seen him in the area that morning.

"He's a good kid," she said. "I hate what the cops are doing to him."

"That's the case that I'm involved in, but when Cooper heard that you might be a witness to the murder, he wanted me to check to make sure it wasn't Isiah."

"Definitely not. I'd swear to that in court. I don't even think he's the one who broke into Hattie's shop."

"Neither do I."

I reached into my pocket and pulled out one of Luke's business cards that I had grabbed earlier and handed it to Harper across her desk. "That's Det. Luke Morgan. He's in charge of the homicide investigation. He also happens to be my husband. I'm sure he'll want to speak to you to firm up the timing of what you heard and when, even if you can't identify anyone."

Harper took the card and looked at it. "Isn't it challenging to have to work at cross-purposes to your husband?"

"Luke's only been my husband for about a month, but yes. Challenging may not even be a strong enough word for it if we disagree." I thought back to some earlier cases where Luke and I had gone head-to-head. In truth, I was more difficult to work with if my mind was made up about something. I told Harper as much.

"We are too much alike. It must be the New Yorker in us." Harper set the business card near the phone on her desk. Then she leaned to the side to look out her doorway then leaned into the desk. "Tell me all the good gossip about Dan. He's such a closed book. Was he as bad at dating then as he is now?"

"Dan date? I can't even imagine it." We both giggled like kids. I relaxed back in my chair and Harper and I shared stories about growing up in New York, the challenges of living in the south, and funny stories about Dan.

CHAPTER 16

L uke hung up after speaking to Purvis and turned around to see Chance staring at his back. He shoved his phone into his pocket and walked over to where Chance remained sitting on the tree stump. Luke stood with his hands on his hips ready to pounce. He was done playing games.

"What time did Holly leave on Sunday morning?"

Chance opened his mouth then thought better of whatever quippy annoying thing he was about to say. "About five-thirty."

"Was she stopping anyplace first before going to the shop?"

"Not that I know of." Chance looked away as he answered the question.

Luke knew there was something he was holding back. "You said you were online at eight. What about before then?"

"I woke up when Holly got up. We had coffee together in the kitchen and when she left, I went back to bed. I got up about seven and got ready for my meeting online at eight."

"Can anyone confirm what you did from five-thirty to eight?"

Chance raised his eyes to Luke. "I was here alone."

"Did you go online during those hours, make any calls or texts?" Luke pressed.

"I was mainly asleep, Det. Morgan." Chance stood and smiled at Luke. "I guess our chess match continues."

Luke stepped toward him and got in the man's face enough to make Chance step back. "Did you kill your wife?"

Chance smirked. "If I did, do you think I'd admit it, especially to you? I wouldn't give you the satisfaction."

Luke didn't rise to the taunt. "What did you think of the comments your wife made recently that caused her a good deal of backlash?"

"Holly and I were similar in our beliefs if that's what you're asking. Those who are not leading a healthy and appropriate lifestyle should be shamed for it until they make a change."

"Appropriate?" Luke asked, putting the word in air quotes. "Who determines that?"

Chance looked Luke up and down. "If you have to ask the question, you are woefully out of step. I told you before you'd be paying for your behavior. I can only imagine it's coming soon."

Luke stepped toward him again. "You then? You and Holly determine what's appropriate for everyone else – is that what you're saying?"

He shrugged. "There are those of us who have been given gifts to help others get on the right path and then there are others, like you, who will never understand."

"What's your deal, man?" Luke asked, his voice tinged with anger. "Do you even know what you believe? I could understand if you were out here quoting the Bible or rambling on about the devil. I could wrap my mind around it if you thought you were some guru life coach or spiritually enlightened."

Chance didn't respond to Luke's tirade, which only spurred him on. "You're none of those things. You are a middle-aged loser who doesn't want to get a real job who thinks he's better than everyone else and is out to prove it to the world. You're all about feeding that ego because you are desperately insecure. That's what I remember most about the last time we met – the stink of insecurity and desperation for someone to pay attention to you at all costs."

Luke's heart thumped in his chest so loudly he could hear it pounding in his ears. He turned to walk toward the house and then stopped himself and spun back around. He pointed his finger at Chance. "Let me tell you this. If you killed Holly, I'm going to make sure you spend your life rotting in a cell. If I find out you are abusing any more young women..." Luke didn't finish his thought. He stopped himself in time before he went so far as to threaten bodily harm to a suspect.

Chance stood there smirking at Luke and then he brought his hands up in a slow clap. "Excellent, Detective. That's some real emotion you have there. Do you feel better?"

Luke didn't know how much longer he could control his temper. He rocked back and forth, willing himself to turn around and go into the house. He knew nothing good would come of pounding Chance into the pavement. Then all of a sudden, Luke felt a hand on his shoulder. "Come into the house with me," Tyler said, pulling Luke back. "There is something I need to show you." He squeezed Luke's shoulder and pulled him again.

"I'm coming," Luke said, shrugging him off. He locked eyes with Chance again and then turned and walked toward the house. As they got to the porch steps, he angled his head to look at Tyler. "What do you need to show me?"

"I found Holly's cellphone folded into a sweater in her closet. I turned it on and you need to read the text messages." Tyler explained the explicit nature of the messages. It seemed Holly was texting with a guy named Jason several times a day.

"Didn't you find her cellphone at the scene?" Luke asked.

"We found one of them. I guess she had two." Tyler punctuated each word as he spoke. "If having an affair wasn't bad enough, Holly was having an affair with a married man, which means there's a wife out there probably none too pleased with her."

"If she knows," Luke added. "We don't know that she knows."

Tyler entered the house first and held the door open for Luke. He grabbed the phone from the coffee table and handed it to Luke after he snapped on gloves. "The wife knows. A few weeks back, Jason said his wife saw their text messages and she accused him of having an affair with Holly. She said she'd make both of them pay."

Luke looked down at the phone and scrolled to the beginning of the thread. It went back several months. Tyler was right that the texts quickly turned sexual and referenced several sexual encounters between them. There were also messages detailing the level of lying and sneaking around they each had to do to meet up. Luke didn't read every text but skimming through he saw enough.

Luke got to the end of the thread and noted the date. "The messages end about a week ago."

"I figured maybe since the wife found out they broke it off."

"That's possible and certainly adds them both as potential persons of interest." Luke handed him back the phone and then leaned in and said quietly, "Purvis called and said that the murder happened at approximately six-thirty Sunday morning. Holly was struck on the back of the head with the claw end of a hammer. There were several blows. Find a hammer around here?"

"Not in here, but there is a barn with several items the crime scene techs said they were processing through." Tyler looked uncertain if he should say what was on his mind but he did so anyway. "What did Chance say? It looked tense when I went out there."

"I'm glad you came out when you did," Luke said sighing. "I was close to doing something stupid. I don't know what it is about that guy that makes me lose my cool so easily. There aren't many suspects who get me like that."

"I felt it, too. There's something about him. When have you

ever known me to lose my temper with a suspect?" Tyler asked. It was a rhetorical question because there wasn't one time Luke could remember. "I'd like about ten minutes alone with him with no witnesses. I can't even believe he's out of prison."

"Most of his followers wouldn't testify against him. There were a handful who stood by him during the trial and then most scattered as soon as his hold was broken." Luke rubbed his bald head and then ran a hand down his face. "We can't get distracted by him though. It's easy to lose focus around him."

Luke's phone buzzed and he pulled it out to read the text. It was Riley who said she had a witness who heard fighting from Holly's shop and could pinpoint timing the morning of the murder. He showed Tyler the text. "This might be as good a lead as any."

"Ask her what time the witness heard fighting."

Luke sent off the text and Riley responded almost immediately. "A little after six. That's right around the time of death." Luke and Riley sent a volley of text messages back and forth and she explained the entire interview to him. When they were done, Luke put his phone back in his pocket. "The witness, Harper Ryan, had a previous history with the victim and her aunt's shop is right near Holly's."

Tyler raised his eyebrows. "Are you sure Harper wouldn't be a suspect?"

"Riley said no. Harper is with *Rock City Life* magazine and Dan Barnes who runs the magazine corroborated Harper's version of events. Besides, she came forward with the info." Luke didn't love Riley meddling around in his case, but she wasn't often wrong about a person's character. "Let's go confront Chance about his cheating wife and then let's talk to this witness."

Tyler followed Luke out but stopped on the porch. "I need to tell the crime scene techs to bag and tag every hammer they find. We'll want to get them back to the lab and run tests for blood. Are you good talking to Chance on your own?"

Luke swallowed hard. "Go ahead. I got this."

Luke watched Tyler walk off toward the barn and then he made his way down to Chance. The man leaned back on the tree stump with his face up toward the sunshine. "We need to talk," Luke said, his voice strained.

"Try to control yourself this time, Detective, or I might need to call my lawyer."

Luke rubbed the back of his neck and locked eyes with Chance. "What do you know about your wife's affair?"

"It wasn't an affair." Chance stood and was eye to eye with Luke. "This may be too hard for you to understand, but we had an open marriage. We are not meant to be monogamous people. My wife was free to have sex with whomever she chose."

"Why was Holly hiding a cellphone then? We found it rolled up in a sweater." Luke watched as Chance had the slightest flutter in his eyes. He hadn't known about the affair. More games. More posturing.

Luke pressed on. "I would think if you knew about Holly's involvement with other men and you were okay with it, she wouldn't have to hide it. Why not use her regular cellphone?"

Chance had no answer for that. He remained still and quiet for once. Luke enjoyed making the man squirm, but he didn't enjoy that Chance seemed genuinely surprised about the affair. If he killed his wife, that wasn't the motive.

"How about you, Chance, who were you seeing outside of your marriage?"

Chance tightened his jaw so hard Luke wondered if the man was going to break his teeth. "I don't have to answer your questions."

"No, you don't." Luke took a step back. "It's okay, Chance. Don't tell me. I'm going to find out though and once I do, I'll be back. You and I aren't done talking."

As Chance sat back down looking deflated, Luke walked to the barn to help Tyler wrap up the search.

CHAPTER 17

C ooper found Colonel Jackson Morris raking his front lawn. Fall had descended on the south late that year and lawns were a blanket of brightly colored leaves. Cooper pulled his truck to a stop at the curb and looked over at the man. Jackson wasn't as tall as Cooper had imagined and he had a slight softness to his body that indicated a few years out of the military. He still looked like he could handle himself in a fight though.

Cooper got out of his truck and walked to the edge of the lawn. He introduced himself and Jackson asked if he'd like to go inside to talk or sit on the wide front porch that wrapped around the house.

"Porch is fine," Cooper said.

Jackson dropped the rake into a small pile of leaves and walked up onto the porch with Cooper in tow. Before sitting, Jackson offered him something to drink and Cooper declined.

"Hattie mentioned you wanted to speak to me about Izzy." Jackson kicked his legs out in front of him and wiped his forehead with a handkerchief he had pulled from his pocket.

"I do," Cooper confirmed and found himself staring at the man who had a pleasant face and an affable smile. He seemed relaxed and comfortable.

Jackson patted his belly. "Not what you imagined when you heard Army Colonel, right?"

Red flushed Cooper's face. "I'm sorry. When Hattie told me that you were a Colonel, I flashed to every military movie I ever saw and I was expecting Jack Nicholson."

"We get that a lot." Jackson laughed and his smile was infectious. Cooper relaxed into his chair. "I'm retired so I've had a few years to mellow out. I've also had far too many of Hattie's treats."

"There's something about her, isn't there?" Cooper found himself asking even though he had no idea why he'd confide in a stranger. "I was kind of freaked out going to her shop, but then she made me feel at home the moment I saw her."

"Hattie does that. She did it to me, too. There's a kindness about her – mothering you didn't even know you needed."

Cooper was surprised that Jackson had articulated so well what he had been feeling but hadn't been able to put his finger on. His mother had passed when he was a baby and while he had a series of unfortunate stepmothers, he had never felt connected to a mom.

"How do you know Izzy?" Cooper asked, changing the subject.

"From the neighborhood here. I saw Izzy about a week after they moved in. He was out front and I walked over to say hello. He seemed surprised that I'd go out of my way to speak to him. He said he hadn't had the best reception from others in the neighborhood."

"He came right out and told you that?"

"I'm abbreviating our conversations but that's the gist of it," Jackson admitted, crossing his legs at his ankles and leaning back into the chair. "The kid seemed down to me and I asked what was wrong. Like all boys his age, he wasn't keen on admitting his feelings, but I told him I understood what it's like being an outsider in a new place and he started to open up."

"You became friendly after that?"

Jackson nodded. "As I'm sure you know, his mother travels for work and his dad works a lot at the hospital. He seemed…" Jackson paused as if searching for the right word, "lonely, I guess. Eventually, he told me that he wasn't fitting in and the neighborhood guys were giving him a hard time. He asked me what he should do about it. In the end, it didn't sound like there was anything Izzy could have done. Scott Sawyer is a bully. I've seen him around the neighborhood. His dad's a detective so he has an attitude that he can do whatever he pleases."

"Is that true?" Cooper asked and when he realized Jackson wasn't sure what he meant, he rephrased. "I want to know if it's true that Scott could do whatever he wanted without repercussion."

"It seemed that way. He's caused a good deal of trouble in the neighborhood from stealing holiday decorations off people's porches and toilet-papering trees in front yards to more serious things like smashing Izzy's car window."

"Izzy said that you saw that happen."

"I did," Jackson said evenly. "It was close to ten in the evening. I had the front windows open because there was a nice breeze blowing in. I heard kids' voices first and didn't think anything of it. They were loud and it was late so I wondered, but it was a nice night. I figured they were out taking a walk or something. A few minutes later, I heard glass breaking. I ran to the porch and Scott was standing by Izzy's car. I got out to the front lawn fast enough to see him run up the road and meet up with another friend of his."

"Were they both involved in breaking the window?" Cooper asked, thankful to have confirmation for Izzy.

"I don't see how the other kid could be involved." Jackson pointed down the road toward the end of the block. "From the time I heard glass breaking and the time I got out here, it was a matter of seconds and that kid was clear down the road. I'm not saying he wasn't part of the plan. But no, smashing that window, the act of it, that was all Scott. He looked pleased with himself. He didn't seem to care that he might be in trouble."

Cooper had never met Scott. Had never even seen a picture of him, but he knew the kind of kid he was. Cooper had dealt with guys like that while growing up. "Did you make a police report?"

Jackson sighed deep and frustrated. "Izzy came out of the house right away and I told him we should call the police. He didn't want to. He said it would make things worse for him. All he cared about was that I explained to his father what had happened. Izzy didn't want to be blamed for doing something wrong."

There was something about Jackson's tone that told Cooper there was more. "I'm assuming you didn't let it go at that."

Jackson shook his head. "I couldn't. I heard him break the window and saw him. I had known what was happening between Izzy and Scott. I wasn't going to let it go. I told Dr. Wright what had happened and he assured me Izzy wasn't going to be in any trouble. Then I spoke to Scott's father, Lou Sawyer." Jackson looked over at Cooper and the look on his face said it all. "He defended Scott and told me that I hadn't seen things correctly. He said I was trying to get his son in trouble and that it was Izzy who was causing the trouble between the boys. Lou said he wouldn't have been surprised if Izzy had broken the window himself."

Cooper understood parents sticking up for their kids but Sawyer went too far. "How could he say that given you saw Scott there?"

Jackson let out a rueful chuckle. "He got in my face and told me since I was black that I'd stick up for Izzy and that we had probably cooked up this little scheme to get Scott in trouble."

"What did you do?"

Jackson tugged at the corner of his pants. "I didn't go with my instinct and lay the man out on the pavement. I walked away and went back to Izzy to try to convince him to make a police report. I had taken photos of his car that night and with my statement, he had a solid case. Izzy refused and told me to drop it."

Cooper hoped against hope that Jackson had saved the photos. "Is it too much to ask to see the photos?"

Jackson pulled his phone out of his pocket and scrolled through his phone. Cooper's heart raced with excitement when Jackson handed him the phone. Cooper stared down at the first image and then scrolled to the following ones. Not only had Jackson captured the broken window and glass all over the ground, but the first photo he took showed Scott walking away.

"How did you get this photo?" Cooper asked, not containing his excitement.

"I figured I might need it at some point, and I wanted proof it was Scott."

Cooper handed him back the phone. "Did you show Lou Sawyer this photo?"

"He denied that was his son. Then he accused me of photoshopping it." Jackson pushed himself upright in the seat. He looked over to Cooper with a seriousness in his eyes. "I'm not saying this was a racial thing. I'm not saying that Scott was doing all this because Izzy is black. I know Izzy feels this way, but Scott seems like an equal opportunity offender. There was a new kid in the neighborhood and Scott took advantage."

Hattie had told Cooper something similar. The motive didn't matter to Cooper. He cared that he had confirmed part of Izzy's story. "Can you send me those photos? Please don't delete them. We may need them for court."

Jackson agreed and added Cooper's number to his phone and then texted the photos to him. "What's going to happen to Izzy? I have no proof either way, but I can't believe that he broke into Hattie's shop."

"I don't believe it either. We have an alternative suspect in mind and we are going to prove that it was him. Your information today is a start in the right direction."

Jackson turned to Cooper. "You think it was Scott who did this?" "Scott and some friends. Izzy saw Scott leaving one of the shops one night. What we know and what we can prove are two different things right now." Jackson nodded. "I'll keep my eyes out. If there is anything I can do to help, let me know."

Cooper stood and reached out to shake Jackson's hand. "You've helped more than you know. Those photos will be important in court. I'm hoping it doesn't get that far, but if we can establish a history of harassment that might explain how Izzy's watch ended up in Hattie's shop."

Jackson turned in the direction of Izzy's house. "Go down a block and the second house past the side street on the right you'll find Nolan Smith. He's a good kid, not involved with Scott. He's been around enough to see how Izzy is treated by the boys. He also played basketball with them all so he might have some interesting things to say."

Cooper thanked him for the tip and promised he'd call Jackson if he needed anything else. He set out on foot toward the house that Jackson had pointed out. Cooper checked his watch and was surprised to see that he had been talking to Jackson for more than an hour and it was now nearing three. At least, at this hour Nolan might be home from school.

Cooper got to the house and stepped up on the wide front porch. Someone had lined the steps with baskets of fresh fall flowers. He reached out his hand to use the brass doorknocker but never got a chance. The door opened and he stood face to face with a young man who had a mess of sandy brown hair and was close to Cooper's height.

"Are you Nolan Smith?" When the young man said yes, Cooper introduced himself.

Nolan shoved his hands in his pockets. "What do you want?"

"I want to speak to you about Isiah Wright."

Nolan stuck his head out of the door and looked up and down the street. Then he stepped back inside out of sight. He gestured for Cooper to enter the house. "Hurry up before someone sees you."

CHAPTER 18

"Let's sit in the family room. My parents won't be home for a while," Nolan said, leading Cooper through the house to a family room adjacent to the kitchen. He grabbed the remote control off the coffee table and turned down the volume on the television and then dropped the remote with enough force that Cooper wondered if he had broken it.

Nolan flopped down on the couch and then looked up at Cooper. "I'm not sure my parents would be happy if you were here so let's make this quick."

Cooper wasn't in the mood to deal with angry parents. "I understand you know Isiah Wright?"

"Yeah, I know Izzy. He lives down the street." Nolan looked away. "I heard he got arrested for breaking into those shops."

"He did and I'm helping his defense attorney." Cooper sat down next to him on the couch. "I thought you might have some information that could help me."

"Help you how?"

"I need to know what you know about Izzy."

"Are you asking me if I think he broke into those shops?"

"I'm asking if you know anything about Izzy and what you know about the burglaries."

"I don't think Izzy did it." Nolan tugged at strands of hair on his forehead. "I can't say anything more though."

The way he said it, Nolan knew more. Cooper challenged him. "You can't because you don't know anything or you know things and won't say? There's a difference."

"I can't say because I'm a dead man if I do." Nolan pushed himself up from the couch and stood near the fireplace. He tapped on the mantel with his fist. When he turned back to Cooper, it was obvious how conflicted he was. "I just can't. I wish I could but…"

"You can," Cooper insisted. "Izzy's life hangs in the balance here. If he goes to prison for something he didn't do, that's his life. If he's convicted, he will serve a lot of prison time."

Nolan wouldn't meet Cooper's eyes. "That's the same for anyone who committed the crime."

Cooper stood and took a step toward Nolan. "Right, but at least the right person should go to prison. You're talking about the difference between justice served and a grave injustice. No one should have to go to prison for the actions of another. I understand you don't want to get anyone in trouble. I'm sure you're worried about your friends."

Nolan shook his head. "They aren't my friends."

"Then give me something," Cooper pleaded. "Give me a direction to go in."

Nolan stood silent and shook his head.

Cooper cursed. They were right on the edge of something, he could feel it. "Let's start with something easier then. Tell me about your interactions with Izzy."

Nolan raised his eyes to Cooper. "He's a good guy. I don't know him that well. He only moved here a few months back. I know he's had some trouble fitting into the neighborhood. Izzy has other friends though from his school."

Cooper stepped away from Nolan and sat back down on the couch. He hoped giving Nolan physical distance might take off a little pressure. "Have you spent time with him?"

"A little here and there. We play basketball in the park a couple of streets over. Izzy's a solid player so I've had him on my team a few times."

"Have you spent time with him otherwise?"

Nolan shook his head. "Izzy isn't around much. There hasn't been much of a chance for us to hang out."

Cooper clasped his hands on his knees. He needed to push now but hoped Nolan didn't back off again. "What do you know about Izzy's interactions with Scott Sawyer?"

Nolan rubbed the back of his neck, leaving his hand to linger there. "It's more like Scott's interactions with Izzy."

"What does that mean?"

"Izzy doesn't want anything to do with Scott. He seems to avoid Scott at all costs, which only enrages him more. He told me he wants to take Izzy down for disrespecting him." Nolan left his position holding up the mantel and joined Cooper on the couch. "I don't think Izzy wants to fight. He doesn't do much to protect himself."

"Has it ever gotten physical?"

"Once on the basketball court, but Izzy didn't hit him back. He grabbed his stuff and left. Scott and a couple of the other guys called him a coward for not fighting back. I don't know if he is or not. You could tell how angry Izzy was, but he wouldn't throw a punch."

He was angry or embarrassed enough he hadn't mentioned the fight to anyone. "How long ago did that take place?"

"About two weeks ago. I told Scott he had to lay off him. Izzy never did anything to Scott. I just think they are two different guys who don't get along. I don't know exactly what Scott's problem is though."

Cooper had several questions but he had a hunch. "Did Izzy leave anything behind the day of the fight?"

Nolan rubbed his jaw and then slowly nodded. "His watch. He had taken it off when he started playing. We found it in the grass when we were cleaning up. It had his name engraved on the back."

Cooper tried to make his voice even like he wasn't excited, but inside his stomach churned and his heart beat louder. "Did Scott take Izzy's watch?"

"No. Jimmy Ragone who lives over near the court took it. He said he'd bring it back to Izzy."

"Are you sure he did that?"

Nolan sat still for a moment and then said, "I can't be sure. I assume he did. Izzy never came looking for it. I figured once he got home he'd realize he left it behind. I assumed Jimmy gave it back because Izzy never asked me about it."

"Did Izzy ever go back to the court to play ball with all of you?"

"No." His voice tight, he said, "I honestly didn't think much of it. Jimmy's a good guy. He never had a problem with Izzy so if he didn't return it, I couldn't tell you why or what he did with it."

"Could Scott have asked for it?"

Nolan shrugged. "Anything is possible, but Jimmy saw the fight, too. I can't imagine he'd give it to Scott. You'd have to ask him though."

"I will." Cooper asked Nolan for Jimmy's phone number and address. "How close of a friend is he to Scott?"

"We're all friends. Most of us have been living in this neighborhood since we were little. I think I met Scott and Jimmy when I was five. We all go to school together, too. We aren't best friends, but we see each other all the time."

"It's possible Jimmy gave the watch to Scott then?"

"Anything's possible." Nolan narrowed his gaze. "Is there a reason this is important?"

"The watch was found at one of the crime scenes. It's what directly connects Izzy to the break-ins. It's the only thing. If you're telling me you know that Izzy lost his watch two weeks ago and other people had it and you can't confirm he got it back, then that helps exonerate Izzy."

"And blames Jimmy…" Nolan said, his voice trailing off.

"Not necessarily. I have no reason right now to believe Jimmy was involved in anything."

"I don't think he is," Nolan said sharply. He must have thought better of it because he relaxed back into the couch. "I don't know what Jimmy is involved with. I'm just saying he's a good guy and don't think he'd do anything wrong."

Nolan's tone was so casual that it sparked Cooper's curiosity. He wasn't going to push his luck though right now. "Let's just sum this up. You know for sure Izzy left his watch at the basketball court about two weeks ago and Jimmy was going to bring it back to him. You cannot confirm if the watch made it back to Izzy."

Nolan nodded. "That's about right."

He needed Nolan to make a sworn statement and he wasn't sure the young man would do that. He wasn't going to press the issue right now though. "Have you heard Scott talk about the burglaries?" Nolan looked away, which answered the question for Cooper. "Let me rephrase. What has Scott told you about the break-ins?"

Nolan still didn't meet Cooper's gaze. He looked down at his hands instead. "Scott said it was probably Izzy robbing those stores. He said that Izzy moved into the neighborhood and suddenly there's crime happening here. He said it made sense."

"Does it make sense to you?" Cooper asked, trying and failing to control the anger that seeped into his tone.

"No, sir, it doesn't," Nolan said, his voice stronger now. "I know Izzy didn't break into those shops. He wouldn't do something like that. All Izzy cares about is getting a scholarship to college. He wouldn't do anything to mess that up. Besides, he's afraid of his father."

"Afraid?" Cooper asked.

"Maybe afraid isn't the right word. Dr. Wright is strict and Izzy said all the time that his dad didn't want him to get involved in anything stupid. Izzy never drank with us. He didn't get high with us. He didn't do anything wrong, ever. If Scott started a fight with me, I'd have hit him back. Izzy walked away. I think that's partly why Scott hates him so much. Izzy never joined in. He acted better than everyone. I knew though that wasn't it. He was scared of disappointing his father."

"That's a pretty good reason to make good choices."

"Yeah, but Scott's dad is a cop so he gets away with everything."

"I've heard that." Cooper inched forward a little on the couch. "Do you know who broke Izzy's car window?"

Nolan raised his eyebrows. "You know about that?"

"I do and I also heard Scott is the one who broke it."

"I didn't see it happen, but that's what I heard. I heard Izzy told Scott's dad. I think that's why Scott started the fight on the basketball court."

Cooper held his finger up for Nolan to wait as he mentally connected the dots. "The window happened before the fight?"

"A few weeks before," Nolan confirmed. "Scott didn't get in any trouble so I don't know why he was so angry. He said that Izzy went to his house and ratted him out like a baby, but that Mr. Sawyer denied it was Scott. He was bragging about getting away with it so I know it was him."

Cooper remembered being their age and the worst thing you could be was a rat. "Izzy wasn't the one who told Scott's father. It was another neighbor who had a photo of Scott right after the act. Izzy didn't want the cops called. He protected Scott if anything."

"That's not the way Scott told it."

"I'm sure it's not," Cooper said not hiding the disgust in his voice. "I know you're hesitant but we need to talk about the break-ins. You said you know Izzy didn't do it so who did? You said they aren't your friends so you have no reason to protect them."

"I'm not protecting them. I'm protecting myself. If I tell you what I know, I'm a dead man. It's not worth the risk."

Cooper reached his hand out and put it on the young man's shoulder. He never got to say more though because a door in the back of the house creaked and Cooper heard a woman's voice in the hallway.

"Your mother?"

"You should go."

"Is there anything you want to say before I go?"

"Nothing else."

Cooper pulled a business card out of his pocket and handed it to him. "Call me if you think of anything."

Nolan shoved the business card into the pocket of his jeans and shifted his eyes toward the hall.

Cooper got up, shook Nolan's hand, and made a beeline to the front door, stopping only long enough to look into the hall to make sure Nolan's mom wasn't standing there. When the coast was clear, Cooper hurried to the front door and stepped outside before he was seen.

Cooper didn't understand why Nolan's mother would care that he was there, but it wasn't for him to dig into that right now. As Cooper hit the sidewalk, Nolan called his name. He looked over his shoulder to see the young man standing on the porch just outside the front door.

"The break-ins aren't what they seem. There's a reason for them. Dig deeper." Nolan disappeared back into the house without saying another word or giving Cooper a chance to ask a question.

Cooper watched the door of the house close but couldn't turn away. He repeated Nolan's words over and over again. *There's a reason for them. Dig deeper.*

Cooper had no idea what Nolan meant but had no choice but to go back to his truck and let the words stew. Cooper climbed into the driver's seat and punched the steering wheel in frustration. He wasn't even sure what he was dealing with anymore.

He pulled his phone out of his pocket and texted Riley. *When can we meet?*

CHAPTER 19

Dugan's Pub was a staple in my household. Luke and I had dinner there at least a couple of times a month. Sometimes on a Saturday we'd make our way downtown and sit on the patio eating fattening pub food, drinking beer, and watching a game on the outdoor television.

As I entered, I waved hello to a bartender and took a table in the far dining room near the fireplace. It hadn't been lit yet but the ambiance was enough for me today. I sat down, didn't need to see the menu because I had long ago memorized it, and ordered a soda when the server stopped by. I ordered one for Cooper as I knew he wouldn't be drinking a beer in the late afternoon.

Cooper arrived as our sodas were dropped off. He pulled out the chair and dropped himself in it. He checked his watch. "Too early for a beer," he said more to himself than me.

I pointed to the soda. "I ordered you a Coke." I was about to launch into an update about meeting with Harper, but Cooper's face constricted and I knew whatever he had to say was far more important. "The floor is yours," I said with a wink.

"I don't even know where to start." Cooper leaned back in his chair. He gave me a quick overview of his meetings earlier in the day. "Everything Izzy said checked out. Hattie indicated she was closer to Izzy than he told us but that makes sense. I can see why a young guy wouldn't want to tell us that he chats with his psychic neighbor regularly."

"How was she?" I knew that Cooper hated all things metaphysical.

"I'm still processing. She's sweet and credible. I'll leave it at that." Cooper took a sip of his soda while I digested that he called a psychic credible. "Jackson, the neighbor, told me to speak to a kid named Nolan who lives down the street. That's where it got interesting."

The server interrupted to take our order and then she cleared out, probably sensing the serious conversation. Once she was gone, Cooper said, "Nolan confirmed a few things for me including that Izzy left his watch on the basketball court, which blows Det. Sawyer's case right out of the water. If he can't confirm that Izzy had his watch and we can prove he lost it before that break-in, he's got no case. Nothing else ties Izzy to the crimes."

That was important information, but I sensed something else was eating at him. "I assume that's not all."

"Nolan didn't want his parents to know that I was speaking to him, so I had to leave when his mother came home. As I got to the sidewalk, Nolan popped his head out of the front door to tell me that the burglaries are not what they seem. There is a purpose for them and we should dig deeper." Cooper sat back and stared at me across the table. "Any idea what that means?"

The *more* was probably what hadn't been making sense to me about the break-ins from the start. I took a sip of my soda and thought about what it could mean. I didn't know any more than Cooper did.

"The break-ins never quite made sense to me," I admitted. "Nothing is stolen outside of items that are cheap and meaningless. Izzy thought it was a game, but that's a risky game to play with no reward – other than being able to say you broke into a shop and didn't get caught. Even then the risk far outweighs the reward."

"Right. I thought that, too. That's why it makes sense that we are

126

missing something."

Sometimes the best thing Cooper and I could do was spitball ideas, even if they made little sense. It was why I liked working with him so much.

"Let's take what we know first." I counted off on my fingers the facts we had. "We know the break-ins occur late in the evening based on what Izzy said. It's well after hours for these shops. The Heights closes down relatively early though. I think everything on the street is closed and locked up by eight or nine, except maybe one or two bars that haven't been burglarized. We know nothing of real value is taken and security systems are cut or shut off. We know the majority of those shops have been hit at this point. They break glass usually to get in or jimmy the lock on the doors from the alleyway. No prints have been found and no suspects other than Izzy."

Cooper tapped on the table. "Do we know why, after the first few, no cops were patrolling the area or doing some surveillance?"

I shrugged. "I wasn't here when they started. Do you know for a fact that the cops didn't do any preventive watches?"

"No, I don't. I assumed," Cooper admitted. "Do we know if someone would have to have any tech know-how to cut the surveillance?"

"I would assume so. I think we need to explore that avenue more. Maybe there is more behind cutting the surveillance. Could it be that's why they are breaking in?"

"Just to cut the surveillance?" Cooper asked with a skeptical look on his face. "Why bother?"

"I don't know." It was starting to feel like we had far more questions than answers. "What do these shops have in common?"

"They are small and mostly cash-driven. All are locally-owned, have small staff, and are frequented most by people who live close by given the walking distance from the local neighborhood. They're not on the main road so you're not getting heavy drive-by traffic."

I hadn't considered that. "That's true. You have to know those shops are there to turn off the main road to get to them."

"They aren't the kind of shops that have too much in value to steal. Their cash flow is smaller than, say, a department store in the mall."

"Probably easier to break into though," I countered and Cooper agreed. "Let's set aside that stealing anything is the motive. You said someone left a marble on Hattie's desk and the shop owner of the kitchen store told me she found a marble near the cash register. What's that about?"

Before Cooper could answer, the server dropped off our burgers and fries and asked if we needed anything else. We told her we were all set and then dug into the food. After finishing a bite, Cooper asked, "You think the marbles are more than a coincidence?"

I dabbed a fry in ketchup. "I think it's more than a coincidence if it's more than two. One probably doesn't mean anything. Two is interesting and three tells me there has to be meaning behind it."

"We are going to have to talk to all the shop owners," Cooper said with a grimace.

"We are going to have to speak to them anyway. I want to learn more about each of their surveillance systems and what it would take to shut them off."

"This whole case is so weird."

"At least we know Izzy is telling us the truth."

Cooper threw his napkin down on the table. "He's not though. He's holding back. Nolan told me about a fight Izzy had with Scott. Izzy never told us anything like that had ever occurred."

There was a tinge of hurt in Cooper's voice. He took it personally when our clients didn't trust him. It had been a while since we worked with someone as young as Izzy though.

"You know kids, Cooper. They take time to warm up to people. Izzy has had a lot of change, and it sounds like his dad is hard on him.

I don't think Dr. Wright would be happy to know his son was in a physical altercation. Give Izzy time. He'll warm up to us once we prove ourselves. I'll stop by today and ask him about the watch."

Cooper stared down at his bacon cheeseburger as if trying to decide if what he had to say was more important than a mouthwatering bite. He chose the food. We both ate in silence until we were mostly done. Then Cooper sat back and wiped his mouth with his napkin. "One of us is going to have to talk to Det. Sawyer."

"That's on you. Luke said they have tension, and I won't get anything out of him."

Cooper knew I was right. I could see it all over his face. I also knew how much he didn't want to talk to Det. Sawyer. "I have to get more information before I speak with him. He's not going to tell us much and I need to go in armed."

"I don't disagree with that." My earlier meeting with Lisa gave me an idea. "All the shop owners are meeting tonight to speak about safety and crime in the neighborhood. What do you think about crashing the meeting? They will all be in one place so we can gather more intel."

"You think they are going to allow us in there?"

I shook my head and recalled Lisa's earlier warning that it was *just for business owners.* She had stressed it in the snotty tone she had taken with me. "You are going to speak to Hattie and see if we can tag along as her guests."

"Absolutely not," Cooper said, but I could see he was hedging already. "I don't want Hattie to get the wrong idea that I'm buddies with her. Next thing you know she'll be trying to tell me my future. She already admitted she gets involved with criminal matters too much."

"It's a way in the door, Cooper. We aren't asking her to join our team as a psychic detective."

Cooper groaned loud enough that customers around us glanced over. "I'll ask Hattie if we can go with her but don't be too chummy with her. What was her niece like?"

"A thinner, smarter version of me." I laughed.

Cooper rolled his eyes and took a sip of soda. "Have you heard from Luke on his murder investigation?"

"He hasn't said much. Do you think the two are connected?"

"I doubt it. Probably just a coincidence." Cooper asked for our bill as the server approached. Then he turned his attention back to me. "If there are marbles left at each scene, then it would be interesting to know if one was found at Bell & Bloom."

I hadn't thought of that. "I can ask Luke. He's not happy about this case at all. He's got some history with Chance Bell, so he was dreading this case all the way around."

"I remember that case. I was leaving the Little Rock PD around that time. Luke caught that case right before Det. Tyler became his partner. He hated every second of it."

Sometimes I forgot that Cooper had been a detective with the Little Rock PD. He and Luke worked together for a few years before Cooper struck out on his own. He hated the paperwork and the politics of being on the force. "He seemed stressed this morning when he left, but hopefully he made some headway."

We sat back while the server came over and cleared the table. Cooper paid the bill, claiming it was a work expense and he'd cover it. I wasn't going to argue with a free lunch. We talked over a few pending investigations including a child custody case that might be coming up for us and then we made a plan for the rest of the day.

As we were getting ready to leave, a young woman approached us as we headed for the front door. "Cooper Deagnan?" she asked as she walked up to us.

"Yes," he said, turning to her.

She stuck her hand out. "My name is Danielle. I heard you talking about those burglaries in the Heights. I think I might have some information."

"How'd you know my name?" Cooper asked.

She smiled shyly. "I've seen you around. A lot of people know you."

By the smile on Danielle's face, I wouldn't have been surprised if she had a crush on Cooper. As much as I wanted to stay and hear what she had to say, I excused myself, telling her I had a meeting to get to. I reasoned that Cooper might get more information interviewing her alone. He had a charm that disarmed most women and some men.

CHAPTER 20

"I hate this case," Luke said as he pulled out of Chance's driveway. He had been saying the same thing to himself over the last two hours. They found three hammers and had bagged and tagged each of them. They'd have to get them back to the lab to test for blood. On its own, it wasn't evidence. Luke was sure just about every home in Little Rock had a hammer.

Their more pressing lead right now was to locate the man Holly Bell was having the affair with. They had run the phone number found on her cell through the database and came up empty. They were on their way to speak to some of her employees again and her best friend, Courtney Murphy. She had already called Luke several times wanting to speak with him.

He had called her back and asked if they could meet in person. She had readily agreed and gave Luke her address. He hoped she'd be able to shed some light on what was going on and a possible suspect. Luke wasn't sure why but he hoped it wasn't Chance. Not that he wanted the guy to be innocent, he just didn't want to interact with him anymore than was necessary.

"You seem lost in thought," Tyler said across the car.

"I was thinking about how I don't want to deal with Chance so much that I'm hoping he's innocent of the murder." Luke turned his head slightly to look at his partner. "Messed up, right?"

"I'm not sure if I'd rather him in prison or as far away from Little Rock as possible. Either would be fine with me." Tyler glanced down at the name written on the case note file. "Tell me about Courtney." Luke tapped on the steering wheel with his thumb while he took a right into his old Hillcrest neighborhood. He had grown up there and then bought a house a few blocks from his parents' house before moving in with Riley. Luke made a mental note to go visit his parents now that he was back. He had called but it wasn't the same.

"Courtney left me a few messages and said she was Holly's best friend. She claims she can help the investigation." Luke shifted his eyes toward Tyler. "I have no idea what she knows. She is married and has three kids and at one point worked as a teacher at a local elementary school. That's about all I know right now."

The information must have been good enough for Tyler because he didn't ask anything else. They drove the rest of the way in silence except for the soft hum of the radio playing so quietly Luke couldn't make out the song. He checked the GPS one more time for the address and then turned onto the street. Courtney's house was the third in from the left.

Luke pulled to a stop at the curb. "I don't have an agenda with this interview other than to find out as much as we can about Holly. I'm going to let Courtney start talking and then fill in the gaps with questions when she's done."

"Sounds like a plan," Tyler agreed and then they hit the pavement. When they reached the front door, Tyler knocked and a squeal of children calling for mom could be heard from inside. A moment later, a short-haired woman yanked open the door and looked ready to yell at them.

Luke flashed his badge and introduced himself and Tyler, hoping to stop her from saying something she regretted. He confirmed she was Courtney and then reminded her about what she had said earlier in the day. "You told me to stop by when I could. We're hoping to speak to you about Holly Bell."

"I'm so sorry, Detective. It's been a long day. Come on in," she said, stepping back into the house so they could enter. She shooed the children upstairs and then over her shoulder said, "Let's go in the kitchen. We'll have some quiet in there."

Luke and Tyler stepped around a maze of toys and followed her into the kitchen, which looked only slightly more cleaned up than the living room. It looked like Courtney had been in the middle of making cookies. She sat down at the table but Luke pointed at the counter. "You might want to put the eggs away."

Courtney blinked like she didn't understand and then followed to where he was pointing. She jumped up from her chair, thanking him over and over again. "The kids get me into such a state I forget where I am sometimes." She pulled the eggs and a bowl, which looked like it had the batter in it, from the counter and put it in the fridge. She offered them something to drink but they declined.

Luke and Tyler sat down at the table with Courtney finally joining them. "I didn't mean to push you off earlier when you called," Luke said. "We needed to get our interview with Chance out of the way first."

"What did you think of him?" Courtney asked but her tone indicated she wasn't a supporter of his.

"I've had dealings with him before," Luke admitted. "I was the one who arrested him years ago."

Courtney sucked in a breath. "He couldn't have been happy to see you again."

"He wasn't." Luke didn't elaborate further. He wanted to get down to the meat of why they were there. "You said you were Holly's best friend. You mentioned you had information you thought we should have."

"I am...was Holly's best friend," Courtney said, correcting herself. "I don't know who killed her, but I have a suspect in mind. Surprisingly, it's not Chance."

"Who is it?" Luke asked.

Courtney swallowed hard and hesitated. "I feel disloyal for telling you this. Holly was having an affair."

"We know that. We found a cellphone in her bedroom rolled up into a sweater. We've read the texts. Do you know his name?"

"Jason Manning. He's a local contractor."

Tyler scooted his chair forward and it scraped loudly along the kitchen floor. "You think Jason killed her?"

Courtney shook her head. "I think Jason's wife, MaryBeth, killed her."

That didn't shock Luke, but he couldn't run on the word of one person who suspected something. "Why do you think that?"

"MaryBeth went into Holly's shop three days before the murder and told Holly that she was going to kill her. MaryBeth didn't know that I was in the back office at the time. It was before closing, and Holly and I were meeting for dinner. She hadn't locked up yet. I was in the back hanging up some dresses from a recent shipment. I heard everything."

"MaryBeth knew about the affair then?" Luke asked, remembering the texts he had read on Holly's phone. This was confirmation.

"She did. From what Holly told me, MaryBeth had suspected before and they had cooled off for a few weeks, but then started back up again." Courtney took a breath and let it out slowly. "I told Holly that getting involved with him wasn't a good idea. I know she shouldn't have been having an affair at all, but that was the worst guy she could have picked."

Luke thought Chance was the worst guy she could have picked so it must have been a trend. "Chance isn't exactly a stellar human being. Did Holly have a type?"

Courtney broke into a wide grin. "You'd think so, but Jason was a bad guy in a different way than Chance. He was up to something and always a little shady. Holly said that he was waiting for some money to come in and then he was going to leave his wife. I don't know what he was waiting for though. If Holly knew, she never told me."

"Did Jason have a criminal record?" Tyler asked.

"Not that I know of, but he was up to something. Even Holly seemed concerned about it."

Luke locked eyes with her. He was sitting on the edge of his seat and would kill for any kind of solid lead at this point. "What did she say specifically?"

Courtney pursed her lips. "Holly said that back in May, Jason was talking about coming into a lot of money. He told her that he had a plan and that once he had the money, he could get a divorce. Holly said that it was at least a million dollars."

Several things flashed through Luke's mind, but it was all so vague he couldn't even pinpoint a theory. "Did Jason ever get the money?"

Courtney shook her head. "Not according to Holly. She said there was a delay and that the money was gone."

Tyler toyed with the pen in his hand. "What does that mean – *gone?*"

"Holly said that Jason made it seem like he got double-crossed by his partners. He told her that he was trying to sort it out and that his plan to leave his wife was on hold. Jason said MaryBeth knew about the money and he had to keep her quiet."

None of this made sense to Luke. If anything, it sounded like an elaborate story a cheating man would tell his mistress to delay leaving his wife. Luke suggested that to Courtney but she was adamant that's what Jason said and meant it. "How can you be sure of that?" he asked.

"Holly didn't care if he left his wife or not. She wasn't sure that she wanted to leave Chance so she was more concerned about Jason getting divorced than not. She told Jason that so he'd have no reason to feel pressured to leave. The whole affair…" Courtney didn't finish her thought. She stood and grabbed a glass from the counter and went to the fridge. She pulled out a pitcher of tea and poured herself a glass. She held it up offering them a glass but they declined.

After putting the pitcher back, instead of sitting, she leaned against the counter. "The affair was out of boredom. Chance was always going on and on about how he wasn't important anymore. He lost his following when he went to prison. He desperately wanted it back and Holly wanted a normal life. She was growing tired of his drama. Holly was bored enough she started looking for attention elsewhere, but it was never as serious for her as it was for Jason. He was in love with her, according to Holly."

Love could lead to rage and that could lead to murder. "When did all of this take place?"

"It was about a week ago that MaryBeth found out the affair was still happening. Now, Holly is dead." Courtney blew out a frustrated breath. "Look, Det. Morgan, it could be Jason or MaryBeth or both, but that's where I'd be looking if I were you. I just think MaryBeth has more motive."

Luke thought back to something Chance had said. "When I confronted Chance about the affair, he suggested they had an open marriage so he'd have no reason to be angry about the affair. I got the sense he had no idea though."

"That's right. He's clueless." Courtney chuckled to herself. "Chance squirrels himself away up in one of the bedrooms he turned into an office. He makes YouTube videos all day and goes live on Facebook ranting and raving about the end of the world and his brand of religion or philosophy or whatever you want to call it. He paid no attention to Holly at all – in or out of the bedroom." She leaned in stressing the last few words.

"Their sex life wasn't what it used to be?" Luke asked.

"Nonexistent. Chance felt irrelevant and emasculated. Holly told me he couldn't even get it up anymore. She suggested little blue pills and he shut her out completely." She sat down at the table again. "The bottom line is Chance was a washed-up cult leader without any followers and no hope of getting any in the future. He was completely irrelevant and that was fine with Holly. It wasn't fine for him though and that's what destroyed them."

Luke let that sink in. He fought the urge to feel bad for Chance, but still, a little pity snuck in. "What about the drama Holly had recently? We heard there was a protest at her shop?"

"You mean the fat girl rage?" When Luke nodded, she laughed. "Holly thought that was hilarious. She was having a good time with the hate. That's how Holly was. She loved the attention – both good and bad – and she'd do anything to get it. It was a laugh to her."

"What about the protest? Jordan Collins had it out with her."

"It was all worth it to Holly."

Luke didn't understand people like that. "Then you don't think that had anything to do with her murder?"

"Well," Courtney started, drawing out her words. "It could have pushed MaryBeth over the edge. I heard she's not exactly thin. Maybe she took offense to that and that Holly stole her husband."

Luke considered that motive enough. He asked her a few more questions and turned to Tyler, but he had nothing else. When they were done, Courtney walked them to the door and told them she hoped they found Holly's killer quickly. Luke hoped the same but he had his doubts.

CHAPTER 21

"I have some news about your watch," I said to Izzy as I stood on his front porch. He was half-in the house with a leg dangling from the doorway. "Can I come in and speak with you?" Izzy didn't look too happy with the idea, but he backed up and let me in the house. "I was doing homework," he said as an explanation for the mess of books and papers near an open laptop on the dining room table. He pushed the books out of the way and I grabbed a chair across from his seat. "What did you find out?"

I folded my hands on the table. "I heard you nearly had a fight with Scott, and that's when you lost your watch."

Izzy's mouth hung slightly agape like he hadn't made the connection before now. "That makes sense. I hadn't considered that. I figured it was when I was playing basketball. Other than taking a shower and at night, that's the only other time I take it off."

I believed he was telling me the truth. It looked like he had just added two and two right in front of me. "What happened with the fight?"

"Scott was always trying to start fights with me. This time he took a swing at me and hit me. I didn't fight back though."

I couldn't imagine the strength that took. If someone hit me, I'd be swinging. "Is there a reason you didn't fight back? I don't think anyone expects you to take a beating and not defend yourself."

"You'd think that, right?" Izzy asked, zeroing in on me. "My father. I'm sure you got a good sense of him when you met him. Here at home, he's tougher. I'm not sure why he expects so much of me, but I try to live up to it. Taking a punch from Scott and walking away from a fight is less humiliating than having to listen to my father tell me how I'm going to end up worthless."

I wasn't a parent, but I couldn't imagine saying anything like that. "You're so accomplished, Izzy. I've seen your grades and your extracurricular activities. Your high school résumé is impressive."

"I need to keep it that way and fighting with Scott isn't on the agenda. So, did he take my watch?"

"No, actually." I pulled out my phone to double-check the name Cooper had given me. I had added it to a note file so I wouldn't forget. "Jimmy Ragone. It seems Nolan found it and Jimmy said he'd give it back to you. Did you ever have a conversation with him about it?"

"No, ma'am. Jimmy is a good guy, but he is friends with Scott. I never got the watch back."

"Cooper and I believe you," I reassured him. "I am hoping this doesn't go to trial, but we have character witnesses for you lined up. Hattie and Jackson, your neighbors, both had good things to say."

Izzy nodded. "Jackson saw Scott break my car window. I feel stupid now because he was right. I should have called the cops then."

"Cooper spoke to him and Nolan. It was suggested to Cooper that you had told Scott's father about the window and that was the cause of the fight."

Izzy shook his head and looked down. "I didn't tell Mr. Sawyer. Jackson did. I had asked him not to, but he said it was important. If that's why Scott hit me, I guess that's as good a reason as any."

"There's no good reason, Izzy. Are you friends with Nolan and Jimmy?"

"I don't know them too well, but I've never had an issue with them.

I don't think they had any issues with me either, at least from what I know." Izzy slumped down in his chair and looked across the table at me. The way the light hit his face, he looked younger than his age. "It's going to be okay, Izzy," I said, trying to reassure him which I try not to do with clients. I couldn't guarantee any outcome. He didn't say anything so I pressed on. "Nolan said something strange to Cooper when he left his house. He told Cooper that there was a reason for the burglaries, something more than we know. Do you have any idea what he was talking about?"

Izzy stared off in the distance so long I wasn't sure if he knew more or was avoiding the question. Finally, he turned to me. "I've been thinking about this a lot lately. Like was there a clue I missed? I thought of something, but I don't know if it's important."

"Just tell me what you know and Cooper and I can figure out if it's important or even relevant."

"It was soon after school started that Scott was with his closest friends, including Jimmy, on the basketball court and he told them they were going to do a job for a guy who was going to pay them a lot of money. Jimmy asked them what they were going to be doing and Scott wouldn't say. He said it was real hush-hush. I figured he was being stupid and they would be painting a house or something like that. Now, I'm not so sure. There were a few times he and Jimmy and two other guys would be talking after that and, if I approached the court, they'd get quiet. I wonder if they were talking about the burglaries."

"They didn't take any money from the shops though."

"Yeah, I guess not." Izzy strummed his fingers on the table. "I still think it was weird."

I thought back to what Cooper and I had talked about. "Are any of them good with technology? More advanced than the average person."

"Jimmy can do just about anything. He told us he hacked into the

141

police station database once. He's a smart guy but doesn't come across like it. He dumbs it down in front of people. I know he does some coding for his dad's company, too."

"Do you think one of the other guys you saw that night might have been Jimmy?"

"I don't know," Izzy said, shaking his head. "The last thing I want to do is accuse someone unless I'm sure. Look at how it's messed up my life."

"Fair enough." I asked him a few more questions and he didn't have much more to add. He never heard Scott and his friends speak directly about the burglaries so there weren't any leads to follow. I got up from the table when we were done and thanked Izzy for the information. I promised I'd be in touch when I knew more.

"What am I supposed to do in the meantime?" he asked as he walked me to the front door.

"Lay low and focus on school." I watched his face fall so I reached up and put a hand on his shoulder. "Izzy, you need to stay out of trouble right now. The best way to do that is to let Cooper and me and your lawyer do our jobs. If you think of anything important, definitely call us. Otherwise, keep out of sight and focus on your future."

"I don't even know if I have a future."

I pulled the door open and took a step out. "You have a future. This will all be over before you know it. It won't be anything more than a footnote in your life. Trust me, they can't even prove you had your watch. We have definite proof that you lost it now. That's a huge step in the right direction."

Izzy stayed in the doorway watching me leave. I had hoped that I had raised his spirits a little, but when I turned to wave, he didn't look any happier than when I had arrived. I walked the few blocks back to my house. Cooper texted me as I walked in the front door confirming Hattie would help us gain access to that meeting later tonight.

I texted Luke about the meeting and that there were leftovers in the fridge for him. It was nearing six and I had to get ready for the meeting. Luke had had a long first full day back. I didn't envy him at all. I should have been a good wife and whipped up some dinner for him for when he came home, but I didn't have time. I also didn't have much food in the house. I needed a grocery run. We were lucky we had toilet paper left.

I headed upstairs to freshen up for the meeting, but I only made it to the third step when there was a knock at the front door. I bounded back down the steps and pulled the curtain aside at the front window. Cooper stood with his hands in his pockets.

"I thought I was meeting you there," I said, stepping out of the way.

"That was the plan. We need to talk." Cooper sat down in my favorite chair in the living room and then looked up at me and smiled since he knew he had stolen my spot. He didn't move though. "That woman who came into Dugan's as you were leaving had some information for me."

I stood in the middle of the room like a dog that had been tossed out of its bed. "Who is she?"

"Danielle Mabry. She's a teacher at the high school. She overheard Scott Sawyer talking to a few of the other boys during a study hall a couple of months back. They were all excited about some money-making opportunity. Then more recently, she saw Scott talking to a guy in the school parking lot. He handed Scott a duffle bag. She was concerned about this man, who she didn't know, and tried to speak to Scott's father. He refused the meeting."

"Why did she seek you out?"

"She saw Adele on the news answering questions about Izzy's arrest. Adele told Danielle we were at Dugan's and gave her my phone number, too."

"It doesn't sound like Danielle has anything solid though."

143

"There's more," Cooper said with a smile. I should have known he wouldn't have rushed over to tell me what amounted to speculation. He was leaving the best for last and letting me sweat it out.

"Danielle heard Scott talk about setting Izzy up for the burglaries. It's as good as a confession to having committed them himself. She heard him say, 'We planted Izzy's watch. That's the only person they will suspect now. We are in the clear.' He was speaking to Jimmy and two other of their friends. At first, she didn't know what he was talking about, but then she saw Adele's interview on the news and connected the name Izzy."

"Is Danielle willing to write a sworn statement? It might be hearsay in court, but that's not up to us to decide."

Cooper smiled. "A sworn statement signed and delivered to Adele."

We were far from solving this but at least we had taken a step in the right direction.

As we headed out for the meeting, I told Cooper about my meeting with Izzy. "Jimmy Ragone may be important. Izzy said he's a tech wiz."

CHAPTER 22

L uke got home from work earlier than planned. When he and Tyler went back to the station after speaking to Courtney, they had planned to visit Jason Manning that evening to interview him about Holly. Captain Meadows had other ideas and told them to break for the day and get some rest. He thought it better to track Jason Manning down at work and interview his wife, MaryBeth, separately. Luke couldn't argue with that so he returned home to find an empty house.

He checked his phone when he realized Riley wasn't home. He found her text about attending a community meeting with the shop owners to discuss the recent burglaries and ways to keep the community safer. He had no idea if they'd have law enforcement present, but he wasn't volunteering himself.

Luke jogged up the stairs to the second floor, took a quick hot shower to wash away the stress of the day, and then put on his favorite pair of blue sweats and a tee-shirt that had been washed about a million times, leaving it nearly threadbare but soft and cozy.

All Luke wanted was the leftover pasta, a beer, and to sink into the sofa to watch TV. He didn't even care if there was anything he was interested in. It was the mere act of not having to think about work or Chance Bell. He heated up the pasta, grabbed a cold one, and relaxed back before turning on the television. He ate like a man who hadn't touched a morsel of food in days. To be fair, he hadn't eaten much of anything all day. When he was full, he pushed the bowl away on the coffee table.

Luke clicked through several channels before settling on the History Channel and a docuseries about U.S. presidents. He made the mistake of closing his eyes as he rested his head back against the sofa. The beer and carbs put him right out. He snored peacefully right there in the living room.

"Luke," Riley said, shaking his arm. "I'm back from the meeting. We need to talk about your case."

He opened his eyes to see Riley's sweet face staring down at him. "What time is it?" The house had grown dark and there was only a small end table light illuminating the room. Someone had shut the television off.

"It's just after nine. I thought I'd be home earlier, but Cooper and I stayed to speak to Mike, the guy who owns the pizzeria. He had some interesting surveillance footage from the night of the break-in."

Luke moved over and made room for Riley to sit on the couch. "I thought all the surveillance video was cut?"

Riley sat down next to him and pulled his legs across her lap. "That's what we thought, too. Mike had a backup camera in his supply room. It's one of those basic nanny cam models. He purchased a backup about a year ago when he thought one of the kids working for him was stealing from the bottle beer supply. The normal surveillance cameras cover the hall, but he couldn't see what was happening in the supply room. Mike put the camera in the far back corner of the supply room."

"Did he see something?"

"Mike never caught the kids stealing beer, but on the night of the burglary, he caught someone searching the supply room. They didn't take anything."

Luke sat up straighter. "Was it Izzy?"

"No. It looked like a white guy."

"You texted me earlier about guys in high school. Are you saying it's not them?"

Riley hadn't told him much about the burglaries other than she and Cooper suspected some of the other guys in the neighborhood set up Izzy. Luke knew Izzy wasn't good for the murder of Holly Bell so he hadn't paid much attention at all.

"I'm not sure who it is, but it happened much later than we suspected the burglaries happened. The guy searching the supply room was in there around two in the morning."

Luke ran a hand down his face and pushed himself up against the side of the couch. His head was still a bit foggy from sleep. "Start from the beginning and then walk me through it."

"The first thing you have to understand is that Det. Lou Sawyer's son, Scott, could be involved."

"He's the arresting officer?" Luke confirmed, letting the implications sink in.

Riley nodded. "That's what makes this case a bit delicate, but we have credible witnesses who told us that Scott had it in for Izzy. They confirmed things Izzy has told us. In one instance, a neighbor confronted Det. Sawyer about Scott smashing Izzy's car window. Det. Sawyer denied it was his son even when the picture clearly shows it was Scott."

Riley went on to explain in-depth some of the other things they had uncovered. She finished with the watch – the only evidence connecting Izzy to a crime scene.

"Izzy swears he never got that watch back and I believe him. Besides, who is stupid enough to take their watch off while breaking into a shop and leave it on the counter?"

Luke couldn't argue with her reasoning. "Were the guys that Izzy thinks is involved seen on the surveillance?"

Riley shook her head. "The supply room is out of the way. I assume the boys didn't go in there for anything."

"Where does the guy on surveillance fit into this?"

"That's the thing, Luke. It doesn't make a lot of sense," Riley said, stressing the point. "Mike said that the alarm company indicated the system had been disabled at ten that evening. This guy is on video at two in the morning. We haven't asked Scott or the other boys we think are involved to confirm their alibis, but I can't imagine high school kids are going to be roaming the streets at that time of night."

Luke didn't think so either. "What do you think then – that the boys broke in and then some guy also breaks in after them?"

"He seemed to be searching for something specific. He wasn't there to steal as no money was taken from the safe or the cash register," Riley explained. "He is searching. That's all he's doing, and he was even bold enough to flip on the lights. He's looking around, moving things, and then he started pushing on the wall, looking to see if it opened or if there was maybe a hidden door. It was crazy. Mike is going to send you the video."

"Is there anything distinguishing about the guy in the video?"

"You can see some skin on his arms. That's about it." Riley showed Luke on her arm. "It's the space from where his shirt ends and his gloves begin. It looks like there might be a tattoo on his arm, but you can't make out the design. The image would need to be enlarged."

"I can see what the tech guys at the police department can do."

"What about Det. Sawyer? He's not going to be too happy with you messing around his case."

Luke rubbed his chin. Riley was right about that. He was higher in rank than Sawyer at the police department, but Luke never liked stepping on anyone's toes. "Did Mike tell Det. Sawyer about the footage?"

Riley nodded. "He knew about it before he arrested Izzy."

Luke cursed under his breath. "Did Det. Sawyer know Izzy's watch was missing?"

"Izzy said he told him, but Det. Sawyer said he didn't believe him."

"Did Izzy know at the time that Scott Sawyer was potentially involved in the burglaries?"

"He did," Riley admitted. "Izzy wasn't going to say anything though because he assumed Det. Sawyer wouldn't believe him just like he didn't believe the neighbor that Scott smashed the car window."

Luke didn't like shoddy police work. He inched forward on the couch. "Send me the footage and I'll look into it. In the meantime, get a statement from Mike. We'll have to do the same, but if I can turn over a sworn statement, Captain Meadows will take it more seriously. Undoing another detective's work is like walking a mine field. The more solid evidence I have the better."

"We already did. Adele is going to need it for the defense case." Riley turned her head away from him and remained quiet for too long.

There were only a few reasons Riley ever got quiet – she was angry, uncomfortable or she was plotting. Luke nudged her arm. "What are you thinking about?"

"There's something else bothering me about the break-ins, but it's going to seem silly to you. Cooper hasn't put stock in it either."

"Let me decide if it's silly." Luke ran a hand down her arm, tickling her.

Riley turned to him and smiled. Her eyes were as tired as Luke felt. "Lisa, the woman who owns the kitchen store, said she found a marble near the cash register. Hattie, who owns the psychic shop, found a marble on her desk. I asked tonight if any of the other shop owners found random marbles in their shops after the burglaries and each one of them said yes. They hadn't thought anything of it. Mike found one sitting on his desk in his office."

"What do you think it means?"

"I have no idea. I didn't know if it was Scott and his friends just messing around taunting the shop owners or if it meant something. We also have no way of knowing if each shop was broken into a second time. No other shop owners had the second surveillance system set up."

Luke had worked several burglary cases before working his way up to the homicide unit. He thought back to a few of them and then others he'd read about. A case a few years ago out of San Francisco jumped to mind. "The first and second break-ins might be tied together. The marble could be a marker of some sort for when the second guy goes in."

Riley scrunched up her face, weighing what Luke said. "Are you suggesting that Scott and his friends break in first and cut the surveillance and then plant the marble as some kind of marker for the second guy?"

"That's exactly what I'm saying. Maybe the kids left it there to alert him that the surveillance had been cut. If kids break into a shop first and the cops come, they can play it off more easily than an adult, particularly if the kids aren't stealing anything."

"Why not just text the guy that the surveillance is cut and the coast is clear. Burner phones are fairly accessible."

Luke hadn't worked it all out. He was merely speculating. "I don't know. Maybe it indicates a room Scott and his friends hadn't searched yet or where they found something suspicious."

"That could be it." Riley stared off into space.

"Where were most of the marbles found?"

"In the back offices of all of the shops except for two. Lisa found hers by the cash register and another shop found theirs in a supply room. That shop doesn't have an office and Lisa mentioned tonight she is rarely in her office. She's normally at the cash register."

Luke remembered the details of a case in Phoenix but didn't want to mention it to Riley until he could look up the details and confirm he was remembering correctly. "We'll keep exploring it. Right now, it sounds like you and Cooper are doing a good job of proving that Izzy had nothing to do with the burglaries."

Riley sighed loudly. "Cooper is going in to speak to Det. Sawyer tomorrow. Since he doesn't like you, I figured it was best to leave it up to Cooper. I didn't think he'd talk to me at all."

"He probably won't talk to Cooper either."

"Maybe not, but at least Cooper will be able to see his response after confronting him with some of the evidence we found."

"If Sawyer doesn't listen, then maybe Cooper should set up a meeting with Captain Meadows. He'll listen to reason."

Riley nodded but didn't respond. Luke swung his legs off her and put his feet to the floor. He reached out and took her hand in his. "Come on, sleepy girl, let's get ready for bed. Tomorrow is a new day and we can tackle your case then."

CHAPTER 23

The next morning, I was up before sunrise. I made breakfast from the food I had available and then left for the grocery store at the same time Luke left for the police station. I didn't have anyone to interview that morning, and I told Cooper I wanted to stay home and do some research. I didn't have access to the law enforcement databases that Luke did, but that didn't mean I was without resources.

I knew the marbles meant something and the fact that Luke hadn't laughed it off the night before meant he did as well. At a minimum, he thought it was worth exploring. The one thing Luke and I did not do when it came to criminal cases was humor each other. If he thought I was off track, he would have told me right then and there. He wouldn't want me to waste my time any more than I would want that of him. Time is the most precious commodity in life and criminal cases.

After getting back from the market and putting the groceries away, I went to my home office and fired up my laptop. I started with a basic search in the databases we had access to but didn't find much of anything. Next, I dropped a few different search terms into the search engine. I spent a lot of time reading news articles about other burglaries in other cities but nothing relevant jumped out at me.

I was persistent though. If Luke was right and the marbles were a marker, it meant that Scott and his friends didn't decide to break into the shops on their own accord. Someone had put them up to it – they were working for someone. That matched up to what the teacher at the school had said and what Izzy mentioned to me. What they were doing and who they were doing it for remained a mystery. If someone got the marble idea, it came from somewhere. My only hope now was to hit on a similar case that might give me a clue about what it could signify.

Two hours later, I had grown increasingly frustrated by the lack of progress I was making. I pushed my laptop away and leaned back and growled. I wasn't anywhere closer than I had been that morning. I checked the time on my laptop. Cooper would be meeting with Det. Sawyer in an hour. I had been hoping to have some evidence to give him that would bolster our case. There was nothing.

I pushed my chair back and it rolled to the middle of the floor. I stood and walked out of my office and down the stairs to the kitchen. I needed coffee and a break and to talk over what was stuck in my head. Luke had listened to me the night before, but I needed to process it all again. It's how I worked best.

I found my phone on the table where I had left it earlier and texted Emma to see if she was busy. She responded a few minutes later and asked if I wanted a walk and some coffee from our favorite place on Kavanaugh. Starbucks had been run out of business long ago, but in its place was a smaller local shop that sold coffee, sandwiches, and had an entire ice cream sundae bar. It was far too early for ice cream but their coffee was fantastic.

I grabbed my things and met her on our connecting front lawns. "Where are the kids?" I asked as Emma came out of the house alone.

"Sophie is in pre-school today and the baby is with Joe's mom. She takes him the days Sophie is in school to give me some free time to get things done." Emma smoothed down her dark hair and smiled through recently rouged cheeks and glossed lips. She had on recently pressed tan pants and a navy sweater I'd never seen her wear. She was pulled together like she was going out instead of going on a coffee chat with me.

"Hot date?" I asked, eyeing her.

"I was going to sneak away and meet Bradley Cooper around the corner, but you called so I told Bradley he'd have to wait."

"Tell Bradley I'm sorry but girlfriends come first."

"He'll understand, I'm sure." Emma reached out and grabbed my hand and swung it as we walked like we were schoolgirls heading for recess. It felt good to laugh with her again.

After walking a few blocks, she let go of my hand and shoved hers in her pockets. "I had an interview," she said so quietly I almost didn't hear her.

Emma had been wanting to go back to work for a while. "That's awesome. What kind of work?"

"Writing for a women's magazine. You know I had been freelancing for a while but this would be more of a regular column."

"Sounds exciting," I said and meant it. Some days I missed working at the newspaper as a crime reporter. I missed the deadlines and the creative process of putting words to paper. There was something empowering about digging for information and crafting a compelling article that informed and educated readers. "When will you hear?"

Emma stopped dead on the sidewalk. "I got the job!" she squealed with delight.

I hugged her and we hopped up and down, not caring how silly we probably looked. "Will you be able to work from home?" I asked when we released each other.

"That's the best part. I'll have a regular paycheck and can work right from home. It's five features a month – one a week for their online magazine and then one print. It's going to be a lot of research and interviewing subjects but well worth it."

I asked Emma more questions about the job and we walked the rest of the way with her telling me everything about it through giddy excitement she couldn't contain. We got to the coffee shop, ordered at the counter, and then took a seat.

As we sipped our coffees, Emma said, "I've been going on and on about my good news. What's going on with you?"

I almost didn't want to shift the jovial energy between us by stressing about the case. Emma sat staring at me wide-eyed though, waiting for me to tell her. "This case has me stumped."

"Walk it through with me, sister." Emma reached out and grabbed my hand squeezing it. "Even if we can't figure it out, you'll feel better talking about it."

That much was true. Over the next twenty minutes, I detailed everything I knew about the case to date including the background on Scott and Izzy and the stolen watch. I explained about the marbles found and the meeting with the shop owners the night before. I finished and then took a deep breath. "I'm missing something and I'm not sure what it is. I spent the morning doing some research but didn't get anywhere."

Emma sipped her coffee and then set it down on the table. "It sounds like you're on the right track, and it's a good sign Luke was willing to listen. I think no matter what happens Izzy won't be convicted. If you can convince Captain Meadows that Izzy is innocent, I'm sure he'll talk to the prosecutor and it won't even get to a trial." She reached out and rubbed my shoulder. "That would be a success."

Emma was right as usual. She had a way of seeing the positives when I was taking up residence deep in the weeds on a case. "I know there's more to it. I can't connect the dots though."

"You know it reminds me of an article I read a while back about a case out west," Emma said and then she paused. I knew by the face she was making she was trying to recall the details. All at once, she snapped her fingers. "It wasn't an article. It was *Dateline* or one of those shows."

"What was it?" I asked with interest.

Emma leaned on the table and her face grew animated in her excitement to tell me about what she remembered. "It was about two rival companies in Arizona. One company was trying to get the recipe to the ingredients of the other company's sauces. They had all kinds of sauces for everything you can think of and this other company wanted to cash in on their success and copy their recipes. So, they sent in a team to bug the place. They left a marker in each room a bug was placed. It was to let their inside guy know which rooms to have conversations in. The inside guy was working to get the company secrets for his bosses."

"What kind of marker?" I didn't remember the case at all.

"It was something stupid," Emma said, drifting off in thought, then suddenly yelled, "Stress balls!"

Emma had yelled it a little too loudly and other customers were looking at us. "You need a stress ball to remember?" I asked, not sure what she meant.

Emma shook her head. "No, that's what was left in the black bag job."

"Black bag job," I said, stifling a giggle. Emma had gone rogue spy on me.

"You know that's what they call covert entry into a building to plant surveillance equipment. I don't think it's technically allowed anymore."

"I know what the term means, I was surprised you knew it. It's definitely not allowable to break into shops and plant surveillance equipment. I don't understand how that relates though." I took another sip of coffee and leaned back. "It was high school kids who broke in and left the marbles. We'd have to believe they also planted surveillance equipment to let the guy breaking in after them know where it was. All for what? No one is trying to steal Lisa's secret knowledge about whisks or Hattie's spells or this coffee shop's cookie recipe. I might believe someone was after the pizza shop's sauce because that's legitimately as good as New York pizza, but even still, that's a stretch."

Emma shrugged. "There's only one way to find out."

"Look for the bugs?"

"Look for the bugs," Emma said smugly, hitching her thumb over her shoulder toward the counter. She stared at me refusing to say another word until I pushed my chair back and headed for the counter. I believed it was a fool's errand, but if it made Emma happy, I was along for the ride.

I asked the young woman behind the counter if the owner or manager of the shop was available. She panicked and asked if everything was okay with our order. I reassured her that all was great, I just had a question about the burglary. I pulled a business card from my pocket and passed it to her across the counter.

She read it and then scurried off behind the double swinging doors. A moment later, a woman named Cara walked out and greeted me. I explained to her who I was in case the young woman hadn't explained well enough.

"I need to speak with you about the burglary. I was at the meeting last night."

"I remember you. How can I help?"

I glanced over my shoulder at the shop full of people and then turned back to Cara. "This is sensitive. Can we speak in the back?"

"Sure, come around," Cara said, pointing to the end of the counter. "We can go to my office."

I went around the counter and followed Cara through the swinging double doors and down a corridor to her office. Before we walked in, I tugged the back of her shirt. "Last night, I assume you were one of the shop owners who said a marble had been found. Where in the shop did you find it?"

"On my office desk."

I stuck my head into the office space and pointed to the small gray desk that had spindly legs and a few nicks on the top. "Do you mind if I search it?" I whispered.

Cara folded her arms over her chest. "For what exactly?"

I pulled the office door closed and whispered, "I know this is going to sound crazy, but I think the burglary might have been about planting a bug in your office."

She raised her eyebrows and shifted her head to the side, looking at her office door and then back at me. "I can't imagine anyone wants to spy on me."

"It's a theory I'm trying to disprove. The marble might have been left to indicate where the bug was planted. It will only take a few minutes."

I thought at first Cara was going to protest. She stood there with her arms crossed assessing my sanity. She wavered only slightly and then uncrossed her arms, dropping them to her sides. "Make it quick."

I opened the office door and went inside before she could change her mind. I looked down at the desk trying to figure out the most likely place to plant a bug and then dropped to my knees. I inched myself on my back under her desk and looked up at the underside of it. I gasped when I saw the small black square box with a tiny antenna on it. It couldn't have been more than two inches long. It was stuck to the underside of the desk in the far-right corner.

I inched back more and reached for my phone. I used a flashlight app to illuminate it. I hadn't seen many listening devices but this was one. I snapped three photos and then crawled back out from under the desk. I sent the photos to Luke with a simple message: *I found out why the marbles were left behind.*

CHAPTER 24

Cooper had one stop to make before he could pay Det. Lou Sawyer a visit. He called Jimmy Ragone that morning. Cooper threatened if Jimmy didn't speak to him, he'd be turning over the evidence he'd found to law enforcement. The gloves were off since Cooper found out that Jimmy had reached his eighteenth birthday a few weeks earlier. He was an adult as far as Cooper was concerned.

Jimmy had told Cooper to meet him at the basketball court in the Heights. He didn't want to meet at school, which is where Cooper had suggested. Citing nosey teachers, Jimmy opted for something more private. The court seemed a fitting place given that was where Jimmy had taken possession of Izzy's watch.

Cooper leaned against the fence and checked the time. Jimmy was ten minutes late. He'd give the young man a few minutes more. The area was fairly isolated at the end of a street surrounded by trees and woods on three sides. There was one way in and one way out unless someone took off through the woods, which Cooper assumed was possible. He didn't see any worn path in the dirt to indicate people went that way often. It meant most coming to the court took the road.

Cooper stood upright as he saw a tall guy walking toward him. He had his head down, with a ball cap pulled low over his ears and down on his forehead. His gait was gangly like he hadn't quite grown into his body yet. His weight said the same. Cooper had shot up similarly in his youth – all height and no added weight for a few years making him feel like Lurch. He didn't fill out the rest of the way until college.

When the guy got close, Cooper called out to him. "Jimmy Ragone?"

The young man raised his head only slightly to peer over at Cooper. "Yeah, we don't need to announce it to the whole neighborhood though. What do you want?"

"I need to confirm a few things with you." Cooper waited until Jimmy reached him. They stood nearly toe to toe. Jimmy was a good inch or two taller than Cooper's six feet. He wasn't going to waste any time. "It's my understanding that Isiah Wright left his watch here after a fight with Scott Sawyer. I was told that you offered to bring the watch back to him."

"Is there a question in there?" Jimmy asked, looping his thumbs in the belt loops of his baggy jeans.

"I know what happened. I'm looking for you to confirm that I have the correct information."

He shrugged. "I guess that's how it happened then."

"The watch ends up at a crime scene. Walk me through how that happened."

Jimmy raised his head to lock eyes with Cooper. "I didn't leave the watch there."

"That wasn't what I asked," Cooper said and silently thanked the kid for confirming that *he* wasn't the one who left the watch but he knew who did. "You and I both know it wasn't Izzy who left the watch there, so why don't you tell me whose idea it was to frame him for those break-ins."

Jimmy didn't say anything. He stood there watching Cooper and didn't say a word. He held his resolve for longer than Cooper thought he might.

Finally, Jimmy kicked a rock in front of him. "I said it wasn't me, but I know who did."

"We've established that." Cooper leaned in and bluffed. "I have a witness who puts you and Scott and two other guys on Kavanaugh late at night coming out of one of the shops that were burglarized. We know it was you and Scott. I want to know whose idea it was to leave Izzy's watch."

"Who is the witness?"

Cooper shook his head. "It doesn't work that way. I can't disclose that, but all you need to know is that I know far more than you think I do." It was a risky move, but Cooper needed the information.

"Scott," Jimmy admitted, looking at the ground. "This was all Scott's plan. The rest of us were just along for the ride."

"Who are the other two?"

"Two guys we go to school with," Jimmy told him and Cooper made a mental note.

"Look at me," Cooper said, his voice stern and commanding. Jimmy raised his head and locked eyes with Cooper. "You are going to have to testify to this because Izzy shouldn't have to pay for the mistakes you made."

"I never intended for Izzy to get wrapped up in this," Jimmy said with genuine regret in his voice. "I was going to give the watch back, but then Scott realized I had it and took it from me before I could give it to Izzy. I didn't even know Scott left it in that shop until the next day when I heard that Izzy was arrested and why."

"You could have made it right then."

"I know. Scott told me not to say a word. He said he had a plan."

Cooper shook his head in disgust. "What were you doing breaking into those shops?"

"It was a game," Jimmy said and his voice caught. "We broke in to see if we could. It was a challenge. We didn't take anything."

"A challenge. A game. Are you listening to how stupid you sound?"

Cooper brushed a hand over the top of his head. "I don't believe you. There's got to be more to it than that."

"No," Jimmy said forcefully and a little too quickly, giving himself away. "That's all there was to it."

Cooper let it drop for now because he didn't have any information to even bluff with at that point. "Were you the one who cut the surveillance?"

Jimmy nodded. "We didn't mean to cause any harm."

Cooper reached for him. He had flex cuffs in his back pocket if he needed them. "You're coming down to the police station with me."

Jimmy stepped back out of Cooper's reach. "I can't. Not now. I will but not now."

Cooper wasn't sure what to do. If Jimmy walked away, he could easily recant what he admitted, but if he pushed too hard, he could do the same. "When then?"

"I need to talk to my parents first. I need to be a man and tell them what I did. Then, with them, I'll go to the police department."

"Is Scott's father, Det. Lou Sawyer, protecting all of you?"

"I don't know." Jimmy looked at Cooper and his eyes were sincere. "Scott didn't seem too concerned about what we were doing. The rest of us all had to sneak out, but Scott walked out his front door on those nights. He said his dad was cool with him going out that late. I don't know what his father knows. That's the truth."

Cooper believed him. He reached into his pocket and pulled out his business card and handed it to him. Jimmy took it and read it over. "I don't want to have to tell your parents or force you into court, which Izzy's defense attorney can do. You need to do the right thing, Jimmy. Call me when you're ready to talk to the cops."

Jimmy started to walk off but Cooper called out to him. "Don't protect Scott if that's what you're thinking of doing because he wouldn't protect you. If you know more than you're saying about the burglaries, you need to think about what's going to happen when we find out the truth. Scott may have his father protecting him – but who is protecting you, Jimmy? When the chips are down, it's not going to be Scott. Remember that."

Jimmy held up Cooper's card and waved. "I'll call you if I remember anything else and when I'm ready to go to the cops."

Cooper watched as Jimmy lumbered off. At the end of the entrance to the courts, Jimmy took a right going farther into the neighborhood in the opposite direction than the way he arrived. Cooper wondered if he was going home to tell his parents right then while he had some courage. If not, then he was going to have to tell Jimmy's parents himself.

Twenty minutes later, Cooper found Det. Lou Sawyer sitting at his desk in the Little Rock Police Department's Detective Bureau's bullpen. He had the phone cord twisted around his finger as he barked orders to someone Cooper assumed was a crime scene tech on the other end of the line.

Cooper hung back and waited for Sawyer to slam down the phone and mutter a string of curses the likes of which he hadn't heard in a long time. He was fairly certain Sawyer even made up some words. Cooper approached taking one confident step after another until he reached the man's desk.

"Det. Sawyer," Cooper said with his hand out. "I need to speak with you."

The man looked up from his desk and stared at Cooper's hand as if it were a diseased piece of flesh that he had no intention of touching. "What do you want?" he barked.

Cooper introduced himself and mentioned that he had worked with the Little Rock police as a detective some years ago. Most detectives knew Cooper, but he wasn't sure if Sawyer remembered him. "I worked at that desk over there," he said, pointing to a desk three over from Sawyer's. "I need to speak to you about the burglaries in the Heights."

"Closed case. Suspect caught. End of story." Sawyer turned away from Cooper and picked up a file from his desk.

Cooper didn't leave though. He sat himself down right on the corner of the man's desk. When Sawyer turned to see what Cooper was doing, his eyes showed his anger and disdain. "What do you think you're doing? Get off my desk."

"No," Cooper said defiantly. "I'm not going anywhere until we talk."

"I'm not talking to you. You aren't a detective anymore and you aren't my superior so get lost." Sawyer leaned back in his chair and crossed his arms. "If you don't get off my desk, I'm going to remove you by force if necessary."

Cooper shrugged. "You can try, but you'll only cause a spectacle. I'm here doing you a favor."

"Yeah, what's that?"

"You made a false arrest of Isiah Wright and you need to correct that. I've found evidence that your physical evidence isn't what it seems."

"Why are you trying to protect that kid? Since he moved to the Heights all he's done is cause trouble."

"That's not the way I hear it." Cooper stared right at him daring him to refute it. "From what I hear, it was Scott who had it in for Izzy from the start."

"That's not true. Of course he'd tell you that." Sawyer made no move to follow through on the threat to remove Cooper from his desk.

"Izzy isn't the one who told me that. It was neighbors and even some of Scott's friends."

Sawyer righted himself in the chair. He hitched his jaw toward Cooper. "What gives you the right to be asking around about my son?" Red crept up his neck and flushed his face.

"I wasn't asking about your son," Cooper said calmly. "I was asking about the burglaries and Scott's name came up. I was told that it was your son who planted Izzy's watch at the scene."

Cooper no more than got the words out of his mouth when Sawyer rushed him, shoving him back off the desk and knocking him to the floor. Sawyer straddled his chest, and Cooper's head thumped against the floor as he took a punch to the side of the face, splitting his cheek open. His head spinning, Cooper got his hands in front of his face to protect himself from the next blow and clipped Sawyer on the chin, knocking him to the side enough that he could get himself upright.

Still dazed, Cooper didn't have a chance to go on the offensive. Other detectives rushed them, pulling Sawyer to his feet. The loud din of yelling and cursing drowned out Sawyer's threats. Cooper didn't much care, but the man had taken a cheap shot, and payback would be required. The man glared down and Cooper mouthed exactly what he planned to do to him.

Seconds later, Captain Meadows stood above Cooper with his hand reached out to help him up. "I expect better than this," he said with disapproval written all over his face.

CHAPTER 25

While I waited for Luke to arrive on the scene, I explained to Emma that she had been right about the bugs. The smile that spread across her face told me all I needed to know – she was right and I should listen to her more often. It had been a wild theory that had proven to be right. Emma could gloat all she wanted.

She went with me to two more shops to check for surveillance equipment. Sure enough, it was found exactly where the marbles had been left. I left the devices where they had been planted, snapped photos for Luke, and sent off another text. I didn't bother going to any more shops.

Emma kissed me on the cheek and told me she'd see me later. I stood at the corner of Kavanaugh and N. Fillmore waiting for Luke to arrive. I texted Cooper that I found some information that was of interest to the case and I was waiting for Luke to arrive. I told him I'd be in touch once I knew more.

I didn't tell him what I had found because I knew if I did, he'd stop what he was doing and show up to see for himself. He had important interviews to conduct and the last thing I wanted was to derail him with something I hadn't even confirmed with law enforcement yet.

A few minutes later, Luke pulled the car to the curb and got out. He approached with Det. Tyler, who had a grin on his face as if he'd been up to something. He playfully punched me on the arm and drew me into a hug – completely uncharacteristic of the man.

"Remember when I used to hate to see your face at our crime scenes?"

I pulled back from his friendly embrace. "I didn't realize you hated to see me. I thought you were annoyed was probably more like it."

He laughed. "No, I hated it. You were in the way and hard-headed. Nothing, sometimes not even facts, could sway your opinions. Plus, you'd make Luke grumpy, and that never made for a good day."

I pushed him away. "Good to know."

Tyler reached for me again and squeezed me tighter. "We are new and improved. You married one of my best friends and you're giving us leads on cases. All is well."

I looked him in the eyes. "Are you drunk?"

Luke couldn't hold back the laughter, and I had the sneaking suspicion the joke was on me and it went right over my head. "What am I missing?"

After Tyler released me, Luke reached out and rubbed my shoulder. We rarely had any public display of affection while working. "Tyler and I were talking about how right after you moved back to Little Rock, you'd nose around our cases and how much it annoyed us both. When we got the call from you today, we realized we were both happy to hear what you found."

"Oh," I said feeling slightly foolish. "Can we go look at the bugs I found now?"

Luke looked to Tyler and they both laughed. "I told you if you got mushy with her, she'd change the subject."

I pointed to the coffee shop. "Bugs. Now." I led them into the coffee shop without looking back. We had work to do.

Cara stood behind the counter anxiously waiting for us. She had been completely freaked out when I told her I found the bug. She had no idea why anyone would want to listen in on her conversations. She said her life was utterly boring and all she did in her office was order more supplies, which didn't make for interesting conversation.

Cara and I walked Luke back to the office and I showed him where the listening device had been planted. He got on his back and shimmed his way under the desk. We were still careful not to say anything that could alert the person listening in that we knew it was there. A moment later, Luke slid back out and stood, shooing us out of the office.

"It's what it looks like," he said, raising his eyes to Tyler in a knowing glance. This changed the course of the case. He asked Cara similar questions to what I had asked earlier and found what I had – there was no real reason for someone to bug her office.

"I'm going to leave that there for now. Try to act normal and not say anything to indicate you know it's there. I'll be back later today and take care of it then."

We were assuming at that point no other bugs had been planted. They'd need a team out to check though. When we were back on the sidewalk, I explained, "I went into two more shops and I found the same in both. All of the shops need to be searched. I didn't bother because I don't know all that much about surveillance equipment. Cooper usually takes those cases and he's in the field doing interviews. We'd have to call you guys either way."

"What do you think it is, Luke?" Tyler asked.

"It's high-grade equipment like we use. This isn't some spy shop bug. We need a strategy for how we are going to deal with this. We should go back to the office and make a plan with Captain Meadows. We also have to decide if we are looping Det. Sawyer in on this or not."

Tyler shook his head. "I say we take this under the auspice of our case and run it to the ground."

"Will you check the other shops before you go?" I asked, trying not to sound needy, but I wanted to loop Cooper in after all was confirmed.

"Tell you what," Luke started. "You come with me to check some of the shops and Tyler will check the others. Then you can meet us down at the station. I'm sure Captain Meadows will want to hear firsthand what you found."

"How did you figure out to look for surveillance equipment?" Tyler asked.

"It wasn't me. I went to the coffee shop with Emma to go over the case because a lot wasn't adding up for me. She suggested that the marbles might indicate where listening devices were left. She had seen a *Dateline* episode about a case of insider trading in Arizona and she wondered if that was happening here."

Luke snapped his fingers. "I knew there was a case like that in Phoenix. I was trying to remember it last night when you were going over the case. I couldn't remember the details but was going to research it today."

Tyler nodded in admiration. "Maybe you and Cooper should hire Emma."

"Her husband would kill me." We divided up the shops that we knew had been broken into and Tyler took one half and Luke and I the other.

Before Tyler left, I explained, "The marbles were all found in owners' offices except for the kitchen store – it was found near the register. Lisa will show you."

I wasn't disappointed that Tyler was going to search Lisa's shop. She and I were a bit like oil and water. For whatever reason, she didn't like me. She hadn't been pleased to see me the night before when we crashed the community meeting. She went out of her way to walk up to me to remind me that I hadn't been invited to the meeting. Luckily, Cooper had gotten Hattie to bring us as her guests, and then when I asked about the marbles, the rest of the shop owners were glad we were there. I didn't know what her problem was, but I hoped to avoid her going forward.

Luke and I made quick work of connecting with shop owners and managers. I knew from the meeting the night before where all the marbles had been left and Luke zeroed in on the locations and found a bug at each shop.

I had hoped to see Hattie and thank her for allowing us to attend the meeting, but she wasn't in the shop. One of the women working for her escorted us to her office and Luke found the bug planted nearly in the same spot that I had found the one under Cara's desk.

The young woman working pulled back in surprise and promised to call Hattie for us.

"Just don't call from the office," I reminded her. "We want to keep a low profile on what's been found until law enforcement decides how to play it. The last thing we want to do is alert the person who planted the bugs that they have been found."

We repeated the same instructions at each shop until we had crossed all of them off our list. Tyler was standing on the sidewalk in front of the coffee shop when we got back.

"Each shop has a recording device," Tyler said as we approached. "We need some tech guys to go through each shop and remove them, sweep for others, and tell us what we are looking at here."

"Let's call on the way back to the office. We can have a tech team member meet with us when we speak to Captain Meadows." Luke turned to me. "I'll meet you down at the police station."

I gave a half-hearted wave and then walked back to the house. I texted Cooper again on the way because he hadn't responded to my earlier text. I assumed he was still in an interview. I got back to the house and was about to leave when my cellphone rang. It was Adele.

"I can't reach Cooper," she said instead of hello. "Do you have any updates for me? I need to call Dr. Wright. I also got a call from the prosecutor looking to cut a deal."

When Adele was in work mode, she was singularly focused. I told her about the bugs I found at the shops. "I'm heading down to the police station right now for a meeting with Luke, Det. Tyler and Captain Meadows. Luke wants me to update Captain Meadows about what we have found so far. It looks promising, Adele. I'd hold off on making any deals with the prosecutor. I'd assume we can get all the charges dropped if Cooper was able to confirm that watch wasn't in Izzy's possession at the time of the burglaries."

"What do you think the bugs are about, Riley? That's so strange." Adele told someone in her office to bring her a client file and then she got back on the phone. "This must go beyond a simple burglary."

"I assume that's why nothing was taken," I agreed. "I can't reach Cooper either so when I know more, I'll let you know. He was headed to the police station today to speak with Det. Sawyer."

"Tell him to call me. I'd love to get the charges dropped. Izzy's not going to agree to a plea anyway."

"There's no way you'd convince him to do that." We talked for a few more minutes and then we ended the call. I drove downtown looking at my phone at every stop light to see if Cooper had texted back. It wasn't like him to go this long without a response.

I pulled into the back parking lot of the police station, parked in a designated visitor's parking spot, then made my way into the building and up to Luke's office. The bullpen was quiet this time of day. Desks had piles of papers and file folders, a phone rang several times, but no one was there to answer it. There wasn't a soul in sight. I assumed most of the detectives were out on cases.

Raised voices coming from down the hall caught my attention. I made my way down the corridor to the conference room door and recognized Cooper's voice as I got closer. I knocked once, waited for the okay to enter, and walked in on Captain Meadows, Luke, Tyler, and Cooper sitting around the table. Cooper had a bag of ice up to his eye and dried blood on his cheek.

I pulled back in surprise. "What happened to you?"

CHAPTER 26

All eyes turned to me as I closed the door behind me. I walked to Cooper and touched the side of his cheek. "Seriously, Cooper, what happened?"

"Det. Sawyer didn't like what I had to say and he lunged at me." Cooper removed the bag of ice to show me his eye which had puffed up and turned a bright red with hints of a bruise already forming. "I tried to explain to him that he arrested the wrong guy and that he might want to take a look at his son and he lost it. I only lost the fight because I was sitting on his desk and he knocked me to the ground. Had he taken a swing at me like a man, he would have lost."

Cooper's pride seemed more banged up than his face. "I don't think who won or lost the fight is important here."

"I agree, Riley," Captain Meadows said and gestured for me to take a seat. "Before you came in, Cooper was explaining what he found out this morning. Do you need to be caught up?"

I pulled out a chair and sat next to Tyler. Luke and Cooper were across the table from me and Captain Meadows was in his normal seat at the head of the table. "Cooper and I haven't had a chance to compare notes since last night so that would be great."

Cooper pressed the ice pack back to his eye and rested his head in his other hand with his elbow on the table. "I interviewed Jimmy Ragone and he admitted that four of them broke into the shops. He named Scott and two other guys who he said he was with on those nights. He said that Scott planted Izzy's watch, and he admitted to being the person who cut the surveillance in the shops. He said it was a game and a challenge – he used both words. I don't believe that's all there is to it."

"You told Det. Sawyer this?" I pinned my gaze on him not surprised that Det. Sawyer had hit him.

"I didn't lead with that. It was contentious from the start. He's not going to listen to us."

Luke looked back at Cooper and then angled himself to speak directly to Captain Meadows. "Where is Sawyer now?"

"I sent him home to cool off for the day."

"No suspension?"

Captain Meadows shook his head. "I'm not dealing with the paperwork from his union rep. Besides, it sounds like Cooper antagonized him."

"Is that true?" Tyler asked, not looking all too surprised.

Cooper chuckled. "It's a fair assessment. I didn't think I was going to get anywhere being nice so I went in a little hot. I'm paying for that now."

Captain Meadows cleared his throat and we all turned to him. "If what you're telling me is true, then Sawyer is in enough trouble, especially given his son was involved in the break-ins." He hitched his jaw to me. "Luke tells me that you had a big find today."

I explained about finding the listening devices in the shops. "I thought it was a farfetched idea at first, but I knew the marbles were an odd thing to leave behind. We need to find out what all of those shops have in common and why someone would want to listen in. Is there a way to trace the equipment?"

I had more questions but wanted to start there. There was a lot I didn't understand about that kind of surveillance. As private investigators, we have rules and laws to follow, and even if clients asked us for surveillance like that, it's not something we were prepared to do all that often.

"It can be traced," Luke said, running a hand down his face. "Are we letting it ride in the hopes of investigating further or pulling all the bugs out of the shops and alerting whoever planted them that we know?"

"I'd think we'd have to pull it," Tyler said and then watched Luke's reaction.

Luke furrowed his brow. "I don't know if that's the right thing. I feel like there's an opportunity here."

"For what?" Tyler asked.

"To catch whoever is involved with this."

Tyler shook his head. "Luke, we can't ask all of those shop owners to work under surveillance indefinitely. Someone is bound to slip up and then it will be out there anyway. If we are going to do something, we need to do it now."

"I agree," Captain Meadows said with tension in his voice. He looked around the table. "Got any ideas?"

I shifted in my seat. I had an idea, but I wasn't sure if it was good or not.

"What if," I said slowly, dragging it out, "you have one of the shop owners find the surveillance and make a show of it so the person listening in can hear them. They can act like they aren't sure how it got there. Maybe accuse an employee of spying on management. Then debate aloud if they should call the cops or not. You can then have a surveillance team watching the shops to see if anyone breaks in and removes them."

The four of them sat stone-faced for a few moments. Luke said, "It's as good an idea as any."

Captain Meadows added, "It cuts down on the time it will be dragged out. If it doesn't work then we can remove them all and get on with the investigation."

Tyler and Cooper didn't look convinced.

Cooper looked to Tyler. "What's the range on equipment like that? Does the person listening in have to be nearby or could they be anywhere in the city?"

"There's a good range. With that particular model, a person can log onto the website, type in the code on the bug, and listen in from the comfort of their home or office, or car. Anywhere they can access the website," Tyler explained. He turned to Captain Meadows. "If we are running with Riley's idea then we need to do that now. We told those shop owners we'd have an answer for them today."

Luke looked at me. "Do you have a shop owner in mind?"

"Not Lisa at the kitchen store," I said too quickly and Luke smirked. "She seems difficult."

"Why don't we ask Hattie?" Cooper said, dropping the ice pack on the table. "Out of everyone I trust her the most. She said she's worked with Det. Tyson Granger."

"Det. Granger's a solid detective," Luke said. "He's only worked here a couple of years, but if he knows Hattie, then I trust her to help us. He was headed out on a case when I came in earlier. Let me give him a call." Luke pulled his phone from his pocket and stepped out of the conference room.

Tyler squinted his eyes. "You think a fake psychic is our best bet?"

I couldn't attest to her psychic skills, but Hattie seemed like a sweet woman. I explained my meeting with Harper. "They are involved in the case on multiple levels so it makes sense to bring them in on this."

Cooper echoed what I said and he offered me a smile of appreciation. "Let me talk to Hattie first outside the shop. She can 'find' the bug and then we can talk in her office about what it means."

Tyler seemed to consider that. "It would be much more controlled that way."

"I could convince her to hold off on calling the cops and to let Riley and I investigate. That will probably be more believable than her choosing not to call the cops."

"Sounds like a plan," Captain Meadows said, seeming pleased with the idea.

Luke returned a moment later. "Det. Granger said we can trust Hattie. He cautioned she tends to overstep sometimes but is well-intentioned."

Tyler gave Luke a quick overview of the plan with Cooper and Luke readily agreed. Cooper would visit Hattie after we finished the meeting. I told him I'd stop in all the shops and update them that Luke and Tyler would be in touch in the morning and for now to keep the bugs a secret. I reasoned that if I went that would probably be better than detectives showing up again on the same day going in and out of the stores. We'd be in trouble if anyone had witnessed us earlier in the day.

A thought occurred to me and I turned to Luke. "We never checked Holly's shop for a bug."

"We didn't but the crime scene techs swept that place. If they found a bug, they'd have told us."

"We should check to make sure, Luke," Tyler said, offering to do that.

"We can do that before we go pay Holly's boyfriend a visit." He looked over at Captain Meadows. "What's going to happen with Det. Sawyer?"

"Let's wait to see if Jimmy Ragone comes in with his parents to confess. If not, Cooper can follow up with his parents. There's not much we can do with hearsay which is what Cooper's interview is right now with nothing on paper. I'm going to let it ride with Det. Sawyer right now and give the prosecutor's office a call. I think it's safe to say Izzy is off the hook."

Captain Meadows looked over at Cooper and then across the table at me. "Let's not tell him yet until we know for sure. I don't want to make any false promises but update Adele."

As they stood to leave, Captain Meadows called Luke back. "We need to discuss Jordan Collins. She's called me three times and I've yet to return her call. She's demanding to be cleared and wants to know if she can leave town. She wants to go back to New York."

Luke sighed. "I haven't even had a chance to check her alibi and we haven't received the surveillance footage from the hotel. I wanted another crack at interviewing her, too." He rubbed his bald head and then turned to me. "What do you think about interviewing her? You've worked as a consultant for us before. Jordan might be more open with a woman. She seemed to hate me on sight."

"I'm fine with it, Riley," Captain Meadows said, turning to me. "We need to clear her or formally tell her she's a person of interest. We can't leave her in limbo. I'll call the hotel and get the surveillance footage. I know the warrant has been served already. They might need a nudge."

"Let me call her alibi right now before I leave," Luke offered. "At least one thing will be taken care of before Riley meets with her."

I followed Luke to his desk. He sat down and shoved paper around on his desk until he found a yellow sticky pad. He held it up to me. "I took the note in my phone and then jotted it down. I'm so old I don't trust my phone."

Luke was anything but old. "You never trust your phone. I'll go talk to Cooper while you call him."

I found Cooper in the staff kitchen. He was leaning against the counter and had a fresh ice pack on his face. "You want to take a break? I can go see Hattie if you want to head home for the day."

Cooper shook his head. He handed me a bottle of ibuprofen. "I can't get the bottle open. I'll take a couple and then head over to Hattie's. I'll take a break when that's done."

I popped off the top of the bottle with ease and then pulled out cash from my pocket and got him a soda from the machine. I handed Cooper the pills and drink. "Starting a fight with Det. Sawyer isn't going to do us any good. You never lose your temper like that."

"He's arrogant and needed to be taken down a peg or two." Cooper knocked back the pills and took a big gulp of soda. He set the can down with a clank. "I'll get him back for this."

"No, you won't. Let it go, Cooper. All that matters right now is that we clear Izzy's name and move on to the next case." I walked right up to him until I was standing under his nose and had to tilt my head back to meet his eyes. "Go talk to Hattie and then go home and update Adele. Get some rest and we can be back at it in the morning."

"I need to get Jimmy to confess to the cops."

I patted Cooper's shoulder. "Tomorrow is another day. You can see his parents and tell them what he told you. If they are responsible people, they will do the work for us."

The look on Cooper's face told me he didn't think it would be that easy. I had slightly more faith in humanity at the moment.

CHAPTER 27

Cooper stood on the sidewalk in front of Hattie's shop. The sun had already started to fall and the streetlights cast an eerie glow against the fallen leaves and storefront window lights. There were only a handful of people in the shop, which closed at six. Cooper checked his watch. It was nearing five-thirty.

He stood at the glass door and peered into the shop. Hattie was busy at the counter refilling someone's tea and handing them a pastry. She chatted with Sarah and then wiped her hands on a dishtowel near the register. No one had seen him yet. Cooper pulled open the door, which rang the bell to alert that someone new had entered. Hattie turned in his direction and a smile spread across her face when she saw him. Her hand went to her mouth when she saw his battered face.

Cooper asked her to meet him outside. Hattie said something to Sarah who also turned to look at him and then she made her way out of the shop.

"What happened to you?" she said as she joined him on the sidewalk.

"Let's just say that my meeting with Det. Sawyer didn't go as planned." Cooper reached up and touched his tender cheekbone and eye. "It will heal. We have a plan and it involves you. I'm hoping you're willing to help."

"Anything," Hattie said. "I'm assuming it's about the listening device found in my office today. I've kept out of that room all day and didn't

180

mention anything to my other staff. Sarah was the one who spoke to Riley."

"Good." Cooper smiled and then appraised her. "How well can you act?"

"I spent a good portion of my life pretending not to be a psychic while in polite company. Fairly well." She giggled and placed her hand on his arm. "What are we doing?"

Cooper explained the plan and why it was important. If he was asking this of her, Cooper wanted her to understand what it meant for the case. "I don't know that anything will come of it. But we will send the message that at least one of the bugs has been found. Then tonight the cops will watch the shops to see if they try to remove the others before they are found."

"I don't know if that will work," Hattie said with skepticism in her voice.

"I'm not so sure either, but it's all we've got right now. I'll give the bug to Det. Tyler and Det. Morgan and they can trace it to determine who might have purchased it."

"My niece, Harper, has a gift where she can hold an object and get impressions. Do you want her to do that?"

Cooper didn't believe that such a thing was possible but it was sweet of Hattie to offer. He told her as much and then added, "I don't want you to touch it at all because there might be fingerprints on it and we need to preserve those if we can. I'll put on gloves when I remove it and then slip it into a crime scene bag." He pulled the bag out of his back pocket to show her.

Hattie tapped the side of her head. "Smart thinking. This is why I'm always getting in trouble with Det. Granger."

"Ready?"

"Let's put on a show!" Hattie giggled again and her infectious laugh made Cooper smile too.

They went into the shop and Hattie waved to Sarah who was behind the counter. "I'm going into my office and don't want to be disturbed." They walked through the shop and behind the red velvet curtain. Cooper had wondered earlier what was on the other side.

He followed behind Hattie down a short hallway and she opened a door on the right. Before stepping in Cooper pulled on gloves. Hattie sat behind her desk and then Cooper sat across from her. They sat chatting like old friends for a few minutes and then Cooper asked her more questions about the burglary, things they had discussed on his earlier visit.

"Let me show you some photos of how things looked when I came in that morning," Hattie said and reached for her phone, which sat on the desk. She grabbed it and then the phone slid from her hands to the floor and bounced under the desk. Hattie groaned. "My hands don't work quite the way they used to."

"Do you want me to get it for you?" Cooper asked, inching forward in his seat.

"No, I got it," Hattie grumbled and made some noises as if trying to reach for the phone. She paused dramatically for effect and then said, "Cooper, what's this thing under my desk? I can't get down here to see and you know my eyes aren't too good anymore."

Cooper stood and went around to the back of Hattie's desk. When Hattie moved out of the way, he got down on the floor. They hoped the whole scene was real enough with the noises to match.

"I'm not sure," Cooper said at first and then ran his gloved finger over it. "It looks like some kind of recording device. Is there any reason someone would have that kind of surveillance in here?"

"None that I can think of," Hattie said dramatically. She played up her shock and speculated about what it could be doing there. Then she reached for the phone on her desk. "I'm going to call the police."

"Let's hold off on calling the cops if you can," Cooper said, detaching the listening device and palming it as he scooted back out. "Riley and I can look into this and then turn it over for you."

"Are you sure? That doesn't sound like something we should do."

"I'm sure. I'll talk to Riley and if we can't figure it out, we'll go to the cops in a couple of days with it. Det. Morgan is Riley's husband so he'll know what to do."

"If you think that's best," Hattie said, her voice giving away uncertainty.

Before they left the office, Cooper asked, "Are you sure there's no reason you'd have this in here?"

"None," Hattie assured him. "No one even comes into this office but me."

They walked to the front of the shop and then Cooper sat down at a table. He flipped over the small device and popped open the small latch in the back and removed the round flat battery, effectively stopping all transmission. He slipped it into the bag, sealed it, and borrowed a pen from Hattie to make a note of where it had been taken from and the date.

Hattie waited until they walked out of the shop to show her excitement. "Did I do okay?"

"You did great," Cooper said and meant it. It couldn't have gone better. He hoped it did the trick. "I'll get this to where it needs to go and then I'll be in touch."

Hattie told him to wait right there. She opened the door and shouted to Sarah to pull some treats from the display case and insisted that Cooper take them. "You've been knocked around today and some sweets will make you feel better." Cooper tried to pay her but Hattie refused his money. Sarah brought the box to the door and handed it to him. Cooper thanked Hattie for all of her help.

She reached up and touched his cheek. "You need to let someone mother you once in a while. You deserve to be taken care of too."

Cooper choked back the emotion that swelled up in him. He had no mother growing up and it had been the one hole in his life. He nodded once and left, hoping to keep it together until he got to his truck. He crossed the street nearly stepping in front of a passing car because he wasn't paying attention. He stepped back just in time as the driver shot him a dirty look and honked.

Cooper waved him off mouthing an apology and then crossed the street to his truck. He tossed the baker's box in the passenger seat, started the engine, and pulled away from the curb before the tears streamed down his face. He didn't know what was wrong with him or why he was so emotional lately. The case wasn't even all that difficult in comparison to many they'd had in the past. There was just something about Hattie that tugged at his heartstrings in a way that no one had ever done before.

Cooper pulled into the parking lot of the police station and gave himself a moment. He checked his reflection in the rearview mirror and grimaced. His face was puffy and red and his cheek and eye were forming a terrible-looking bruise. It wasn't one of his better days.

Once he got upstairs, he put the evidence bag in Luke's side drawer under a stack of folders, tucking it away out of sight. There was only one detective in the bullpen when Cooper had arrived. It was someone he had worked with before. He waved as he went in and then yelled goodbye on his way out.

When he finally got home, he found Adele sitting on the couch with a blanket wrapped around her and scattered papers in front of her. Her glasses were perched on the end of her nose as she chewed on the capped end of a blue highlighter.

"What's all this?" Cooper asked, joining her on the couch.

Adele leaned over and kissed him on the cheek and then held his chin, turning his head side to side as she checked out his face. "Riley told me you were banged up. Sawyer got you pretty good. Are you okay?"

"Better now that I'm home." Cooper snuggled into the couch. "Hattie sent me home with some sweets. I put them over on the counter if you want any."

Adele gathered up her papers and stacked them in a neat pile on the coffee table. She tossed the highlighter and her glasses on top and wrapped her arms around Cooper, pulling him into her. "I spoke to the prosecutor's office today. They want me to come in for a meeting tomorrow afternoon to discuss some options. I told them outright that Izzy wasn't going to take a plea. They assured me that wasn't the reason for the meeting. I assume Captain Meadows called them."

"He talked about calling them at the meeting today." Cooper went through his day and all the evidence that both he and Riley had found. He explained about the listening devices and the plan. "Luke and Tyler are going to sit out there tonight. Hopefully, the people responsible will get spooked enough to try to remove the others from the shops."

Adele crinkled up her face. "You think that will work? That's a lot of breaking and entering for one night."

"That's what I thought. It's only one night wasted if it doesn't work. Maybe they will get curious enough to come back to the scene."

"Now that the scope seems to have expanded beyond a simple burglary, did Luke say anything to indicate he thinks it might be connected to the murder?"

Cooper shook his head. "I don't think so. He thinks whoever killed Holly was someone she knew. She turned her back on the person."

Adele hugged Cooper closer. "That doesn't mean it's not all connected," she said absently as she ran her fingers through his hair.

CHAPTER 28

I stood on the sidewalk outside the Capital Hotel and read Luke's text. He had called the number Jordan Collins had given him for her one-night stand. Instead of a man, a middle-aged woman answered. She said she had never heard of Jordan Collins. The woman assured Luke that she was the only one who had access to her phone. She wasn't married and didn't even have a boyfriend. Jordan had either lied about her alibi or she had been given a fake number when her lover slipped out of her bed that morning.

It wasn't looking good for Jordan. No one stopped me as I made my way past the desk on the first floor and went right up the center staircase. When I found her room, I knocked once and then again.

"Hang on," a woman shouted from inside. The chain squeaked as it moved across the mechanism and the deadbolt clicked open. Jordan stood in the open doorway barefoot wearing a tee-shirt and sweats. She raised one perfectly arched eyebrow. "I asked for more towels like an hour ago."

"Can't help you with the towels, but I need to speak with you." I introduced myself and barely finished speaking when Jordan waved her hand in the air like she couldn't care less who I was and then let me in the room.

"I'm stuck here I might as well have someone to talk to," she said, sitting down on the couch. I took a chair on the other side of the small living room space.

"You don't seem surprised to see me."

"The cops have talked to me. I assumed there'd be others." Jordan shrugged and tugged on her tee-shirt that clung to her middle. "I don't know anything so I don't have anything to hide. This will make for some good posts on social media."

The woman's cavalier attitude shocked me. The fact that she was using it as fodder for Instagram was beyond my comprehension. I didn't get the need to post so much on social media.

"A woman is dead, and you are being looked at as a suspect. Doesn't that bother you?"

"Not particularly. The cops aren't going to find that I did anything wrong so no reason to stress it. One dead hater. What does it matter?"

I inched myself to the edge of the chair. "Jordan, your alibi didn't check out."

She stared across the room at me like she hadn't heard what I said. "Of course it did."

"No, Jordan, it didn't. I spoke to Det. Morgan before I arrived. The phone number you gave him was for a woman who has never heard of you." I watched her to see if there was any recognition or caring that she had lied to a detective.

Jordan sat there for a moment like she didn't believe me and then she shoved herself off the couch and went to the desk in the corner of the room. She pulled a slip of paper from the table and yanked her phone so hard from the charger I wouldn't have been surprised if both had broken. She punched in the numbers and held the phone to her ear. When she asked to speak with the man that she claimed she had been with, her face fell at the response.

"Are you sure?" she barked at the person on the other end. "He's about six-foot-three and had sandy brown hair and green eyes. I met him at Big Whiskey." Jordan listened and then her hand started to shake. Her breathing became shallow and she dropped the phone to her desk.

"I don't understand," she said, turning to look at me. "We had a great night together. Why would he give me a fake number?"

Tears ran down her face and she cried so hard her body shook with each giant sob.

I wasn't good with huge displays of emotion from people I knew let alone someone I had no attachment to. Before Luke, I went on a blind date once with a guy who cried in Starbucks. While everyone stared at us, all I could muster was offering to buy him a cookie. I had wanted to tell him to man up and go home and cry in his beer. I had the same reaction now with Jordan, but there was no cookie to offer her and technically we were in her room. She could cry all she wanted.

"It happens," I said after giving her a moment. "You know men. They are afraid of smart, beautiful women. He was probably intimidated by you." I didn't believe the words coming out of my mouth any more than I thought Jordan would. That's why it surprised me when she sniffed and turned to me.

"You think that's it? He did say a few times that I was smart."

I forced a smile and nodded. "I can't think of any other reason why." Unless of course she was lying and there was no guy. Jordan seemed genuinely shaken up though, as if she'd never taken a man home and then been ditched the next day. I figured stuff like that happened all the time. I wasn't so cavalier in my personal life. I assumed every stranger was a serial killer.

I refocused her attention. "We need to find a way to verify your alibi."

Jordan wiped the tears from her face and plopped down on the couch. "I'm not sure how."

"Det. Morgan said you had a confrontation with Holly. When was that?"

"The night before her murder. I went to the shop late in the evening and confronted her." She looked up at me with her eyes opened wide. "I fought with her. I already admitted that. I left the shop and never returned. That was the last and only time I saw Holly."

Call it a hunch or a deep rumbling in my gut, but I knew there was more. "Tell me about your interaction with her."

Jordan cocked her head to the side. "I'm not sure what you want me to say."

"The truth. You went there to confront her so tell me what happened."

Jordan sighed loudly and picked at her thumbnail with her finger. "Holly was on the phone when I arrived. She was shouting at someone so it seemed like she was already in a bad mood. You should have seen the look she gave me when I walked into her shop. I pretended I was looking through the racks. When she hung up the phone, she came over to me and practically guided me to the door."

"Why would she do that?" I asked even though I was sure of the answer.

"Hello!" Jordan sing-songed loudly and opened her arms wide. "I'm fat and Holly didn't like fat women, especially fat women who dared to enter her precious shop. I'm sure you've seen photos of her. She thought she was perfect – blonde, attractive, thin. I'm sure on the inside she was a raggedy hag."

"Ah, the scandal. I was out of town for that."

"It was bad. Worse than you can imagine. Holly went full crazy on her Facebook page. She didn't have to say anything at all. It's not like she posted a comment on someone else's post and then she started getting hate and had to defend herself." Jordan cackled a high-pitched laugh. "No, the big dummy brought it on herself. She went right to her business Facebook page and slagged off another business for having plus-sized athletic wear. She said fat women don't deserve nice workout clothes. We don't get to look cute and be fat. Holly brought all of this on herself."

"She didn't deserve to die." I didn't want to justify Holly's actions because they were indefensible. Sure, she had a right to her opinion and the community had a right to check her for it. Death wasn't a justifiable punishment though.

"Maybe not, but as I said, that had nothing to do with me."

"Get back to what happened at the shop. She walked you toward the door and then what?"

"I stopped before we got to the door." Jordan smiled. "One of the upsides about being a big girl – if you don't want someone to move you, they aren't moving you. I tried to talk to her about what had happened and why she was getting so much hate. My goal was to educate her, but Holly wasn't having any of it. She went off on me and I went off on her."

Jordan shrugged. "I ended up punching her and then I left the shop."

"You hit her and ran?"

"Not exactly." Jordan pulled her legs under her and sat cross-legged on the couch. "After I hit her, we both stood there stunned that it had happened. She tried to lunge for me, but I ran. She was either going to call the cops or she was going to kill me. I didn't stick around after that."

Seemed like a smart decision to me. "Where did you go?"

"I came back downtown and went to Big Whiskey. I was hyped up after it happened. I didn't even Instagram it because I figured if she called the cops, I needed to find a way to deny it, you know?"

"You're willing to lie to the cops?"

"Well, I wouldn't lie about killing someone," Jordan said, defending herself. "Something stupid like punching a terrible person – a lie might be needed. I shouldn't be in trouble for her being a bad person."

I couldn't reason with the unreasonable. "Was anyone at the shop when you were there?"

"Not that I saw and no one came in as I was leaving. As far as I know, Holly was alone closing up the shop for the night."

"What about the phone call? You said she was on the phone when you came in. What was she talking about?"

Jordan pursed her lips. "Now that seemed a little strange."

"Strange how?"

"Well, she..." Jordan paused as if trying to think back. "Holly was yelling at the person when I first walked in. She seemed hotheaded like she was upset about something. She told the person they had to find it. That they weren't doing a good enough job. Then she saw me and quieted down. I could still hear her though. She said they had to find the money before anyone else did. She glanced over at me and then told the person she'd call them back."

"What money?" I asked aloud even though I was sure Jordan wouldn't know the answer.

She shrugged. "No idea. I wondered if she was talking to a shop investor because people had stopped shopping with her. Maybe she was facing some financial strain because of the protests and stuff."

"That could be it. You didn't hear anything else?"

"No." Jordan looped her hair behind her ear. "Do you think it's important?"

"I don't know what's important."

"What are you going to do about my alibi?"

I wasn't sure what Luke would do. I stood and headed for the door. "I'll be in touch about that."

Jordan groaned and stood. "I still can't leave? I want to go home."

I called over my shoulder, "Stay put for now and Det. Morgan will be in touch soon."

Jordan followed right behind me. "If you catch the killer, will you call and tell me? I'll want to post about it."

I didn't respond and left her room thinking that was the most ridiculous thing that I had heard all day. For what it was worth, I believed Jordan hadn't killed Holly. She may not have had an alibi and she may have even been strong enough physically to pull it off, but I didn't get the feeling she was a killer.

CHAPTER 29

L uke knocked once and then stepped back off the small two-step porch of Jason Manning's home. He and Tyler had been able to locate the man's home address with relative ease. If they had to separate him from his wife, MaryBeth, to interview them in different rooms, that's what they'd do.

Luke stepped up on the porch for the second time and banged his fist against the blue door. The outside of the home had had a recent paint job and looked like it had been recently renovated. Luke would have bet money that the front door had graced the cover of one of Riley's home improvement magazines that she frequently left around the house as a hint for projects they could take on. Luke made neat little piles of the magazines and tried to ignore any unnecessary home-improvement work.

Luke was about to tell Tyler that they should leave and come back another day when the front door cracked open. A woman with a poof of brown hair stuck her head out and appraised them.

"What has my husband done now?" she asked with a pop and snap of her gum.

"MaryBeth Manning?" Luke asked and the woman nodded. He explained who they were and why they were there. "We understand that your husband was familiar with Holly Bell. We need to speak to him."

"Familiar?" MaryBeth laughed. "That's one way to say that my husband was screwing trash."

She pulled open the door and came fully into view, her wide hips blocking Luke's view into the home. Her belly strained her pink top. Luke couldn't help but wonder if Holly's attack on social media didn't have something to do with her boyfriend's wife.

Tyler propped his foot on the first step. "You were aware of the affair then?"

MaryBeth dug her fists into her hips. "Not only was I aware of it, but I also put a stop to it."

"How did you do that?" Luke asked, trying to keep his tone even.

MaryBeth shook her head at Luke like she thought it was a stupid question. "I confronted him about it. I told him he had to stop or I was divorcing him and taking everything including his business. What did you think I did?"

"I wasn't sure." Luke stepped up onto the porch. "I assume your husband isn't home?"

"He's at a job site. Do you want me to call him?"

Luke looked back at Tyler and they communicated a simple message without words. He turned back to MaryBeth. "If it's possible, we can speak with you instead of him. We have a few questions."

"Come on in," she said, stepping out of the way. "Take a seat in the kitchen if that works for you. I have dinner in the oven and will need to check it soon."

The home was warm and inviting. There didn't seem to be an item out of place. No kids were running or yelling and no clutter on the floor. The furniture was new and the living room and foyer looked like it could have been a spread in a recent magazine. Luke had no idea how anyone lived like this. It looked a bit like a show home rather than something lived in. Even the pillows positioned on the couches seemed like they had been placed there professionally and arranged just so.

"Do you have children?" Luke asked as they sat at the rectangle farm table.

"No. We never had kids. Jason was busy building his business and I was busy building mine. The time never seemed right. Now, given the affair, I'm glad we never did." MaryBeth sat down and pulled her chair into the table. "What do you need to know?"

"What do you do?" Tyler asked.

"Interior design. I have several clients I work with here in Little Rock, but my clients are as far away as Georgia." She tugged on her pink shirt. "Don't let appearances fool you. I was about to stain a cabinet when you showed up and didn't want to ruin any good clothes. I clean up better than this."

Before Luke could ask anything else, MaryBeth leaned forward on the table and pointed at Luke. "My husband likes to say that he's the breadwinner of this family but that hasn't been the case in several years. I had a rough couple of years at the start, but I've been making far more than him since that time. He doesn't like admitting it. I wouldn't rub his nose in it if he didn't act like I was a lazy cow sitting at home all day. My business is thriving."

MaryBeth's anger simmered at the surface. Luke could understand it, but she seemed right on the brink of boiling over and they had only just started. "I assume that there have been some issues in your marriage."

"Beyond issues." MaryBeth waved him off. "I said we could divorce, but he said we could work on it. He told people he didn't have the money to divorce. The truth is, he doesn't want to walk away from my money. I pay the mortgage and most of the bills. He's run himself and that business into debt. He'd be homeless if he left." A smile spread across her face. "Want to know the kicker of it all?"

Luke nodded, watching how animated her face had become.

195

"We got married later in life. We were both in our thirties. At the time, Jason's construction business was doing well. I was only getting started. He insisted on a prenup that states we each leave with what we came in with and that neither of us can benefit from the other's business or anything created during the marriage. Jason assumed he'd be making millions and I'd be a flop. Fate gave him a kick in the fanny for that one." MaryBeth smiled at Luke and it was clear she was proud of herself.

Tyler rested his arms on the table. "You have no reason to stay married then."

"Correct. I spoke to a divorce lawyer after I found out about the affair. I haven't served him yet, but we are headed in that direction."

"Did you confront Holly about the affair?"

MaryBeth took a breath. "I'm not proud of it but I did. I wasn't going to because I have more pride than that. Holly posted that stupid message on Facebook about big girls and I lost it. I went to her shop and screamed at her. I might have even threatened her, who knows. I lost it at that point."

"Did it get physical?" Tyler asked.

"No. Never. I've never been in a physical fight in my life. I have a business and a reputation to protect." MaryBeth looked at the both of them, making strong eye contact. "I said some hateful, regretful things for sure. I shouldn't have gone to her shop. It was stupid of me and my temper got the better of me."

Luke didn't have a reason not to believe her. She sounded sincere. "Where were you on Sunday morning around six-thirty?"

"In bed with Jason. We had gone out to dinner the night before and talked about our marriage. He seemed to believe it was worth saving, but I wasn't convinced. We went out to dinner and stayed up late talking. We both slept in." The timer went off on the oven and MaryBeth stood from the table. She slipped on an oven mitt and opened the door and pulled out a casserole dish.

Luke couldn't see what was in the dish but it smelled like lasagna. "Holly was murdered Sunday morning. If I'm hearing you correctly then you and Jason are each other's alibis?"

MaryBeth slipped off the mitt and turned to face him. She had a far-off look on her face. "I guess so. I hadn't thought about it like that. I understand why you'd think Jason could be a suspect, but he was here with me that morning."

"And you were here, too." There must have been something about the way Luke said that because MaryBeth looked at him in confusion.

She pointed to herself. "You considered me a suspect?"

Luke nodded. "We knew you had a confrontation with Holly. You had motive and it was suggested to us that you should be a person of interest."

MaryBeth narrowed her eyes. "Who'd suggest such a thing? Jason?"

"No, we haven't spoken to him yet."

MaryBeth walked back to her chair and sat down. "Then who?"

"I can't tell you that."

MaryBeth shifted her eyes between Tyler and Luke. "If I guess, will you tell me?" She didn't wait for a response. "I'm assuming it was Holly's friend, Courtney. She didn't like me much. She didn't like Jason either so she wasn't supportive of the affair. I'm sure she'd try to pin it on one of us."

Luke pulled back in his seat. He had no idea MaryBeth knew Courtney. The fact that she had guessed it right off raised his suspicion. He didn't confirm or deny though. "Did you have much interaction with Courtney?"

"I've had some. I knew her before I knew Holly so when I found out about the affair, I already knew their little clique." MaryBeth leaned forward on the table. "I have no evidence, but the rumor is that Courtney has a bit of a drug problem and snorts most of her husband's money up her nose. She's had some beef with Holly a time or two as well. She isn't quite what she seems."

Courtney had seemed frazzled when Luke and Tyler were at the house. Luke assumed it was the kids. "Do you have any idea who might have killed Holly? Heard any rumors or talk about that?"

"I don't run in those circles, but Jason and Holly were up to something. I'm not sure what."

That piqued Luke's attention. "Why would you say that?"

MaryBeth got up from her chair. "I'll be right back."

When she was gone from the room, Luke turned to Tyler. "What do you think?"

"She's credible. I'm not surprised what she said about Courtney, but if no one else can confirm that Jason and MaryBeth were home Sunday morning, we need to keep them both on the suspect list."

Luke blew out a frustrated breath. "Agreed."

MaryBeth came back into the room with her hands full of printed-out pages. She dropped them on the table in front of Luke. "My husband's text conversations with Holly. Take them with you. His cellphone is in my name and he was dumb enough to text. All I had to do was request a printout from the provider. I have other copies here and a set with my attorney. I can't quite make out what they were doing, but Jason kept talking about coming into money and he was worried that I'd find out."

She leaned over and separated the pages. "When you get part of the way back, he flat out lies to her and tells Holly that I found out what he was doing and everything is delayed. Jason says that I'm threatening him. I took this whole thing as his way of backing out of the affair. I don't know anything and none of it makes any sense to me."

Luke and Tyler skimmed over the documents and took turns asking more questions for clarity but didn't make any headway. MaryBeth insisted she had no more information. Luke picked up the pages, thanked her for her time, and said he'd be back if he needed to know more. He left the house with more questions than answers.

CHAPTER 30

L uke sat in his car with Tyler in the passenger seat. After leaving MaryBeth's they had stopped to grab a quick dinner and then took up their surveillance spot on Kavanaugh Boulevard within a line of cars. They were shaded by some trees and not directly under a streetlight. A person would have to be on top of the SUV before anyone realized there were people in it.

Luke mulled over the text conversations between Holly and Jason, but so far, not a lot made sense. He had read through the documents that MaryBeth had given them even though he had quickly read the same messages on Holly's phone earlier. Luke was trying to make sense of it. It's not just that they were talking in code, but it was clear they had talked about things in person and much was missing as far as context. Jason never came right out and said where the money was coming from, but it was clear that it wasn't by legal means.

Luke asked Tyler, "Do you remember any crimes where there was a large sum of money missing from about six months ago?"

Tyler put his head back and pinched the bridge of his nose. "Not in Little Rock, but there was a series of bank robberies in Fayetteville, one in Jonesboro and two over the border in Memphis."

"Did they ever catch who did it?"

"No, and they didn't get back any of the stolen money either." Tyler typed something into his phone and then read what he pulled up. He

200

held the phone low so the light wouldn't be too obvious from inside the SUV. He showed his phone to Luke. "It was three people – one main guy who was the leader robbing the bank, his muscle who was with him, and one getaway driver."

Luke scanned the article but didn't see an answer to his question. "How did they know it was the same people who hit all four banks?"

"Same make and model SUV but different license plates. The leader wore the same red ski mask and black tee-shirt." Tyler put his phone back in his pocket. "Jason could have been getting money from anywhere though. Maybe he was into drugs. MaryBeth said Courtney had a cocaine habit. We know that Chance was into drugs back then and maybe Holly and Jason were, too. Maybe all of them got mixed up in some big drug ring."

"Possible," Luke said absently, scanning the row of shops. They had been sitting out there for about an hour and he wasn't sure how long they'd stay. "Do you think the person who planted those bugs is going to risk coming out here tonight? They can't go into every shop and remove the bugs, right? Most of those shops have reinstalled their surveillance."

"That's why I didn't think this was a solid idea," Tyler said, looking over at Luke. "Riley was good-intentioned, but I don't think she completely thought it through."

Luke agreed but no one else had any other ideas. "Cooper left the bug in my desk. Can you give one of the techs a call and see if they can go into my desk and grab it? The sooner we have some specs on it the better."

"Will do." Tyler reached for his phone again and made the call.

While he did that Luke scanned across the street. He turned slightly and looked at the shop behind them and a flash of light caught his eye. Luke fixed the side mirror so he could more easily check it out. It was at the kitchen shop, which sat right on the corner of Kavanaugh and a small side street. There were windows on the side and front of the shop. Light bounced around inside the dark shop. Luke was sure it came from a flashlight.

Luke reached over and tapped Tyler on the leg. "Hang up. We need to go." He unlocked the car doors and stepped out. Tyler was right behind him. Luke crossed the street and stayed close to the building, hoping whoever was in the shop didn't look out the side window and see them coming. He turned to Tyler. "You go around to the back door through the alleyway and I'll take the front of the shop."

"We should call for backup."

"No time now." Luke knew Tyler was right though. He had no idea who or how many people were inside the shop. "When you get around back radio in quietly."

Tyler took off down the side street to the alley and disappeared. Luke unholstered his gun and kept it at his side as he made his way to the front of the shop. The light from the flashlight stopped moving and seemed fixed on one spot as if the person had set it down. The person inside would easily see Luke if they looked out the front window. Luke could only assume they were focused on whatever they were doing.

Luke hesitated for only a second and then rushed to the door. He tried the handle and was surprised that it was unlocked. He readied his gun in front of him and stepped inside the shop. There at the register crouched a hooded figure with their hands under the counter. Their face was shielded by the hood and so were their hands under the counter. Luke had no idea if they had a weapon or not.

Luke planted his feet and aimed his gun at the person. "Hands up and slowly turn toward me."

The person jerked forward, taken by surprise. They made no other move and remained in a low crouched position.

Luke yelled his command again. "I said get up! Show me your hands!" He caught movement on the other side of the shop as Tyler stepped into view.

"We have you surrounded! Get up slowly now!" Tyler shouted and advanced with his gun trained on the person.

The person hesitated for only a moment before they slowly raised their hands in the air. He stood to his full height and then turned toward Luke with an angry scowl written all over their face.

"Sawyer?" Luke said slowly, showing his confusion. He wasn't sure whether he should drop his gun or not. "What are you doing in here?"

Tyler was as surprised as Luke. He lowered his gun as his mouth fell open. "Sawyer, come on, man, what are you doing in here?" He moved to join Luke at the front of the shop.

Det. Sawyer lowered one hand to take off his hood and then raised it again. "Can I put my hands down now, Det. Morgan?" There was a sarcastic tone to his request.

"Not until you tell me what you're doing in here." It didn't escape Luke that Sawyer had been searching in the exact spot that the bug had been planted.

"Lisa told me that a bug had been planted, and I came to see for myself. She knew I had been on the case and didn't understand why Det. Tyler came to her shop earlier and told her not to remove the bug."

Luke lowered his gun and cursed under his breath. The strategy, as much as it was, had been blown. Now, whoever wanted those bugs planted knew what they were doing. "Lower your hands and come around the counter."

As Sawyer did that, Tyler went behind the counter to disable the bug. Luke patted Sawyer down. He had his service weapon on his hip under his sweatshirt as Luke anticipated. Other than that, he didn't have anything more on him.

"The keys to the shop are in my pocket. I didn't break in."

"I don't want to have to call this in but you need to help me understand why you're sneaking around this shop in the middle of the night looking for the surveillance equipment. You could have retrieved it from Lisa in the morning."

Without missing a beat, Sawyer said, "You could have removed it by morning. This is my case. I'm the one that should be livid right now. You've got Captain Meadows twisted around your finger and he lets you do whatever you want to do."

Luke shook his head. "That's not what's going on here. We wouldn't have even known about the listening devices if it wasn't for Riley and Cooper working on a case to defend the kid that you falsely arrested."

Sawyer shut up at that. Luke was sure that at this point he had figured out this was more than a burglary. "You arresting me?" he asked.

"Give me Lisa's phone number." Sawyer rattled it off and Luke placed the call. When she answered, Luke asked her if she had given Sawyer permission to enter her shop. The woman confirmed she had and seemed rather put out that Luke had called her about it.

"You don't have permission to be in my shop so get out," Lisa said and then hung up. He had wanted to explain that he thought he was stopping a burglary in progress, but he didn't get the chance. Lisa didn't seem like she'd care either way.

Luke shoved his phone back in his pocket. "You can go," he said to Sawyer. "We all need to meet with Captain Meadows in the morning and make a plan for what we are going to do with these cases. It's more than simple burglaries committed by a kid."

"The kid is still guilty," Sawyer sneered. "He's smarter than we gave him credit for."

Luke wasn't going to take the bait. "Make sure you lock up."

Tyler followed Luke out of the shop and they both turned to watch Sawyer as he closed and locked the front door and then crossed the street toward his house.

"That was shady," Tyler said as they started walking back toward the car. "Since Lisa asked him to be at the shop, he had no reason to sneak around like that. As you said, he could have gotten the listening device in the morning. He's hiding something."

"I know," Luke said, even though he had no idea what it was. "I don't trust him. I'm calling Captain Meadows tonight and filling him in. This can't wait until morning."

"I think he's covering for his son. Based on what Riley and Cooper said, his son, Scott, is knee-deep in this."

Luke nodded. "That wouldn't surprise me. I know it's technically his case but one of us is going to have to bring his son in for questioning. We can only hope Sawyer doesn't lawyer him up right away."

"We both know he will if he's smart."

Luke couldn't argue with that. He'd never let his future kids talk to the cops without a lawyer present no matter what they did or didn't do. Luke ran a hand over his head. He wasn't sure of his next steps on either case, which frustrated him to no end. As they were getting back in his SUV, Luke said, "Call me if the tech gets back to you about the bugs. That's the only way we are going to know more at this point. I'm ready for this day to be over."

Tyler yawned. "You and me both."

CHAPTER 31

The next morning, I loitered around the coffee shop on Kavanaugh. I had it on good authority that Amelia liked to grab an espresso before school. Izzy didn't want me to speak to her and begged me to keep her out of it, but I didn't see any other option at this point. She'd be able to tell me more not only about her relationship with Izzy but about her relationship with her brother and father. She was Izzy's alibi. The only one with definitive proof of where he'd been during at least one of the burglaries.

Luke had told me that he caught Det. Sawyer in Lisa's shop the previous night. It came as no surprise to me that she wouldn't have followed directions. I had no idea at the time that she knew Sawyer well enough to call and tell him though.

My plan for the night hadn't paid off. No one came to the shops other than Sawyer. In the end, both Luke and Tyler had been glad they were out there, but it didn't get us any closer to finding out the truth. That was the way it went sometimes.

I sipped an iced mocha latte even though the fall temps had me wearing jeans, my favorite gray sweater, and flats. I had fixed my wild auburn hair that morning and it fell in soft waves on my shoulders. I don't know why but something about meeting a teen girl got me a bit nervous. I was waiting to be judged.

Izzy had sent me a photo of Amelia and she looked like the kind of young woman who never had a hair out of place. Her blonde head of curls laid perfectly around her heart-shaped face. She had big blue eyes and a perfect row of white teeth.

As scheduled, Amelia walked into the coffee shop texting without looking up. I always wondered how people did that. I trip over my own feet for no reason at all. I always had to watch where I was going. Otherwise, I was like a cartoon character falling off a cliff. Amelia walked right up to the counter and placed her order.

"Amelia," I said after she paid and stepped to the side. I introduced myself. "Do you have a few minutes to talk to me?"

She looked toward the door and then down at her phone. "I have to be at school soon."

"It shouldn't take long, but if there's another time you can meet, I can make that happen."

Amelia shook her head. "I shouldn't talk to you at all, so let's do this now." She looked around for a table and chose one in the far back corner of the shop. The wall jutted out and blocked half the table from view. That was the seat she took.

I retrieved my coffee from the table I had been sitting at and joined her. "As you know, Izzy has been arrested for the burglaries. He claims he was with you when a few of them happened."

"I don't remember the dates specifically," she said, frowning. "Izzy and I are together most nights though. I tell my parents I'm studying at a friend's house and I meet up with Izzy instead."

"He mentioned that you usually meet in your car rather than his house."

Amelia averted her eyes. "That's true."

"I'm not judging. I was in high school once. I understand not being able to hang out with your boyfriend when you want to. It's hard to get privacy at your age."

Amelia didn't comment further on that. When I asked about the burglaries, she said, "You don't know him very well if you think he'd do something like that."

Amelia pushed her phone and espresso to the side and leaned her arms on the table. "Izzy would never do something like that. He cares about his future too much. Besides, his father would kill him."

"Do you know who was involved in the burglaries?"

Amelia locked eyes with me but didn't say a word. She swallowed hard. "I'm not sure I should say."

"Do you care about Izzy?" I asked not hiding my frustration. I leaned on the table. "If you care about Izzy at all, you're not going to let him get in trouble for something he didn't do."

Amelia reached for her espresso and I saw a brief shake of her hand. She brought the cup to her lips and took a sip and then held the cup against her chest. "You don't understand the situation I'm in."

"You don't want to rat out your brother so you're hoping by some chance that we can get Izzy out of trouble without you having to implicate your brother?"

Amelia closed her eyes. "So, you do understand," she said quietly.

She stayed still like that for several moments. I knew this was asking a lot. She was essentially having to choose between her boyfriend and her brother. I didn't envy her position, but the truth had to win out.

I told her as much. "We have evidence. You're not going to be the lone voice getting your brother in trouble, but I need to understand what's going on because a lot of things aren't adding up for us. If your brother is in some kind of trouble, we might be able to help him, too."

Amelia raised her eyes to me and smirked. "My brother lives for trouble. This is of his own doing. I shouldn't have a problem telling you because Scott and I do not get along at all. We never have. He's my father's favorite and he can do no wrong – except all he does is do wrong."

I could tell her resolve was building. "I understand. I have a younger sister and she's been a handful my whole life. We are both in our thirties now, and I'd like to say that it gets easier. In some ways it does, but in other ways, she is who she is. She also happens to be my mother's favorite. I recently found out why. It's because she needs so much more help than I ever needed. I was an independent kid and an independent adult."

Amelia nodded her head as I spoke. "That's exactly it. Scott always needed help. I was a straight-A student, played sports, and never got into trouble. Scott was always getting in trouble in school. He's a guy with a lot of anger that I don't understand." She looked down at the table. "I still feel disloyal talking about this though."

I reached across the table and touched her arm. "Amelia, I understand. I do, but we have to know what's going on. If you have information, you must share it. If not with me, then the police."

"My father would never believe me." Amelia looked over at me and the sincere look on her face broke my heart. "I tried to tell him when this all started, but he wouldn't listen to me. He told me I was jealous of Scott and trying to get him into trouble. I tried to tell my mom, too. She wouldn't hear a word against her favorite child. I've kept it to myself."

I couldn't push her for the information any more than I had so I played the best trick I had during an interview. It was also the hardest. I sat back, clasped my hands in my lap, and let the silence hang between us. Amelia wanted to tell me. It was written all over her face. She had been carrying around her brother's burden for too long now. She just had to pick her moment.

Amelia stood from the table and stepped around my chair and looked out into the shop. When she determined there was no one there she knew, she sat back down. She took a sip of her last bit of espresso and then locked eyes with me.

"Scott worked at a construction site last summer. My dad wanted him to get some work experience so he made him take a summer job. Scott didn't complain because a few of his friends worked with him, too. When school started, he stopped working. One of the guys he met there contacted Scott and asked him if he and his friends would like to make some money. I think they were going to be paid something like ten thousand dollars each."

Amelia took a breath. "I overheard all of this so you know. Scott never told me directly. Our bedrooms are connected by a bathroom and he's loud on the phone and when his friends are over. That's how I heard."

"It's okay," I said, waiting for her to get to the good part. "Who was the guy?"

"That I don't know," Amelia said with force. "Scott called him JB. I don't know if that's the guy's initials or a nickname. That's the only name Scott has ever used. JB told Scott that something was hidden in one of the shops on Kavanaugh and that he needed to find it. He didn't trust Scott and his friends to search for it because he didn't want to tell them what was missing. Scott assumed drugs or money. Scott's only job was to break into the shop, cut the surveillance, and then leave some listening devices. My brother's friend, Jimmy, knows everything tech-related. I'm sure he was directly involved in all that. The goal was to plant the listening devices and JB would go in after and search the shops."

It seemed like an elaborate plan to me. "Why didn't JB break into the shops himself?"

"I guess he didn't want to risk getting caught. If Scott and his friends went in and got caught, then it would be less of a big deal and JB would be protected."

There was a lot of risk to Scott and his friends. Then again, ten thousand dollars to seniors in high school would be significant. "Wasn't Scott concerned about getting into trouble?"

Amelia shook her head. "I don't think it ever crossed his mind. Listening to them talk about it was like listening to someone talk about playing a video game. They were having fun talking about the strategy of getting in and planting the listening devices. They thought it was some cool challenge – like they were playing spy or something. They dismissed the idea of it being wrong because they weren't stealing anything and JB was trying to get back something that was his. I don't know if Scott considered it a crime – at first."

I raised my eyebrows. "At first? That changed later?"

"Yeah," Amelia said with a sigh. "My dumb brother realized my father was investigating the burglaries and what a big deal it was. Scott and all his friends were completely freaked out. That's when Scott mentioned framing someone else. They didn't use the word *framing*. I don't think Scott's that smart."

"Is that when they mentioned Izzy?"

"No. No," Amelia said shaking her head. "They never mentioned Izzy or I would have been more forceful in warning him. I didn't know what to do at that point. I had already tried to speak to my parents. I tried to talk to Scott, but he brushed it off and then threatened me not to tell anyone. He said he had a secret of mine and I wouldn't like it if it got out. I thought he was talking about me and Izzy."

"Someone would have a problem with you dating him?"

"My father and my brother, but Scott couldn't do anything because I knew what he was doing."

Amelia pulled back in her chair and crossed her arms. She checked her phone again. "Are we almost done? I've already missed my first class and if I miss the second, the school will call my parents."

I let the subject slide and asked her a few more questions trying to determine who JB might be but didn't get far. "How should I reach you if I need to ask you anything else?"

"I'd rather not," Amelia said, standing. She hesitated at the table. "I guess here is fine, like you did this morning. Just show up and we can talk." She rested her hand on my shoulder as she passed, tossed her cup in the garbage, and left the shop without looking back.

CHAPTER 32

"Captain Meadows, we need to remove Det. Sawyer from this case," Luke insisted as he sat down across from his boss. He had practiced the speech during the hour he laid in bed before he needed to get up for work. Riley had slept soundly beside him while he ruminated how to get Sawyer tossed from the case. When it came right down to it, the direct approach had been the best.

"Give me your argument," Captain Meadows said, leaning back and watching him.

Luke laid out his reasoning from the quick arrest of Isiah Wright to not finding the listening devices on his initial search and the biggest reason of all – his son was a suspect.

When Luke was done, he said simply, "I don't see how Sawyer can continue. It's nothing less than a conflict of interest."

Captain Meadows gave nothing away with his expression. "You think Sawyer is knowingly protecting his son?"

"I can't be sure of that. I don't know whether Sawyer knows about Scott's involvement or not, but I suspect that either he knows and is protecting him or he's subconsciously avoiding the truth. No one wants their kid to be a criminal."

Luke had sent Captain Meadows a message early that morning detailing that he and Tyler had found Sawyer creeping around one of the shops and he had been told about the listening devices. Captain

213

Meadows still hadn't told Luke his thoughts on that.

"I don't trust him," Luke said, driving the point home. "He could have gone to Tyler and asked about the listening devices after Lisa told him. He could have come to you and asked why we were involved. He didn't do any of those things. Instead, he crept around after hours in the dark and is still insisting that Isiah Wright is involved."

Captain Meadows sighed heavily. Luke knew he hated any kind of drama among his detectives. "Sawyer had a right to go into Lisa's shop. I can't dispute that. It's his case after all. You're right though, he's compromised and didn't do a good job investigating. He rushed to judgment. As much as I like Riley, I hate that she's one-upping us. It's not a good sign that a private investigator is making more headway in our cases than we are." Captain Meadows pointed at Luke and chuckled. "Don't you dare tell her. Her head is big enough."

"That's my wife you're talking about," Luke said and then broke into a grin. Captain Meadows wasn't wrong. "Do you want Tyler and me on the burglary case?"

"If you can handle it with the murder investigation and not compromise either."

"We can handle it," Luke assured him.

Captain Meadows leaned back in his chair. "The prosecutor's office isn't quite ready to drop the charges on Izzy, but go ahead and start investigating like a suspect hasn't been found yet. As far as I'm concerned, this is far from a closed case."

Luke left the office and waited until he was outside the captain's office before he breathed a sigh of relief. Sawyer hadn't been seen in the office yet that morning, which was fine by him. Luke sat down at his desk and Tyler turned around in his chair to face him.

"Sawyer off the case?"

Luke nodded. "Went better than I expected. The case is ours now."

"Good." Tyler spun back around to his desk, grabbed a stack of papers, and then turned back to hand them to Luke. "The tech got back to me while you were in your meeting. This isn't spyware from a basic spy shop. You're not buying this off Amazon or even a local store. This is high-grade surveillance equipment. There are only a handful of places that it can be purchased. The closest place is in Dallas. It's voice-activated and has a battery life of nearly a month. I don't know if they planned to swap out batteries or remove the equipment. Some of the shops were broken into longer than a month ago."

"Maybe they decided if they can't get the info they wanted within a month, they weren't going to get it," Luke scanned down the page taking in the information in bites. He didn't have a specialty in this kind of high-grade surveillance. When he finished reading, he handed the report back to Tyler. "Are you following up with the Dallas store?"

"I've put a call in for a warrant already in case they balk and don't want to share their client files with us."

That was a good call. Shops like that could be hesitant to share purchase information without a warrant. Luke couldn't blame them, but it held up the investigative process. "Speaking of that, I need to call the Capital Hotel to see if we can pick up their surveillance footage. Riley said Jordan seemed surprised that her alibi didn't check out. Even without a solid alibi, Riley doesn't believe Jordan killed Holly."

Tyler pointed to Luke's laptop. "Captain Meadows got it yesterday. The link should be in your email. The files were already uploaded for us."

Luke gave his partner a thumbs up and then clicked his keyboard until he found the email with the link. He clicked it and a new screen popped up with a video of the hallway of the Capital Hotel. He scanned through with his eyes focused on the timestamp. He stopped at the time when Jordan said she came home with the man who spent the night. Sure enough, at close to eleven on Saturday night Jordan walked out of the elevator arm in arm with a man. She stumbled once in the hall and he helped her steady herself. They were both laughing and smiling.

Luke hit fast forward on the video and scanned through the overnight and well into Sunday morning. Just as Jordan described no one left her room until late on Sunday morning. Her alibi checked out. He clicked it off and picked up the phone and called Jordan. It rang right through to voicemail.

"Jordan, this is Det. Morgan with the Little Rock Police Department. We have confirmed your alibi and you're free to leave the city. We will be in touch should we need anything further." He hung up the phone without saying more. Luke never liked confirming that anyone had been released as a potential person of interest until the case was solved to his satisfaction. He'd seen too many cases where detectives cleared someone only to find evidence later that linked to the person. Luke was comfortable enough to let her leave and that would have to be enough for now.

He waited until Tyler wrapped his phone call and then called to him. When Tyler turned around, Luke said, "I called Jordan. She's off the list for now. Her alibi checks out. Who is left?"

"Chance hasn't been cleared. Jason and MaryBeth haven't been cleared, and we should probably explore Courtney a little more although I can't imagine she'd kill anyone. With Jordan out, that's all we are left with for now. That's assuming it's not someone who we haven't explored like one of the other shop owners or a random person not tied to the case yet."

Luke checked his watch. "Let's give it an hour and then talk to Jason at his work site. What did you think about MaryBeth yesterday?"

"She wasn't what I thought when we first arrived," he admitted. "I don't know why, but I assumed she might be completely out of the loop. She didn't immediately come across as astute. I was surprised by what she said and all she knew. Do I think MaryBeth could be the killer? I don't know. It's plausible especially since she and Jason alibi each other out. It would be easy enough for one to protect the other. She certainly had enough anger to do it."

"I don't see MaryBeth protecting Jason though. It sounded like she would have handed Jason over to us on a silver platter if she had the information."

Tyler considered this. "I wasn't sure from her tone if she wanted to be rid of him or if there was still a soft spot."

"Ahhh...I don't know," Luke said his frustration evident. "What I do know is we are getting nowhere fast with this case. Any information come back yet on the hammers pulled from Chance's barn?"

"Not yet," Tyler said and then raised his eyebrows looking over Luke's shoulder. He pointed. "Looks like the devil himself has arrived."

Luke craned his neck to the side and sure enough, there stood Chance Bell. "He's got some balls to come in here," he muttered.

Luke got up and walked over to the man who watched from the corner of the room. Chance had cleaned himself up from the last time Luke saw him. He had cut his straggly beard all the way down to a thin layer of stubble across his face and he had cut his long hair. His crisp button-down shirt and dress pants made him look like a normal human being for once.

"Can I help you, Mr. Bell?" Luke asked as he approached.

"I need to speak with you."

"Follow me." Luke walked down the hall to one of the interrogation rooms. He could have picked a nicer room, one used for witnesses and the family of victims, but he chose interrogation on purpose. Luke had no idea why Chance was coming to visit. Confess, hopefully. He wanted to throw the switch on the surveillance in the room and record the whole thing. Luke also hoped to intimidate. The cozier rooms with comfortable chairs and light-colored paint on the walls were too good for Chance.

Luke opened the door wide. "Take a seat on the far side of the table." Chance did as he was told and then raised his eyes to Luke. "I'm not a criminal. There isn't a need for the interrogation room."

Luke sat across from him, pulling his chair to the table with force. "I'll determine that. What do you want? If you're here to ask about the items we took from your barn, they are still being processed."

"I wasn't here to ask about that." Chance leaned back in his chair and looked around the room. A smile spread across his face as he nodded his head as if bobbing in time to the music in his head. "This place looks different when you know you're leaving at the end."

Luke crossed his arms over his chest. "Let's get on with this, Chance. I don't have all day."

Chance watched Luke for several moments. A pit of anxiety grew in Luke's gut with each passing second and his palms began to feel damp. He had no idea why this guy affected him so much.

When Chance was good and ready, he leaned into the table. "Det. Morgan, as much as you'd like to arrest me for killing my wife, I didn't do it. If you're spending time on me, then you're wasting time. I came here today to help you out."

"Really?" Luke asked sarcastically. "I've never known you to be helpful to anyone but yourself."

Chance chuckled. "You could say the same about why I'm here. I don't want to go back to prison. I've been doing everything I can to not go back to prison, and that's why the relationship with my wife was never going to work out. So, in essence, I'm here to avoid prison again."

He blew out a breath and admitted, "I don't care if you solve this case or not. I don't care who killed my wife. As I'm sure you've figured out, I don't even care that she's dead – only that it doesn't impact me."

There were so many reasons to hate this guy, Luke stopped being so hard on himself for how he felt about Chance. "How romantic and loving of you. So," Luke locked eyes with him, "what have you got?"

Without missing a beat, Chance dropped a bomb that made the burglaries and the murder start to make sense. "Holly was involved in a series of bank robberies. One of her accomplices was in charge of hiding the money that was stolen and now won't give up the location because he's in prison. All he said was he hid it in one of the shops on Kavanaugh. He assumes, and rightly so, that Holly and her partner will cut him out of his share. That's what sparked the burglaries and what got my wife killed."

CHAPTER 33

Chance's statement rendered Luke speechless. Each part of the case started to make a certain amount of sense. All the pieces that separately weren't adding up fell right into place. "You believe her partner killed her?"

Chance shrugged. "That I don't know. I was serious when I told you I have no idea who killed Holly. I'm fairly certain that's what led to her death. How could it not?"

"It's an avenue we haven't explored," Luke admitted. "Who is Holly's partner?"

Chance rolled his eyes. "I might as well get a badge and gun. I'm doing all the work for you. Jason Manning, my wife's lover. Jason wants out of his marriage, but he can't afford to get a divorce. He's flat broke and his wife is a ball buster. MaryBeth has her own money. Jason needed fast cash and cooked up some scheme to rob some banks."

Luke had so many questions he didn't know where to start. "How do you know all this?"

"You get savvy in prison, man. You are always keeping your eyes and ears open and you learn to lay low and bide your time. That's what I was doing with Holly." Chance took a breath and blew it out slowly. His voice had a hint of disgust. "I thought she was forever. In the beginning, life was good. Then she got hungry. She wanted more. Holly wanted Prophet Chance Bell the all-powerful. I wasn't that guy

220

anymore and she wasn't interested in who I was when I got out of prison. All I wanted to do was enjoy my freedom and live out my life quietly."

"She had an affair," Luke said, a statement not a question.

Chance nodded. "With the guy who did some repairs on her shop. That's how she and Jason met. When you were at the house, I said we had an open marriage. We didn't, and I wasn't having an affair. I was trying not to do anything that would cause me trouble or bring more drama into my life. Holly was all about big drama as you can see by the drama she ginned up with her business. She didn't need to do all that. She was bored and wanted a reaction. Holly got more than she bargained for though. That's the risk you take when you do things for attention."

Luke tapped his index finger on the table. "You don't know then who killed her – if it was Jason or someone else?"

"It wasn't the partner that's for sure. He's in prison. Davis Smith – that's the guy's name. From what I understand, he never got caught for the bank robberies. He was picked up on something else and it threw off their whole plan."

"You overheard all of this?" Luke asked. He still didn't understand how Chance had come by this information. He could see how Chance would be more aware coming out of prison and more suspicious but that didn't give Luke a clue as to how he knew.

"Overheard. Snooped through her phone. Followed her," Chance admitted and then waited for Luke's reaction. When he had none, Chance softened his tone. "Det. Morgan, I don't know if you've ever been cheated on, but it doesn't take a rocket scientist to figure it out. You get a vibe. There are clues that your spouse isn't being straight with you. Too many late nights. Too many hushed phone calls. They don't have sex with you anymore. There are small lies you catch them in. It all adds up. I wasn't just going to let her continue to lie to my face. I had to find out."

"While you were looking for evidence of an affair you stumbled on the bank robbery scheme?"

"It was shortly before Holly was murdered. I came to that info late. The store burglaries had already started and Holly didn't seem concerned at all. I told her a few times she shouldn't open or close her shop alone. She wasn't worried. That didn't make any sense to me. Then I started seeing messages about the burglaries from Jason and that piece of the puzzle slowly fell into place."

Chance threw his hands up. "At the time, I didn't know how they were pulling it off. Then I saw they arrested some kid for the burglaries. You can think whatever you want of me, but I've been to prison. It's no place for a kid who seemed like he has his life together. The interview his father gave to the media got to me."

Luke assessed Chance and took in his relaxed open body language. For the first time since Luke had the displeasure of meeting the man, he believed what Chance told him. "Do you have proof to back up this claim?"

"I can't do all the work for you. I guess you could find the money. I have no idea where it is and no idea why some dummy would hide it in one of the shops. Seems kind of risky to me, but then again, I'm not a bank robber."

Luke asked him a few more questions and then let him go, promising to be in touch. Chance asked if he was cleared off Luke's suspect list. While Luke wouldn't go that far, he did shake the man's hand. He had earned at least that for coming forward voluntarily with the information. Chance took what was given with a curt nod of his head and he left the station.

As Luke made his way back to his desk, he heard Riley's voice and found her perched on the side of his desk talking to Tyler.

"What brings you in?"

"I met with someone who I think can shed some light on the case." Riley looked around the room. "Where is Det. Sawyer?"

"He hasn't come in yet." Luke gestured toward the conference room. "Why don't we go in and have a chat. I have some information, too. Let me run it by Captain Meadows and I'll see if I can share it with you."

Riley looked down at Tyler. "He's always by the book. Here I thought after I was willing to marry him that I'd have easier access."

Luke didn't bite because he knew she was teasing him. Her playful voice told him that. He knocked on Captain Meadows' door and gave his boss a quick overview of the information Chance provided.

"If that's the case, by all means, share it with Riley as it will impact the case against Izzy." Captain Meadows pushed his chair back and stood. "I'll join you in the conference room."

Together they walked down the hall to the large conference room where Tyler and Riley sat at the table chatting. They both turned their heads to look at Luke when he entered.

"Sounds like you both made some headway today," Tyler said, reaching for a cup he had on the table in front of him.

Luke sat down at the table and hitched his jaw toward Riley. "You start first. What I found out today is complex and I'm not sure how reliable Chance is as a witness." Luke thought he was extremely reliable in this case but refused to put himself on the line promoting information that he hadn't vetted yet, even if it was Riley and his team.

"I met with Amelia today – she's Det. Lou Sawyer's daughter and Isiah Wright's girlfriend. She told me she heard Scott and his friends talking on several occasions about the burglaries and their role in them."

Captain Meadows' head snapped in her direction. "Is she willing to give a formal statement?"

"Not yet," Riley said resigned. "If pushed, she might. I think if she had her father's support, she definitely would. Amelia said she tried to talk to Det. Sawyer a few times about what she heard but he wouldn't listen to her. She said she tried to speak to her mother as well. Apparently, in their family, Scott can do no wrong."

Tyler sat up straighter in his chair. "Any chance she's lying to protect her boyfriend?"

Riley looked over at him. "I believe her. I don't think she'd implicate her brother. I ambushed her this morning. I waited around the coffee shop she goes to and spoke to her then. She was hesitant and even took a back table shielded from view of the rest of the place. It was difficult for Amelia to tell me. That was clear in the way she hesitated and her body language."

Tyler nodded as if he agreed. "What did she say about the burglaries?"

"That's where it gets interesting," she began. "Amelia said that Scott told his friends that they would go into the shops first, cut the surveillance, and plant the bugs. That was their only purpose. Amelia said it was someone Scott knew from a construction site he worked. Someone with the initials or nickname JB. He was going to pay Scott and his friends ten thousand dollars each for their help. Amelia said JB wanted them to break in first because if they got caught, they'd get a slap on the wrist since they didn't take anything. It all spiraled out of control once Det. Sawyer started investigating. Scott freaked out and pointed at Izzy figuring he might get in trouble."

Captain Meadows jotted a few notes on a pad he had in front of him and then raised his head. "Riley, I don't understand why JB wanted them to do this."

Luke knew and it confirmed what Chance had told them, but he kept quiet and waited for Riley's answer.

Riley shrugged. "I don't know. Amelia said she thought something was hidden in one of the shops. Scott thought it might be drugs or money, but they didn't know for sure."

Captain Meadows rubbed his fingers across his forehead before jotting down another note. "Why would these kids take the risk?"

"Amelia said Scott and his friends treated it like a video game, a challenge. It was exciting to them. The money, of course, was motivation. I think they got a thrill out of it. The more break-ins they got away with, the more emboldened they became."

"That makes sense," Tyler said. He smiled over at Riley. "Good work."

It was time for Luke to reveal what Chance had told him. He was sure now all the pieces had come together. He leaned back and looked at each of them who were watching him in return. "Chance Bell came in willingly to speak to me today and what he said fills in many of the gaps in Amelia's statement."

Luke went on to detail what Chance had told him about the bank robberies and the hidden money. He finished by saying, "I'd bet money that JB is Jason Manning. Holly knew about the plan and they were working to find the money. How else would they search all of those shops undetected? Holly's shop was never broken into. She never filed a report like the other shops."

Tyler rubbed at the back of his neck. "Luke, do you think it's the bank robberies I mentioned the other night?"

"I would assume so. We are going to need to follow up in those jurisdictions to see what we can find out."

"Where's the money?" Riley asked Luke.

"We don't know. We don't even know for sure that the accomplice who is in prison was telling the truth about where he stashed it."

They all started talking at once, but Captain Meadows quieted them down. He stared down at the pad in front of him while they waited. Then he tapped his pen and said, "Riley, have you spoken to any of Scott's friends?"

"Cooper was close to getting a confession from Jimmy Ragone," Riley reminded him.

Captain Meadows gestured with his hand as he spoke. "Tell Cooper to go interview him again and talk to his parents. I'd like one of the kids on record before we go after Scott. If he has a rapport with the kid, that's better than a detective showing up."

He turned and looked at Luke and Tyler. "Let's find out the details of those bank robberies and then get Jason Manning in for an interview."

"What about searching for the money?" Tyler asked.

Captain Meadows shook his head. "Waste of time right now. Let's keep this between us for now. Don't alert the shop owners or we'll start a frenzy with them ripping up their shops to find the cash. We don't even know if Jason found it yet. Someone killed Holly in the process and we can't jeopardize bringing that person to justice for the sake of finding the money. That will come later."

They all agreed and got up from the table and left with their collective assignments.

CHAPTER 34

I followed Luke out of the conference room and back to his desk. I texted Cooper and told him he should probably head to Jimmy's house as soon as he could. I put my phone back in my pocket and sat on the edge of Luke's desk. I realized then I had been the only one not given an assignment.

"What do you want me to do?"

Luke looked over at Tyler and both seemed unsure if there was anything for me to do. I didn't want to get in the way, but it seemed like the burglary case had wrapped up and there wasn't much more we could do to help Izzy. The case had taken a turn in another direction.

"Is there anyone in Holly's life that might know about her involvement in the bank robberies? Sometimes people will admit things to a private investigator they won't tell detectives. That's proven true countless times over."

Luke looked at Tyler. "What do you think about sending her to speak to Courtney? They were best friends and we both felt that she wasn't being completely honest with us. Riley can follow up like she's asking about the burglaries and see if Holly ever said her shop was robbed. Then once she's in the door, she can steer the conversation to other topics?"

"Fine by me," Tyler said, turning back to his desk. "Can't hurt either way."

"That's hardly a ringing endorsement for my work."

Tyler chuckled but didn't turn back around. "It hurts me to have to admit you're good. Take the fact that we let you stick around as endorsement enough."

"He means it," Luke said and wrote down Courtney's address and gave me a few details about their previous interview with her. "Courtney pointed the finger at Jason's wife, MaryBeth. We haven't ruled her out yet. Although given this information today, she falls lower on my person of interest list."

I thanked him for the information and hopped down from his desk.

Luke grabbed my hand. "We heard Courtney might have a drug problem, but I didn't see any signs of that. Just be on guard."

"I'm always on guard when I'm interviewing someone." I turned to leave but only got a few feet when I got a text from Cooper, letting me know he was on his way to Jimmy's house in a few minutes. I told Luke and then added, "Cooper said he'll call you as soon as he knows anything. He is going to encourage Jimmy to come to the police station with his parents to give a formal statement."

"If we aren't here, tell him to ask for Captain Meadows. Don't let him anywhere near Det. Sawyer, who still seems to be missing in action."

I saluted and left with my marching orders. I texted Cooper when I got to my car confirming I saw his text and let him know my plan. As I drove out of downtown Little Rock, I turned the radio up loud and opened the sunroof even though the air had a chill. The sun was shining and leaves had finally started turning glorious colors. Even a few minutes of fresh air while I drove reminded me that life was good.

I took side streets out of downtown up to Hillcrest and found Courtney's house without needing directions. Her house was modest but landscaped well. The bike lying on its side and two soccer balls on the lawn advertised Courtney had kids. Luke said she seemed frazzled when they interviewed her the first time, and I expected the same.

I parked in front of the house, walked to the porch, and knocked once. The door opened and a small boy stood on the other side.

"Who are you?" he asked with his eyes wide. Before I could answer, he screamed for his mother loudly, more loudly than I realized a child of that size could scream. I pulled back in horror. I wanted to reassure the kid I wasn't there to hurt him but his scream stunned me into silence.

From inside the house, I heard a woman scream back to him. "Stop yelling! I'll be right there. Close the door."

He didn't close the door but he did stop screaming. He looked up at me. After a few moments, he asked me who I was again.

I crouched low to his level. "My name is Riley. I need to speak to your mommy." For good measure, I added, "I like the giraffe on your shirt."

He pointed to the animal with his stubby finger and said something I didn't understand. Whatever it was sent him into a fit of giggles. He ran in place with his little legs bouncing up and down. He shouted, "Mommy!" in a high-pitched giggle with each step.

Finally, a woman came to the door and dragged the little boy back from it. "Scoot," she said pulling him back into the house. She raised her eyes to me. "Can I help you? It's been a day so excuse the mess."

I explained who I was and why I was there. "I won't take up too much of your time. I'm hoping you can help me clear up a few things about Holly."

Courtney looked at me skeptically. "Who hired a private investigator to look into her murder?"

"No one," I admitted. "That's not what I'm here about. I'm investigating the burglaries that happened on Kavanaugh. I was wondering if Holly ever spoke to you about them."

"She did," she said slowly, "but I'm not sure I can help you." Courtney started to close the door, but I held my hand out to stop it from closing in my face.

"Courtney, I know you don't want to get your friend in trouble. This is important. It might hold a clue to her murder." When she still didn't seem convinced, I added, "If something happened to my best friend, there isn't anything I wouldn't do to help get justice even if that meant spilling some of her secrets. Nothing can happen to her now."

"It can destroy her reputation."

I wasn't going to stand there and debate. "Was Holly's shop burglarized?"

"No," Courtney said softly and then watched my face. "You know something, don't you?"

"Can we talk please?" She opened the door and let me enter. Two of her children were plopped down on the floor in front of the television. The one that had come to the door was sucking his thumb and his eyes were glued to his show.

Courtney walked me to the back of the home and pointed to the kitchen table. "You should know I already spoke to the police. I gave them some information but not everything. I don't want to get in any trouble."

She wrung her hands around a dishtowel that she had picked up from the table. "I was trying to give them information but protect Holly at the same time. Do you know Det. Morgan?"

I would have garnered more trust if I had been able to say no, but there was no point in lying. I needed to put a positive spin on it. "Det. Morgan is my husband. I can say with confidence that he's not looking to do anything other than find Holly's killer."

She raised her eyes to me. "Did he send you here to interrogate me?"

I laughed and shook my head. "No one is here to interrogate you."

Courtney dropped the dishtowel and relaxed her posture. She pulled out the chair across from me and sat down. She asked me a few questions about what it was like to work as a private investigator and to work so closely with my husband. Courtney admitted that she would never be able to work with her husband. She hated even having him at home.

"It's like having a fourth child. I worked for a while but then with three small kids, I wasn't even making enough to cover daycare so it's better that I'm at home. I can't stand it most days though. Any children?"

"Not yet, maybe one day." I paused and waited to see if Courtney wanted to keep up the banter. It seemed to be relaxing her. The more relaxed she was, the more eager to talk she seemed. When she didn't add anything else, I broached the subject. "Given that Holly's shop was the only one not broken into, I assume she knew what was going on."

Courtney looked away but nodded her head. "She knew." After a moment, she turned and looked right at me and told me the story of Holly and Jason and the bank robberies. "Every time they'd rob a bank, they'd stash the money above the tiles in the ceiling in Holly's office. But then Davis Smith was sent back to prison on a parole violation. One of them called his parole officer. I don't know what was said, but it got Davis sent back to prison. Davis found out though and moved the money before he went back in."

"How did he find out?"

"No idea." Courtney smiled as if amused. "I guess the moral of the story is never try to outwit a real criminal. When Holly went to retrieve the money after Davis was in prison, it was gone. That's when Davis told them it was in one of the other shops. He said when he got out, he'd split the money. Jason and Holly didn't have time to wait."

It was as wild a story as I had ever heard. "I assume Jason and Holly believed Davis about where he hid the money?"

"They didn't have a choice but to believe him. Davis was in prison and stopped letting Jason visit and it's not like they could call the cops and say the guy they robbed banks with hid the money."

"Holly knew the shop owners. Couldn't Holly have asked the shop owners if anyone had been broken into? If Davis hid the money, he broke in to do it."

Courtney slid forward on her chair and rested her arms on the table. "Davis had some serious lock-picking skills. That's how he got into her shop to steal the money. Holly tried hinting around to some of the other shop owners, but she didn't get anywhere. She didn't come right out and ask if they were robbed, but she asked if they had seen or heard anything suspicious. That's when she and Jason came up with their plan."

"To use the local kids?"

"I don't know who they are – possibly some guys who worked for Jason on a job site. Holly didn't share the details with me, but she said they had a solid plan in action. Holly had surveillance equipment in her shop to listen in on the other shops, too. She let me listen in but no one talked about anything important. Holly said she knew where the bugs were planted if they needed to change the batteries or get them out of the shops. She said she could easily distract the owner and take care of it."

There was something I was missing still. "Why plant the bugs at all? It seems riskier than searching the shops."

"Believe it or not, that was Holly's idea," Courtney said like she couldn't believe it herself.

"Holly said searching the shops would be one and done. Having a bug in each shop allowed them to keep an eye on things. She felt like a shop owner would start talking about finding money if it was found."

"Let's say a shop owner found the money. What would Jason and Holly do then?"

"I don't know. Steal it back, maybe. Holly never shared that with me."

"Why did Holly implicate you in this mess?"

Courtney shrugged. "We tell each other almost everything."

"Who did you think killed Holly?"

"I told Det. Morgan that I think it was Jason's wife, MaryBeth. I stand by that." Courtney exhaled a breath. "MaryBeth was jealous of Holly for several reasons including the affair. I believe MaryBeth also found out about the burglaries and that sent her over the edge. When she confronted Holly, I think she lost it."

I asked a few more questions but Courtney held firm in her suspicion of MaryBeth. No matter what evidence I suggested or how I reframed the question, Courtney stuck to her belief. She was unflappable in that regard. I didn't see any indication of drug use in the short time I was there. I uncovered the information I had come for though, so I took my win and went on my way.

CHAPTER 35

Adele wanted to go with Cooper to interview Jimmy Ragone, but she was needed in court for another case. Cooper didn't mind. He didn't want her to go because he figured he'd get more information without her present. Instead of contacting Jimmy first, he went directly to his house, expecting him not to be home. Cooper wanted to speak to one or both of his parents alone first.

Cooper pulled to a stop at the curb in front of Jimmy's house. The last thing he had wanted to be forced to do was rat Jimmy out to his parents. The kid needed a push. One of the four would surely flip and tell the cops everything when push came to shove. Why not Jimmy?

Cooper cut the engine and grabbed his keys and phone. He walked the short distance up the concrete path that cut through the landscaped front yard. Even before he put his foot on the first step, a woman pulled open the front door.

She was a petite lady with short blonde hair. She wore an emerald green sweater and jeans that looked as if they had been ironed. She told him her name was Mary, Jimmy's mother.

"Are you Cooper?" she asked, stepping out onto the front porch.

"I am," Cooper said. He wasn't sure why the woman would know of him already unless Jimmy told her. "Is Jimmy home?"

She folded her arms across her chest. "My husband, Bob, told me to tell you to leave Jimmy alone. He had hoped to be here when you showed up because Jimmy said you would. I don't understand why you're bothering him."

It was clear that Jimmy had told his parents a much different story. Cooper had no choice. "With all due respect, ma'am, I'm here to help your son. He's in a great deal of trouble with the cops. I'm here to give him the chance to turn himself in and cut a deal. If he does that, he might even save himself some prison time. He promised me he'd tell you and your husband what was going on."

Mary's eyes grew wide and she hesitated ever so slightly. "What kind of trouble?"

Cooper explained about the burglaries and that Jimmy had admitted to being involved. He watched her face contort in the way of a mother hearing that kind of news. "Your son got involved in something over his head. It's going to come out one way or the other. All I'm trying to do is give your son a fighting chance. We believe that Scott Sawyer is the one responsible for starting all of this. Jimmy was recruited into it for his tech skills."

"Scott Sawyer, the detective's son?"

Cooper nodded. "You and I both know Det. Sawyer will do anything to protect his son, including blame the three other boys involved." Cooper took a step toward her and they locked eyes. "Scott has already tried to shift the blame to an innocent party. His father arrested an innocent young man and that's how I'm involved. The cops know he didn't have anything to do with it. It's only a matter of time before Scott tries to do the same with your son."

Mary took a breath and exhaled slowly. "I never liked Scott. Even when the boys were young, Scott would cook up all sorts of trouble and get the other boys involved. All his father does is protect him so he's never faced any kind of punishment. I even had the school move Jimmy to another classroom to get him away from Scott."

This was the best news Cooper had heard. "You understand what

I'm saying. This goes beyond elementary school trouble. Jimmy could be looking at jail time, and I know he's supposed to be going off to college. He has his whole future in front of him. It's time you get out in front of this and stop Scott and his father before they can turn the tables on Jimmy."

Mary didn't even hesitate. "Come with me," she said and turned and walked into the house.

Cooper followed right behind her, not believing his luck. Mary escorted Cooper into a large living room to the left of the front door. It was decorated like something out of a catalog. Even the beige carpet looked pristine as if it had been recently shampooed.

"Sit please and let me call my husband. He can be home from work in less than ten minutes." Mary walked out of the room and Cooper could hear her on the phone in the other room. Her calm demeanor had given way once she was speaking to her husband. She told him in a rushed frantic tone that he had to come home as soon as possible – that Jimmy was in serious trouble.

Cooper did not doubt that she took what he said seriously. When Mary came back into the room, she sat down in a straight-back chair and folded her hands in her lap. "My husband will be home any minute now."

"Is Jimmy here?"

Mary shook her head. "He's at school. I want you to tell us what's going on first and then we will call him home. I don't want him to have any chance to argue or intervene. It sounds like he's not been honest with us and that's a huge problem." Her eyes watered and she wiped away a tear. "My son is smart. I hope he hasn't done something so stupid that his entire future is destroyed."

When Cooper started to speak, she held her hand up. "Wait until Bob gets here. There's no point explaining this multiple times."

Cooper sat back on the couch and got comfortable. He wasn't

sure if he was glad or not that Jimmy wasn't there. He understood the reasoning, but there were still things Cooper needed to know. While they waited for Bob, Mary asked Cooper how long he'd been in business and what brought him to that work. She seemed to have a renewed sense of confidence in him after he explained that he had once been a detective with the Little Rock PD.

Cooper gave her a sympathetic smile. "I know the detectives investigating this case. That's why I'm sure Jimmy can work something out if he's willing to be honest and tell them what happened."

"He'll be honest. I'll make sure of it," Mary said with a certainty that Cooper hadn't heard from her before.

A moment later, Bob Ragone came charging down the hallway into the living room. Cooper heard his heavy booted steps even before the man entered the room. He stood about six-three and had a brush of closely cropped gray hair.

Cooper hadn't been sure what to expect from Jimmy's father, but the concern in the man's dark eyes told Cooper everything he needed to know. This family wouldn't sweep anything under the rug.

Bob took a few steps with his hand outstretched to Cooper. He stood and clasped the man's hand in his. Bob's mouth set in a firm line, he assessed Cooper and then said, "Let me say first that I apologize for telling Mary not to speak to you. My understanding was that you were harassing Jimmy about a watch he had taken from the basketball court. He assured me he had given that back so I didn't understand what you were doing."

"Understood," Cooper said and waited for Bob to sit down on the couch, and then he sat back down with him. "I can understand why you'd think that. That's initially why I spoke to Jimmy. I had heard he had taken Isiah Wright's watch from the basketball court after it was left there. I'm not sure if you realize, but that's the watch that ties Isiah to a crime scene. I needed to establish that the watch wasn't even in Isiah's possession when the burglary occurred."

"I understand why that would be important," Mary said softly.

"Jimmy assures me he gave the watch back," Bob said, looking at his wife and then back to Cooper. "Did he not?"

Cooper softened his gaze. "I believe Jimmy intended to give it back. I don't think for one second that Jimmy intended in any way for Isiah to be caught up in all of this. I think he feels bad about that. Scott intercepted Jimmy before he could give the watch back and he took the watch from your son."

Bob cursed. "Then Jimmy played a direct role in some innocent kid getting arrested. Whether that was his intent or not, that's what happened."

"Correct," Cooper said, feeling bad for both of Jimmy's parents.

Bob gave Cooper a leveled look. "Tell us what you believe Jimmy has done and what we need to do."

Cooper appreciated that the man cut straight to the point. "Jimmy got caught up in something that Scott got himself involved in. Scott, Jimmy, and two other guys were the ones breaking into the shops on Kavanaugh. My understanding is Jimmy helped to cut the surveillance and planted bugs – listening devices. They didn't steal anything."

"I can't even argue with you. My son has all the tech know-how to do that. He probably could have done that at ten years old. I don't understand why he'd do something like that though. He knows right from wrong." Bob lowered his head and looked to the floor, clearly upset by even thinking his son could have committed a crime.

Cooper wasn't sure how to explain this. No words seemed right. "They didn't take anything so they probably thought it was less of a crime than stealing. Also, they were encouraged to do this by someone who was paying them."

Bob's head snapped up. "They were paid? By whom?"

"The detectives on the case are looking into that right now." Cooper positioned his body so he was looking right at Bob. "I'm not saying to go easy on your son because what he did was wrong. There were several factors at play here. This wasn't something your son cooked up. It wasn't something that was his idea. Right now, though, Jimmy has an opportunity to cooperate with the cops and tell them everything he knows. He needs to do that before Scott or one of the other guys does that first in order for him to get the best deal from the prosecutor's office."

Cooper finished telling Bob and Mary everything he knew about the case so far, including Scott's involvement and Det. Sawyer's rushed investigation. He had to avert his eyes as he spoke because both Bob and Mary looked horrified that their son could be involved in something like this.

"The bottom line," Cooper said in closing, "is that Jimmy needs to step up and take responsibility for his actions. He can't worry what Scott or his other friends will think. If he wants to go to college and still have a future, he has to think like an adult now and protect himself. You know that Det. Sawyer will attempt to do the same for Scott. He will shift blame to your son and the others."

Mary pushed herself off the chair and stood. "I've heard enough. I'm not going to allow Scott to bully my son further." She turned to her husband. "Let's get Jimmy out of school and take him to the police station."

Bob stood. "Who should we speak to at the police station?"

Cooper had already written the information on a small orange Post-It. He pulled the slip of paper out of his pocket and handed it to Bob. "Det. Luke Morgan is on the case right now, but he is out running down leads. Call Captain Meadows directly, and I'll let him know you're on your way. Remember time is of the essence. I wouldn't delay if I were you. You want Jimmy to be proactive in this and not on the defensive if one of the other guys comes forward first."

Bob reached out and shook Cooper's hand. "I can't thank you enough for coming to speak to us. Please apologize to Dr. Wright and his son for us. I'm horrified that they had to be caught up in this."

"They will be happy to hear that," Cooper said and then followed Mary to the front door. She thanked him and even reached out and hugged him. Cooper did not doubt that they'd do exactly what they said and get Jimmy right to the police department.

Once Cooper got to his truck, he placed a call to Captain Meadows and alerted him that the Ragones were on their way after they picked Jimmy up from school. He told Captain Meadows how receptive the Ragones were to speaking with him and in getting Jimmy to speak to the police. Captain Meadows assured Cooper that if Jimmy shared the truth that they'd go easy on him.

When Cooper hung up, he texted Riley and asked her to meet him at Adele's office. They needed to regroup and see what else they could do now.

CHAPTER 36

By the time Luke reached Jason Manning's construction site, he had heard from both Riley and Cooper with updates on their respective interviews. He hadn't been surprised by the information either of them had obtained. Luke was glad to know that Jimmy Ragone would speak with Captain Meadows because they needed every bit of evidence they could find when the time came to confront Scott Sawyer. The Sawyers would not go down without a fight.

The information that Riley had obtained from Courtney had come as a shock. While Luke thought that Holly knew about the bank robberies, he wasn't expecting to hear that she had been involved. That put a whole new spin on her murder. He and Tyler were ready to make an arrest if they had the slightest hint that Jason was lying. It didn't matter to Luke that MaryBeth could give him an alibi. Alibis were easily bought or faked.

Before they left the police station, Tyler had pulled up all the information he could find about the robberies. Luke had spoken to each of the detectives involved. Because the bank robberies had taken place in different jurisdictions, there hadn't been much cross-sharing of information among them. They believed it was the same suspects in all the cases, but they hadn't done much work beyond that. It was no wonder they weren't anywhere close to solving them.

One detective sent Luke surveillance video from inside the bank. It didn't mean much though because the suspect, who was calling all the shots, was covered from head to toe – black non-descript long sleeve shirt, jeans, and red mask. There was no skin visible at all. The other person, most likely a man, was similarly dressed. He hadn't said a word during the heist but constantly looked to the main guy for direction.

While the newspaper had called the silent guy the muscle of the operation, Luke didn't think that was true. He was unsteady and not sure of himself. Every move he made he looked at the man calling the shots. If Luke had to guess, Jason was the silent suspect. Davis Smith had been the one in control – which made sense given his criminal background. They found no criminal background on Jason. Right out of the gate, bank robbery was a leap for a first-time criminal.

"Lots of hammers at a construction site," Tyler said, drawing Luke's attention from his thoughts.

Luke asked him to repeat what he said and then he agreed. "If it's Jason, he probably got rid of it or washed it and tossed it back among the supplies at his various construction sites."

Tyler pointed out the car's front window. "They are building a subdivision and have tools and supplies in each one of those framed houses. Most of the employees have their own tools. There's nothing to say Jason didn't make a switch. I don't know that we'll ever find it, if that's the case."

"There are many things that can go wrong right now. Let's focus on what could go right." Luke shared Tyler's pessimism but didn't want to walk into an interview with that kind of burden hanging overhead. He told his partner as much.

Tyler looked at him wide-eyed and grinned. "You're getting soft in your old age."

"Not soft," Luke corrected although he wasn't sure that was true.

"Come on, man, let's get this done." Luke opened his car door and hit the pavement. Tyler came around to the other side and joined him. Together they walked the short distance over a stone-paved area where there was a smattering of work trucks parked. At the far end was a double-wide trailer Luke assumed served as the construction site office.

Luke approached the door and put one foot on the metal step up to the door. He knocked once and heard a woman yell for him to enter. He pulled open the door and was hit with a wave of cigarette smoke. He coughed and shook his head but entered. Luke had no idea how anyone worked in such poor air quality. He was never a smoker and dreaded the stench it would leave on his clothes. Tyler followed right behind him grumbling about the same.

The office space was sparse with a few desks, a coffeemaker, and a table with snacks on it. A copier was pushed against the far wall.

Luke flashed his badge and introduced himself to the woman sitting at the desk closest to the door. She was the only person in the place. "I'm looking for Jason Manning."

"You want the boss," she said with a puff of her cigarette. "He's on-site. Let me call him for you."

Luke held his hand up to get her attention. "Don't mention it's the cops if you can."

She looked at him wide-eyed and then tapped at her temple. "Smart thinking. He's probably done something stupid and you don't want a runner on your hands."

"She doesn't seem surprised that Jason might be in trouble," Tyler whispered to Luke.

Luke waited as the woman picked up a walkie-talkie and radioed to Jason that he had two men in fancy suits in the office talking about a large investment in the construction firm. He said he'd be right there. She dropped the walkie on the table and had a good laugh at herself.

"That will get him running in here real quick." She stood from her desk. "Do y'all want some privacy?"

"That would be appreciated," Luke said evenly. "You don't seem to be surprised that we are here to speak to Jason."

As she gathered up a few things, she angled her head to look at Luke. "I've been working with Jason since he started this firm. He's had affairs and had some shady business dealings. Some days I don't even know how we are still in business. Your visit is par for the course of what I've seen." She scooted past Luke and Tyler and reached the door just as Jason pulled it open.

"Good luck, sweetie." She laughed as she brushed past Jason on her way out.

He turned to look at her but didn't say anything. He climbed the two steps into the trailer and then finally swiveled his head to see who was there waiting for him. He got one look at Luke and Tyler and backed up. His face registered a shock that Luke couldn't believe the man felt. He had to have known they'd track him down to speak to him eventually.

Jason stood about five-eleven and had sandy brown hair that fell over his forehead in a messy wave. His jeans had a rip in the knee and his plaid shirt stretched over his biceps. He regained his composure quickly. "Can I help you with something?"

Luke introduced himself and Tyler and then got down to business. "We understand that you were having an affair with Holly Bell." Luke could have started with a question about how the man knew Holly, but he wanted to go in with a show of force and make Jason wonder what more he already knew.

"That's right," Jason said, the color draining from his face. He shuffled past Luke and Tyler in the small space and sat down at a desk. He gestured with his hand for them to pull up a chair. "I assume this is going to take a while. You might as well get comfortable."

Tyler sat but Luke remained standing. "How long were you involved with Holly?"

"First," Jason said, raising his head to make eye contact with Luke, "I had absolutely nothing to do with Holly's murder. I was home in bed with my wife. I didn't even know Holly had been murdered until it hit the news."

Luke didn't say anything in response. Instead, he asked his question again. "We'll get to that. I want to know how you met."

Jason looked up at the ceiling. "I don't remember exactly how long ago it was, but she wanted some work done in her shop. She hired me. Right off the bat, we had a certain chemistry."

"The affair started immediately then?" Tyler asked with a judgmental tone Luke knew he couldn't help. The man had been married for longer than Luke could remember and the thought of being unfaithful to a spouse was abhorrent to him.

"It wasn't the first day but the second. It was that fast." Jason swallowed hard. "I'm not trying to defend myself, but I was going to leave my wife anyway. I was waiting for the right time."

He had opened the door so Luke was going to walk through. "What was the delay?"

"Money, man." Jason shrugged. "Divorce is expensive and I knew my wife would want a fight. It would cost me more than I had."

"What did you do about that?" Luke asked and stared down at him waiting for any sign of deceit. He didn't have to wait long because Jason crossed his arms and ankles and stiffened his posture.

"I tried to get the money together."

Luke smirked. "By any means necessary, right?"

Jason didn't say anything for a few beats. He looked to Tyler who had an even angrier expression on his face. "I don't know what you mean," he said to Luke, his voice catching.

"Oh, I think you do, Jason. I think you know exactly what I'm talking about." Luke waited while the man squirmed in his seat. "Do you want to tell me or should I lay out the evidence we have?"

Jason held his hands up in surrender. "I have no idea what you're talking about. I still don't have the money together for a divorce, which is why I was with my wife when Holly was killed."

Luke pulled a chair from a nearby desk and rolled it right in front of Jason. He took a seat and leaned forward resting his hands on his knees, inches from Jason's face. "I believe you don't have the money – yet. That's only because you were double-crossed and can't find it."

Jason shifted his eyes back and forth and sweat beaded on his forehead. "I don't know what you heard, but it's not true."

"If you don't know what I heard – how can you know if it's true or not?"

Tyler inched forward in his chair. "Jason, there is no point lying to us. Don't you think we gathered all the evidence before coming to see you? We have enough to arrest you right now. You might as well help us out."

"What...what do you want to know?" he stammered, looking at Tyler with his eyes wide.

"First, whose idea was it to rob banks? Forgive me for saying so, but you don't seem smart enough to pull that off on your own."

Jason sucked in a sharp breath and seemed to hold it like a child about to have a temper tantrum. Tyler and Luke didn't budge, just sat there staring at the grown man who looked like he was about to cry.

"I, well, we..." Jason wiped the sweat from his forehead.

"That's what I thought," Luke said. "You're wasting our time."

"It wasn't me, I swear," Jason said finally. "It was Holly's idea. She knew Davis Smith and she had the idea to rob banks so I'd have enough cash to get divorced. I went along with it and then Davis double-crossed us when he went back to prison on a parole violation."

Luke couldn't believe what this guy was saying. "You expect us to believe that Holly Bell contacted a known criminal and orchestrated bank robberies? She doesn't even have a hint of a criminal record."

"You didn't know her. She didn't have a criminal record because she was good enough to have never gotten caught. Believe it or not, that's what happened," Jason said with fear in his voice. When Luke didn't respond, Jason continued, "You said it yourself, I don't seem smart enough to pull this off and you're right. I've never committed a crime before and had no idea what I was doing. It was all Davis and Holly. I was along for the ride. Davis needed money. He was having trouble finding work after getting out of prison and Holly's shop was in trouble. We all needed the money."

Luke considered what Jason said and it wasn't that farfetched. Holly had married Chance in prison so as far as Luke was concerned, she wasn't operating at full good-decision-making capacity. "We have a lot to discuss. On your feet." Luke stood and waved Jason up. He read him his rights and then turned the man around to slap the cuffs on him.

As they walked to the door of the trailer, Luke said, "You might as well tell us while we're here, where's the hammer that killed Holly?"

"I didn't kill Holly!" he yelled. "You got me, I robbed some banks, but I didn't kill Holly. Go ahead and search the construction site. I'll give you keys to my office and my house." There was full-blown panic in Jason's voice. Then more softly, he said, "I loved her. I'd never hurt her."

Luke turned to Tyler. "You heard him. Call the crime scene investigators. We just got verbal permission to search. But let's get a warrant in case he changes his mind later." Luke had a hold of Jason's arm and shoved him out the door of the trailer. "I'm guessing your divorce is going to be fairly easy now since you'll be spending a long time behind bars."

Jason let loose a current of tears as he pled for Luke to give him leniency.

CHAPTER 37

"Looks like Luke made an arrest in the burglary case," I said, reading his text. He added that he'd update me on any progress interviewing Jason Manning. He said he hadn't explored the totality of the burglary cases yet, but now that they were back at the police station, Jason was willing to talk. That eased my mind. I hoped this meant that Izzy would finally be free from the charges.

Cooper and I had arrived at Adele's office while she was still in court. We ordered lunch to the office and sat at the small table in the conference room eating and chatting about other cases we had pending. There was a cheating spouse case that had Cooper following a woman in circles through the city. He assumed she had figured out she was being followed. It turned out she had been lost and twenty minutes later, she pulled into a hotel parking lot in North Little Rock. Cooper shot a video of her embracing her boyfriend up against her car.

The following day Cooper had shot video of a man who had claimed he had pulled his back and could no longer work. His office had suspected he was lying and hired us to catch the guy so they could deny the disability claim. During the first few days following the man, Cooper found nothing. It was the fifth day that Cooper followed the guy to an electronics store and watched him carry out a big-screen television on his own.

All in all, Cooper was catching the evidence the clients had paid him for and all were happy with the results. It meant more work for us.

Cooper had already given me our next case. It would require me to do surveillance, which I hated. I'd rather go undercover, create a fake backstory, and trick someone into giving me the information I wanted. The fact that Cooper was even asking me to do surveillance meant he was desperate.

He tapped the file. "It's one weekend and it's easy work," he said with a grin.

The case wouldn't be difficult but it would require both of us to sit in our vehicles watching a house for the weekend. We'd trade off in eight-hour shifts. All we had to do was make sure no one entered the home while the owners were out. They suspected that their college-aged daughter would throw a party or invite her boyfriend to the house.

"So, basically we are making sure a college-aged girl doesn't have any fun?" I asked. "It sounds like these parents need a better relationship with their daughter. She's an adult after all."

Cooper shrugged. "He's a big-time defense attorney and could bring us more work if we do a good job. Let's humor him, okay?"

"Yeah, sure," I said with a pout. Who was I kidding though – work was work and it was an easy gig. I never fancied myself a rat though so I hoped the young woman didn't do anything wrong while we were watching the house.

"Did Luke say anything about Jimmy Ragone and his parents speaking to Captain Meadows?" Cooper asked.

I grabbed my phone off the table and sent Luke a quick text. I didn't want to bother him during an interrogation and knew if he was busy, he wouldn't respond. "He'll get back to me sooner or later."

"Have you talked to Luke at all about Holly Bell's murder?"

"Not much other than the conversations you were a part of. I've spoken to Courtney, Holly's best friend, and Jordan Collins. She and Jordan had a confrontation before the murder. Luke wanted to rule her out."

My phone chimed and I picked up my phone and read it. "Luke said Jimmy Ragone confessed to everything. They didn't learn anything they didn't already know. Captain Meadows has instructed Jimmy not to talk to anyone. The prosecutor is going to let him off with probation and a clear record if he stays out of trouble for a year. Might not look too good for college, but at least he won't serve any time."

Luke sent another text before I could put my phone down. I locked eyes with Cooper. "Captain Meadows wants to wire us up and try to get a confession from Scott Sawyer. He believes that Scott will have his guard down thinking we are stupid. Captain Meadows thinks that together, we'll be able to push enough buttons to trip him up."

Cooper's face gave away his uncertainty. "How are we going to get Scott away from his father? Don't you think by now he would have instructed him not to talk to anyone?"

"Det. Sawyer doesn't believe that Scott has anything to do with the burglaries. He's in total denial according to Amelia. She said she tried to tell him and neither he nor her mother would listen. If we can get Scott alone and confront him with what we know, he might get cocky enough to give himself away."

Cooper considered what I said and made a suggestion. "What would you think of interviewing on your own? He might think he can intimidate you. You can say you've spoken to a few people and tell him what you suspect."

"I don't know if that's a good idea." I've interviewed countless suspects in my time and even a few hardened criminals, but something was intimidating about a teenage boy. Add to that Scott Sawyer's sense of entitlement and the anxiety grew more.

251

"You're overthinking," Cooper said, wagging his index finger at me. "It's possible that Jimmy told Scott or some of the other guys about my interview with him. If I ask to meet Scott or even attempt, he'll shut me down right away. Besides, my interview with his father landed me a black eye."

That much was true. Cooper's slight bruise had turned into a full-blown ugly purple and black bruise under his eye and down his cheek. He looked like he went ten minutes in the ring with a heavyweight boxer and barely escaped alive. Cooper had a logical argument and I was coming from emotion. I had to give this round to him.

"I can do it," I said and watched as Cooper smiled over at me in the condescending way he did sometimes. It was a brotherly "I win" kind of smile. I checked my watch. "When do we expect Adele back from court?"

No sooner had the words left my mouth than I heard her down the hallway giving instructions to her administrative assistant. Her voice was rushed but there was a tinge of excitement underlying it.

A moment later, Adele appeared in the doorway with a beaming smile stretched across her face and an envelope in her hand. She rushed in and kissed Cooper and then sat down at the table. "The prosecutor has dropped all charges against Izzy and there won't even be so much as a hint of an arrest on his record. It's been expunged completely from the system."

I clapped my hands. "That's wonderful news. Have you called Izzy and his father?"

"On the way back from court. Dr. Wright is pleased and Izzy had the same nonchalance he always has. I'm sure he didn't want to show me how excited he was with the news."

Cooper asked, "What pushed them to get it done so quickly?"

"It was the interviews you both conducted." Adele reached for a bottle of water on the table, uncapped it, and took a big sip. She set

252

it down when she had drained half the bottle. "Riley, I don't know what you said to Amelia but it worked. This afternoon she went to the prosecutor's office and asked to speak with whoever had the Isiah Wright case and she told him everything she knew. She even said she'd be willing to testify against her brother if it was needed."

I pulled back in surprise. "Amelia didn't give me any indication she'd be willing to do that. If anything, she played down her willingness to get involved. She had compelling evidence though."

Adele nodded. "Well, she is willing and provided great information. It was what ultimately got them to close the case against Izzy. It was too compelling to disregard. It also provided corroborating evidence to everything Jimmy Ragone told Captain Meadows. Amelia showed up at the prosecutor's office about an hour after they got Jimmy's statement. They worked out a deal with him for his testimony against Scott and the others. They want a confession from Scott, but at this point, I'm not even sure it's necessary."

Cooper looked across the table. "Maybe this is why Captain Meadows wants us to interview Scott."

Adele hadn't been in the loop on that so Cooper and I spent a few minutes catching her up to speed on everything, including that I'd do the interview alone. When we were done, Adele turned to me. "Are you sure you want to go alone? I was talking to the prosecutor and Scott sounds like a dangerous guy. I'd venture to say he's a budding sociopath. He has no regard for anyone else and he's been empowered to be this way by his father."

"I'll be fine," I said, reassuring her even though I wasn't sure myself. "I'll be wired and Luke and Tyler won't be far. I don't even know that Scott will speak to me."

"I don't know," Adele said, her face giving away her displeasure. "It sounds too risky, and they don't even need it for the case."

"It's probably because Det. Sawyer will fight it so hard," I said. "I wouldn't be surprised if Det. Sawyer provided a false alibi to keep Scott out of trouble."

Cooper rubbed a hand down his face, wincing when it hit the bruise on his cheek. "That's probably why they want some kind of statement from Scott. Det. Sawyer was Izzy's arresting officer and if this case goes to court, all the corroborating evidence in the world might not hold the weight of a detective who alibis his son."

Adele tapped the table. "I can't argue with you there. When are you going to speak to him?"

"I'm not sure. Cooper and I haven't even spoken to Luke yet about me interviewing Scott alone. I'll talk to him tonight and go from there."

"Sounds like case closed on our end." Adele looked at the both of us as she handed the envelope she had come in with to Cooper. "You'll see a nice bonus in addition to your regular fee. Dr. Wright was happy with your work."

Cooper opened the envelope and peered down at it and then slid it over to me. I looked quickly and raised my eyes to him. "Can we accept this?" It was a five-thousand-dollar bonus. I didn't feel like we had done all that much on the case to warrant it.

Before Cooper could respond, Adele did. "Take the money and don't insult Dr. Wright. In a matter of days, his son went from looking at ten plus years in state prison to being free. You earned it."

I guess the matter was settled then. Adele and Cooper asked me if I'd like to join them for dinner, but it had been a long day and I wanted to get home. Even if Luke was late, I could at least cook some dinner. I said goodbye and left them in the office making plans for later.

CHAPTER 38

Luke had spent the late afternoon well into the evening getting the story from Jason Manning. The man insisted that the bank robberies had been Holly's idea. He pointed the finger at her for everything – from connecting them with Davis Smith to planning each heist and hiding the money in her shop. Jason tried to convince Luke that it was Holly who made the plan to bug the shops and break into them to search. He admitted to being the one who broke in after the boys left.

When pressed about who set up the deal with the high school boys, Jason refused to mention them by name. He swore up and down that he didn't know. Luke went so far as to pull photos from social media of Scott Sawyer, Jimmy Ragone, and the two others. He had shown them to Jason who remained emotionless. He said that maybe they had worked at one of his construction sites over the summer, but he'd need to check his employment records. He had too many laborers to know everyone by name. Jason explained one of his three foremen might know better.

While Jason fully admitted to being a part of the bank robberies, he denied killing Holly. He swore up and down to Luke that he had nothing to do with it. Jason told a similar tale as MaryBeth had when they questioned her.

They had gone out the night before for dinner and came home and crashed. He slept late on Sunday morning. MaryBeth had already been awake and cooking breakfast by the time he woke up. He had been surprised that he slept that late, but he'd had a rough time at work the week prior. Jason explained he had been stressed about finding the money.

He and Holly had also been arguing constantly. She claimed that he wasn't doing enough to find the money and free himself from MaryBeth. By that point, Jason wished he had never met Holly and had never robbed the banks. His only goal was to live as low-key as possible and hope they wouldn't get caught. Then Holly was murdered.

Jason had held his head in his hands and looked up at Luke. "When I found out that Holly was gone, I felt relief. I know that sounds horrible, but it meant I could stop looking for the money and get back to my normal life before this all started. I didn't even care about the money at that point."

Luke hadn't been sure he believed him. When pressed about it, Jason held firm. No matter how Luke asked the question, Jason didn't waver. It had been an exhausting interview in that regard. With an airtight alibi and no forensic evidence tying Jason to Holly's murder scene, Luke had no reason to hold him for anything other than the burglaries. He'd be charged for those outside of Little Rock's jurisdiction and held until a transfer to the other counties could be made. Even if Luke had charged Jason with murder right now, the case would go nowhere due to lack of evidence.

The only lead Jason provided during the interview was that he had started to believe that the money wasn't in any of the shops. He swore up and down that he had searched everywhere.

With his eyes locked on Luke, Jason had admitted his biggest fear. "Holly was diabolical. I've never met a woman whose mind worked like hers. I got to a point where I started to think she was having me break into the shops so that I'd get arrested and thrown in prison.

Then she could keep the money for herself. I think Holly knew exactly where the money had been stashed. Ask Lauren, Holly's niece. She was like Holly's little puppy at the boutique. Holly was having an affair with someone else. There was another man. I'm sure of it."

That was the last thing Jason had said before he invoked his right to counsel. He didn't say a word after that and Luke had to end the interview. It didn't matter because the bank robberies had been solved, but they were no closer to finding the cash or who killed Holly.

After officers came to the interrogation room and left with Jason to officially book him into jail for his preliminary hearing the next morning and eventual arraignment, Luke went back to his desk. He had already sent Tyler home for the night. One of them might as well get some sleep.

Now exhausted, Luke sat slumped at his desk. He texted Riley and told her he'd be late and not to wait up for him. Then he pulled a large accordion-style folder from his bottom drawer. He knew the name Lauren was familiar to him, but he wasn't sure how. Luke spent the next hour going through the initial statements Tyler had taken from Holly's staff. Luke found the statement he'd been searching for – the person who found Holly's body. Her name was Lauren Baldwin.

Lauren was twenty-two and had worked at the shop since it opened. She hadn't disclosed any relation to Holly when Tyler first interviewed her, but that didn't mean anything. Tyler might not have asked. It was common for traumatized witnesses not to offer information – even if later it seemed odd that it wasn't mentioned.

Luke jotted down her address, put the file back in the desk, and got up. He gathered his phone and keys and headed out of the office into the cold November air. Although it was nearing eight in the evening, he figured he might get lucky and Lauren would be home. She lived in an apartment community in West Little Rock near Pleasant Ridge Town Center, which was full of shops and restaurants – about a twenty-minute drive away.

Once Luke got past the gate, following another car, he found his way through a maze of apartment buildings. In the last parking lot, he found building eight. Nearly every apartment in the building had lights on – at least from his vantage point.

He made his way to the apartment and knocked on the door. Luke heard a television on and movement behind the door. "It's Det. Morgan with the Little Rock Police Department," he said.

The door opened slowly and a young woman peeked out. "Can I help you?" she asked cautiously.

Luke flashed his badge and repeated his name. He confirmed the young woman was Lauren and then explained, "I'm investigating the murder of Holly Bell. I had a few questions that couldn't wait until tomorrow. Can I come in and speak to you, please?"

Lauren closed the door and Luke heard the slide of a chain. She pulled it open and allowed Luke inside. "Take a seat on the couch. I need to save a document I was working on." Lauren disappeared down a hallway.

Once Luke sat down, he felt a bit foolish to have come at this time of night. The questions could have waited. Luke had run out of patience for this case, mostly because the more he found out about Holly, the less he liked her or felt sympathy for her. That was never good in a murder investigation.

Lauren was in her pajamas and the remnants of her dinner were on a plate sitting on the coffee table. Otherwise, the apartment was clean and well-kept. She returned a moment later with her hair piled on top of her head. She grabbed the plate off the coffee table and headed for the kitchen which Luke could see from the living room.

"I'm sorry for bothering you so late," he said.

"It's fine," Lauren responded, running water over the dirty plate. She wiped her hands on a dishtowel and then joined him in the living

258

room. "I'm not sure how much I can help you beyond what I already told the other detective."

"I read that statement. It must have been difficult finding Holly like that."

Lauren sat back on the couch and tucked her legs under her. "It wasn't easy. I wasn't even supposed to be working, but she had called me the night before and asked me to meet her there to do some inventory."

Luke's suspicions rose when Lauren's voice hitched at the word *inventory*. He had more important things to get out of the way first. "Are you and Holly related? I had heard that she was your aunt."

"That's correct. Holly was my father's sister." Lauren expelled a heavy sigh and leaned back on the couch. She clasped her hands on her lap. "Truthfully, my father wanted me to work at the shop to keep an eye on Holly and report back to him."

"Why would he want you to do that?"

"Holly wasn't reliable. My father invested in her business because he wanted her to have stable work and be able to support herself. She always had an eye for fashion and had a good business sense. But she was prone to making poor decisions in her personal life. Look at who she married."

"Holly started the business after Chance got out of prison."

"Right," Lauren said and then explained, "My father knew Chance couldn't support her and wanted Holly to have some autonomy. Opening the shop was something she had talked about for quite a while. He invested in the hopes that eventually it might draw Holly away from Chance."

"Did you know Holly was having an affair?" Luke asked and watched her expression carefully. It was obvious by the lack of shock on her face that Lauren knew.

"Jason wasn't the first guy Holly had an affair with since she married

Chance. As you know, Holly married him while he was still in prison. She never stopped dating. We don't know why she married him if she wasn't going to be faithful. My father tried to talk to her about it, but it wasn't something she hid very well."

Lauren paused and scanned her eyes around the room as if searching for the right words. She refocused on Luke. "Holly wasn't doing well in the weeks leading up to the murder."

Luke tried to be as gentle as possible. He didn't want to get down in the weeds of it though. He wanted to stay on track. "Why did you go into the shop on Sunday morning?"

Lauren offered a half-smile. "I'm sure this won't come as a surprise by now. Holly was spying on the other shops. I had been helping her. Well," Lauren paused, "not so much helping her, but trying to get her to stop. She told me an elaborate story about her boyfriend, Jason, and money that was hidden. She said he'd been double-crossed and she was trying to help him make things right. I thought she was a bit delusional."

Luke's expression turned to surprise. "You didn't believe there was money?"

"I didn't know what to believe. I don't want to say that Holly was a liar, but she was prone to being dramatic. If there was money, why would someone hide it in one of the shops? The whole story didn't seem to make a lot of sense to me."

"Did you consider that spying on other shops was illegal?"

Lauren lowered her head and nodded. "I told Holly that. I tried to get her to stop, but it's not like I could turn Holly in to the cops. I hid it from my father, too, because he would have. I thought I could get her to stop." She raised her head and looked at Luke. "There's no point holding anything back now because Holly is dead."

"Do you have any idea who killed her?"

"No," Lauren said and softly started to cry. She wiped a tear from her eyes. "I'd have told you by now if I knew. I'd have told that first detective who interviewed me. I don't even know who the other guy was that she was having an affair with."

"There was another guy then? I heard that there was someone other than Jason but I wasn't sure it was accurate."

Lauren nodded. "It's true unfortunately and he was young. That's all I know."

"How young?"

"Holly wouldn't say. I asked if he was my age and she said younger but legal."

The legal age for consent in Arkansas was sixteen. "Could he have been a senior in high school?"

Lauren gasped. "I'd hope not. I don't know anything else about him. I never met him or heard his name mentioned. I never saw a photo of him. I wondered if she was telling me the truth. Holly bragged about a guy that young being interested in her, but I thought it was kind of sick."

Luke asked a few more questions to make sure that Lauren didn't have anything to identify the young man. When she insisted that she knew nothing, he moved on. He went through a series of other pressing questions, but Lauren didn't offer anything he didn't already know.

Luke had one final matter to address. "Do you know if your aunt committed any bank robberies?"

"Absolutely not," Lauren said with strength in her voice that made Luke believe her. "I don't understand. What are you talking about?"

Luke explained that the money Jason was looking for came from a string of bank robberies. "Jason pointed the finger at Holly and said she spearheaded the whole thing. Was Holly capable of orchestrating something like that?"

Lauren remained quiet for several moments and then took a deep breath. "Holly was incredibly manipulative and devious. My father constantly tried to keep her on the straight and narrow. I hate to say it, but yes, she had the devious mindset and capacity to do that. Holly was in control at all times. She thought she was smarter and could outwit anyone. Mostly what she did was cause trouble for herself. Holly thrived on drama. If there wasn't any, she'd create some."

That certainly sounded like the woman Jason had described.

Lauren looked to Luke. "Holly could have done anything she set her mind to do. There were very few people who got one over on her."

"Someone did in the end," Luke said.

CHAPTER 39

The next morning, I sat in the conference room at the police station with Captain Meadows, Luke, Tyler, and Cooper. Between the murder and the robberies, Luke felt like we needed a meeting to ensure we were all on the same page and to discuss things going forward.

When he arrived home the night before, hungry and exhausted, I held off on asking him about Cooper's plan of letting me interview Scott Sawyer alone. I knew his immediate reaction would be to tell me no. He needed food and a good night's sleep before I could broach it. He had eaten like a man who had been starved for days and then he slept like a rock.

When Luke woke refreshed and ready to take on a new day, I eased him into the idea over a morning breakfast of scrambled eggs, bacon, toast, and coffee just the way he liked it. By the time he left for work, Luke wanted all of us to meet and had been convinced that Cooper's idea was sound.

"Does anyone feel like this case is small in location but all over the map at the same time?" Tyler asked.

"That's exactly how I've been feeling," I admitted. "There are many players involved for something we thought might be simple and straightforward from the start."

"What do we know to date?" Captain Meadows asked.

Luke got up and went to the whiteboard at the end of the room. He needed a visual when mapping out a case. It also gave him something to do with his energy, which tended to be high during a case review.

He opened the cap on the marker and made some initial notes. "We know for sure that all of the shops along Kavanaugh Boulevard were burglarized and that listening devices were found in each one. We know that there were two break-ins – the first when Scott and his friends broke in and cut the shops' surveillance and left the bugs and then later when Jason came in and searched the shops himself. We know the names of all four boys who were involved and that Scott was the ringleader."

"Davis Smith was named as an accomplice who double-crossed Holly and Jason and hid the money," Tyler added. "While we've not spoken to Davis yet, we know he's been arrested previously for bank robbery and that he currently sits in state prison. He's not going anywhere. We know that the money from the heists is still missing."

Tyler pulled a page out of a file and glanced down at it. "In total, there was $2.3 million stolen. Both Jason and Holly believed that Davis hid the money before going back to prison on a parole violation. Jason also blames Holly for orchestrating the burglaries and the aftermath."

"What was the parole violation and how did Davis have time to move the money?" I asked. It just occurred to me that it was odd that Davis had enough time to hide the money before going back to prison unless he knew there was the threat of that pending.

Luke looked over at me. "That's a good question and one not answered yet. To be honest, I hadn't even given it much thought. I was so focused on who could have killed Holly, I haven't paid much attention to Davis' role in this at all."

Luke drew a line down part of the board and labeled that area "questions." He numbered the first and wrote out what I had asked. He turned back around. "Let's move on from the burglaries if we've noted all the facts."

"I have a question before we move on," Cooper said, drawing Luke's attention. "We know that Holly and Jason were having an affair, which started when he did some work for her. Do we know how Davis is connected to them? We also believe that Scott was connected to Jason because they worked for his construction company last summer."

"That's in dispute," Tyler said, correcting him. "We've confirmed that Scott and his friends worked for Jason's construction firm, but we aren't able to connect them conclusively. Scott and his friends were hired as part-time help. This morning I spoke to the foreman who hired them and they worked under. He can't state that they never met Jason, but he assured me they didn't have contact on the construction site. The foreman told me that Jason wasn't there because his time was spent on another site. Jason also denies having met them last summer. He told Luke he only got to know them once they were involved and he put that on Holly. He said that Holly knew them, which isn't out of the realm of possibilities, given how close her shop is to where they all live."

Luke added, "I was also told by Lauren, Holly's niece, that Holly was having an affair with a younger guy. I'm not saying it's one of the boys since they are all in high school, but he could have known Scott and his friends. Jason also thought that Holly was seeing someone else."

"Add the question to the list," Captain Meadows instructed, pointing to the board.

Luke added three more questions concerning Davis' and Scott's connections and the unknown affair.

"Luke," I said, interrupting his concentration. "You said that Jason blamed Holly. Her best friend, Courtney, suggested she took a lead role in it, particularly the surveillance."

Luke wrote it on the board and added, "Lauren also supported the idea that Holly could have been the mastermind behind the bank heists.

She said that her aunt was always in control and was capable of such a thing. It sounded to me like her family knew she was a bit unstable and was trying to keep an eye on her."

We went through a few more things we knew and questions that were still pending. Then Luke turned to all of us and asked the big question. "What do we know about Holly's murder?"

"That's all you and Tyler," Cooper said. "Riley and I have been pretty much hands-off on this one."

Luke ran a hand over his bald head. "I hate saying it, but we don't have much. We've ruled out Jordan Collins. Jason and MaryBeth alibi each other out. We still aren't able to confirm an alibi for Chance, but he claims to have been asleep and then on a Zoom call well after the murder. Davis Smith was in prison."

"I think we can safely rule out anyone she worked with at the shop," Tyler said. "The few employees she had are young women and all have alibis. The only one who doesn't is her niece Lauren who said she was at home before meeting her aunt."

Luke played with the marker in his hand. "I don't see that Lauren would have any reason to kill her aunt. If anything, she was trying to protect her. Now, Holly's brother is a possibility. It sounds like he was working to keep Holly's shop up and going. If he found out what she was up to, he could have snapped." Luke added his name to the list.

Captain Meadows cleared his throat. "The unknowns are Holly's killer and the hiding place of the money from the heists."

"And getting Scott Sawyer to confess," I added, not wanting them to forget what I thought had been important to them. "Adele told us the prosecutor said they had enough information to take it to court. Are you sure you want to go after a detective's son?"

"Yep," Tyler said without missing a beat. "I don't think we have a choice if we want to ensure justice. If we don't get Scott to admit to any wrongdoing, his father will protect him."

"I'm in, too," Luke said and locked eyes with me. "It sounds to me from everything you and Cooper found that Scott has been bullying kids for a long time and that's not going to stop unless he's held accountable for his actions. Det. Sawyer isn't going to do that. He will work to protect Scott at all costs."

"Are you feeling conflicted, Riley?" Captain Meadows asked, looking over at me in the fatherly way he could sometimes.

"No. There's not going to be blowback on me. I was worried about Luke." He had to work with Lou Sawyer. While I agreed that it would be best if Scott confessed, I didn't want to make life difficult for Luke at work.

Captain Meadows shook his head. "I'll handle that."

Luke looked at me and his expression was soft and loving. "You don't need to protect me. I can handle Sawyer on my own. He should have been doing his job all along."

"I'm sure you can handle it. It wasn't a question of that. I just don't like to kick the hornets' nest unless necessary."

When the words left my mouth, everyone in the room laughed and turned to me like it was the craziest thing I'd ever said.

"What?" I said offended.

"Did you suddenly get soft after getting married?" Cooper asked, teasingly. "You love kicking hornets' nests."

"My own maybe but the backlash will be felt here." Cooper was right though. After going through everything I did around the time I got married, I was feeling a little softer – less willing to take unnecessary risks.

"We're fine," Captain Meadows assured. "When do you think you can interview him?"

"I need to track down his schedule. I assume the interview should happen far away from home."

"Preferably," Luke said. "Does anyone have his schedule?"

"I can ask his sister Amelia." I reached for my phone and sent off a quick text requesting Scott's schedule. I was sure that if she was willing to speak to the prosecutors that she'd be willing to give me his schedule and keep it a secret.

While we waited, Luke and Tyler made a plan for the rest of their day. Cooper was going to start tackling some of the other cases we had pending but would be around if we needed him.

A few minutes later, Amelia texted back with a detailed agenda of Scott's day. She didn't know all of his classes but knew on Mondays he was out of school at noon. He was supposed to be working on a senior project during the afternoon, but he rarely stayed on the school campus to do that. I got the name of the diner where he ate lunch most days and hung out with friends who were also MIA from school.

"Scott should be at Fred's Diner in Hillcrest by noon." I read Amelia's text to them and we decided on a plan. I checked the time and we had about an hour, which would be enough time to wire me up and drive over there.

The meeting broke up and we said goodbye to Cooper. Luke told me to wait in the conference room and he'd get what we needed to wire me for sound. I didn't feel nervous, but it had been some time since I'd been wired for an interview.

"You ready?" Luke asked, returning a few minutes later. He had the black wire and tape. He closed the conference room door and wedged the doorstop under it. Then he turned around to face me with a mischievous grin on his face. "Take off your shirt."

"What kind of girl do you think I am? Not even going to buy me dinner first," I teased. "Is that why you secured us in here because you want to get fresh with me?"

"Right over the conference room table." Luke took a few steps and reached for the hem of my shirt and raised it. Then he tickled my tummy, which made me squeal. He kissed me to quiet me down and then got down to work.

He secured the wire around under my bra line, leaving the mic right between my breasts but hidden down into the left bra cup. Luke added more tape and then made sure everything was secure. I smoothed my shirt down impressed with how it looked. Unless Scott stuck his head between my breasts, he'd never tell I was wired.

Luke put his hands on my shoulders. "You got this," he said with a reassuring nod. "Tyler and I will be right down the street listening in." He kissed me sweetly before we left the room together.

CHAPTER 40

I arrived at Fred's Diner ten minutes after twelve. From down the road, I had watched Scott park his car in the adjacent parking lot and walk into the diner alone. He had a few books under his arm but seemed like a kid without a care in the world.

Luke and Tyler were out of sight but could hear me on the mic. We had tested the range a few times and then I entered the diner. The hostess asked me how many were in my party and I told her I was meeting someone. I pointed to Scott who was sitting in a far back booth with his head down focused on the menu. The hostess raised her eyes to me.

"Tutor," I said, brushing past her. I was at the table before Scott even glanced up. He had a head full of brown hair and a pleasant enough face. He had jeans and a blue button-down shirt with the tails untucked from his jeans.

I cleared my throat and he finally looked at me.

"Can you get me…" he started but then trailed off when he realized I wasn't wearing the green polo shirt and black pants like the other servers. He dropped his menu on the table, leaned back in the booth, and appraised me. "Who are you?"

I didn't wait to be asked. I slid into the booth across from him and rested my hands on the table. "I'm here to help you."

"Help me? With what?" he asked with the same cocky attitude that everyone had described. They weren't wrong. Scott came across like he could do no wrong.

"The police are looking for you and want to arrest you."

Scott laughed and leaned forward on the table. "Honey, you don't know who my father is. If the cops were looking for me, I'd know."

"Det. Lou Sawyer has been taken off the case. He wasn't looped in on the meeting."

Scott locked eyes with me. "What are you talking about? Who are you?"

I introduced myself as a private investigator but left it vague. "The prosecutor's office dropped all the charges against Isiah Wright. They know he didn't commit the burglaries, Scott. And they know who did."

He didn't seem so cocky now. By his surprised expression, he hadn't heard about Izzy. "What does this have to do with me? How do you even know who I am?"

"Come on, Scott. Don't play dumb. You know exactly what this has to do with you." I couldn't be bothered to tell him how I knew him and he didn't press it further. He didn't say a word but sat there watching me. I could tell he was unsure but too interested to tell me to leave.

I relaxed back into the booth. "Your friends have been talking to the cops, Scott. They know you were the ringleader. You planned those burglaries and got your friends to help. Jimmy Ragone has already confessed. I figured I could help you."

Scott didn't refute anything I said. "Why would you want to do that?"

"Everyone is entitled to a defense. You tell me what happened and I'll work my magic." I leaned into the table and batted my eyes at him. "I'm friendly with the cops involved in the case. I can make sure that it's your friends who go down for this."

"What do I need to do?"

"I'm not doing it for free. You've got money from what I hear. I have to know the truth though to know how to spin the story."

"I don't need to pay you for anything. My father can take care of whatever I need. I'm untouchable in this city."

"Oh, Scott," I said, laughing. "Listen, kid. You're a bit naive. Your father is off the case because they think he's protecting you. He might even lose his job over this. He's not going to be able to protect you when he's lost his job. You can kiss that big house goodbye, too. Even college maybe."

Scott reached for his phone, which I figured he'd do. "I'm calling my father."

"And tell him what, Scott? Are you going to admit you broke into those shops? Are you going to ask him if he's off the case? He'll get suspicious about why you're asking. You think he's going to risk his whole career if he knows you're guilty?"

When Scott didn't answer me, I shrugged and started to move out of the booth. "It's your call, but if you call your father, you can forget my help. I'm not dealing with him."

Scott didn't set his phone down, but he didn't bring it to his ear either. He palmed it. "How do I know I can trust you?"

I turned back to him. "You don't. I don't see anyone else around here offering to help you out. The way I see it, you've been hung out to dry. Holly is dead. Jason has been arrested. It's only a matter of time before he rats you out. Jimmy has already made a deal to testify against you."

I had hoped speaking like I already knew everything would get him to talk. Scott wasn't denying or correcting anything so I assumed I was taking the right approach.

After a moment, he asked, "How do you know all this?"

"I told you. I know people." I punctuated each word. I slid back into the booth and stared at him from across the table. "I was down at the police station this morning hanging around after bringing in a guy who skipped bail. I hear things, and the way the cops were talking, they are going after you big time because you're a detective's kid. Plus, I heard you can be a real peach. I heard about some of the things you've done to Isiah Wright including setting him up. It made your father look like an idiot, and cops don't like wasting their time or having to admit they are wrong. That Izzy thing burned them all."

I pointed at him. "They got a real hard on for you, Scottie. I wouldn't be surprised if they tried to stick you with Holly's murder."

Scott held his hands up, palms facing me. "I didn't kill Holly. I'd never do that."

"But you knew her." It was a shot in the dark and out of left field, but I went with it. "Intimately," I said with a wink.

Scott looked past me and then to the side. It was a few moments before he locked his eyes on me again. "How'd you know that? No one is supposed to know. Holly said she'd never tell anyone."

"Come on, Scottie. She's got a husband and she was having an affair with Jason Manning. You didn't think one of them was going to be suspicious? Even her family knew she was involved with a young guy. When did it start?"

Scott took a few breaths and red crept up his face. If he were any older, I would have been concerned he'd have a heart attack.

"A few months ago," he said, tugging at his collar. "We ran into each other near her shop. Then, she asked me to carry a few things to her car. We'd see each other from time to time and wave. It went from there."

"Who made the first move?" With a kid like Scott, I wasn't going to assume anything.

"She did but I might have if she hadn't. I was into her as much as she was into me." Scott went on to tell me how she'd text him that she needed some help in her shop when she wanted him to meet up with her. He'd go there and they'd have sex in the back of the store. Most times the place was closed. It also happened a few times during the day though, and Holly would close and lock her office door.

"I assume she told you about her plan with Jason to look for the stolen money from the bank robberies?"

"I didn't know about that at first," Scott admitted. He took a sip of his drink and gnawed on his lip. He still looked worried and uncertain if he should tell me. I wasn't going anywhere though.

"Holly didn't give me too many details," Scott admitted. "She said if I got in trouble, I'd be able to get out of it because my dad was a detective. But she didn't trust me enough to give me the full story. She said she had a friend who needed help. She was going to pay me. I couldn't do it alone though so I got my friends to help."

I raised my eyebrows. "Holly was okay with more people being involved?"

"No," Scott said, stressing the point. "There was no way I could do it on my own. I had to have help. I didn't know anything about the kinds of stuff she was asking me to do."

"Cutting the surveillance and dropping the listening devices? I know that was Jimmy's specialty."

"Yeah," he said. "You seem to know everything."

"I've got connections. I told you." I needed to keep him talking. He admitted it more easily than I had assumed he would. "How did it go down? I counted twelve shops in all that you broke into."

"Yeah, twelve." Scott explained how Jason had showed up one day when he was at Holly's shop and asked him to do them a favor. Scott explained he listened as Jason and Holly described a plan for him and his friends to break into the shops, cut the surveillance, and plant the listening devices. Later, Jason showed up in the parking lot at school to give him the listening devices.

Scott said it was his idea to leave the marble so Jason would know where the listening devices had been planted. Jason was supposed to take the marbles when he went into the shops after them, but he left them because the shop owners would assume it was kids that way. Holly didn't like that and they fought over it, but Jason won out. Scott thought it was a dumb idea.

There was something I didn't understand so I interrupted Scott. "Why did they care where the listening devices were planted? Couldn't you have told Holly later?"

"Sure, yeah, later. Jason wanted to know where they were before he went into the shops, and I was told never to contact him. Holly and I never met up a few days before or after we broke into a shop. Even when we were together, Holly didn't want me to talk about it. We made the plan and stuck to it and that was it. She told me that if anything went wrong, she wouldn't pay us."

I guess that made sense. "Why did you decide to frame Izzy?"

"I didn't know my dad was going to be on the case. I had to throw him off. Besides, Izzy deserved it. He thinks he's better than everyone else. He doesn't even belong in my neighborhood."

For the sake of getting information, I had to let that go. "Who else knows about this?"

"No one," Scott said, his cocky attitude returning. "The only people who know are Jason, Holly, and me and my friends."

"No other family?"

"My sister, but she ain't telling anyone," Scott said dismissively. "How are you going to help me?"

I didn't answer his question. I knew I had what Luke wanted. It was a full confession, but I wanted to push harder. "You said you didn't hurt Holly. I believe you. Do you know who did?"

Scott blinked rapidly three times. "No."

"You're lying to me. I can tell by the look on your face."

"Holly complained that Jason's wife had been hassling her."

"About?"

"You know how girls can be if a guy has a female friend," Scott said. "I figured it was about that. Holly told me that she and Jason were friends and nothing more. I believed her."

I hitched my jaw toward him. "What about you? Did you have a girlfriend?"

"At the time. Not anymore though."

"Why? Did she find out about you and Holly?" When Scott refused to answer me, I pressed, "Did your girlfriend find out what you were doing?"

Scott reached for his phone and I got the sense that he was done talking. I waited a few minutes to see if he'd make a call or look at me again. When he didn't do anything other than look at his phone, I slid out of the booth.

"You know how to reach me if you want my help," I said and walked away.

Luke and Tyler wouldn't make an arrest while I was sitting there, but they were both standing on the sidewalk at the front of the diner. They had ear-to-ear grins and Tyler slow clapped for me as I walked by.

I walked to my car without looking back at the diner. *Little Rock Police detective's son arrested for the Heights burglaries* – that would probably be lead on the evening news. I started my car and drove down the road wondering if Luke would plan a perp walk.

276

CHAPTER 41

Luke paced back and forth in the interrogation room. Tyler had left to get Scott a soda, not that the young man should be rewarded for sitting at the table stone-faced. They had heard enough when they were in the car outside the diner and brought Scott in on the spot. Luke couldn't believe how easily Riley had been able to get him to talk. He credited Riley's approach almost as much as he assumed Scott thought he was untouchable.

Luke looked down at Scott, sitting slumped back in the chair. He still seemed like a guy with no worries in the world. There had only been a brief moment when Luke and Tyler walked into the diner and over to Scott's table that he even seemed to understand that he was in serious trouble. He hadn't even made the connection that Riley had recorded him until they were back at the police station and Luke played it back to him.

Scott had stared at Luke with a blank expression on his face. "You can't bug a diner. This isn't going to be admissible in court," he had said with an air of arrogance.

"I didn't bug the diner," Luke had responded. "Since you're aware of the laws, then you know full well that planting listening devices in the shops was illegal. Arkansas is a one-party state and no one in that shop involved in those conversations was made aware of the bug."

Scott had no response for him other than to look away.

Now Luke paced while he waited for Scott to understand how they had gotten the recording of him speaking to Riley in the diner. Luke had no idea how anyone could be this dense.

When recognition took hold a few moments later, Scott looked at Luke. "No, that isn't fair. She said she wanted to help me. She can't record those conversations. She promised she'd help me."

Luke sat down at the table. "She is helping you. This is going to go much better for you if you tell me what you did and plea this out. If you make the prosecutor go to trial, it's going to be harder on everyone. We have witnesses and now your own words."

Luke was surprised that Scott hadn't asked for a lawyer or his father at that point. He checked his watch. They had been in the room for more than an hour. No matter how Luke tried to press him about the burglaries, he didn't budge.

"Scott," Luke said softly, drawing his attention. "I didn't realize until you told Riley that you were involved with Holly. I don't believe you killed her, but I'm curious to learn more about her so we can catch who did."

"What do you want to know?" Scott asked with his voice calm and even.

"There's quite an age difference between you. What did you have in common?"

Scott raised an eyebrow as if to ask Luke if he was an idiot. "What do you think we had in common?"

"I'm not talking about sex, Scott. If that's all Holly wanted, she could have done so with someone who didn't have a cop for a father."

Scott laughed. "Maybe I'm just that good."

Luke doubted it but didn't feel a need to debate the point. He tried another angle. "What did the two of you talk about? Did she ever mention friends or family?"

"It wasn't like that. We weren't boyfriend and girlfriend holding hands in the hallway talking about what we were doing after school."

"So, it was just sex?"

Scott shrugged. "We didn't talk much otherwise. She didn't confide in me. We didn't date."

"Do you know if Holly was seeing anyone else besides her husband and Jason?"

"I don't know," Scott said and seemed on the brink of saying something else but then he got quiet again. "I thought Holly and Jason were just friends. I didn't realize."

Luke didn't have time to address his hurt feelings. "Scott, the more helpful you can be with me, the more I can put a good word in with the prosecutor. You know something you don't want to tell me."

Scott sighed. "Is my dad here?"

"No, he's not in the office right now." Luke was being honest. He hadn't seen Det. Sawyer all day. "Does your father know about your relationship with Holly?"

"No way, man. He'd kill me if he knew." Scott looked to the door and then up at the ceiling. He chewed on his bottom lip.

"Did anyone in Holly's life know about your affair?"

Scott looked away. "Her husband knew what was going on. Even if he said he doesn't, he caught me with Holly one night. She explained it away that I was doing some work at her shop, but I know he didn't believe her. The way he looked at me. I thought he was going to kill me."

Luke remained quiet wanting him to go on.

"There was another time we were in Holly's office and her cellphone rang. She said she had to grab it because it was her husband. I could tell by the way Holly was trying to convince him there wasn't any money that he knew. I couldn't hear what he was saying but he didn't believe her. She kept saying 'it's not true, there's no money. I don't know what you're talking about. There's no money.'"

Luke had long suspected Chance knew more. "What did Holly say when she hung up the phone?"

"She rolled her eyes and said that if Chance thought he was getting any money, then he was out of his mind."

"Was Holly going to divorce him?"

"She had said so but who knows."

Luke asked more questions about Scott's relationship with Holly, but it didn't sound like he knew much of anything. Scott had been a patsy. Holly had reeled him in with sex and then used him and his friends to do her dirty work.

"When were you supposed to get paid?" Luke asked.

"After they found the money."

Luke sat back and tapped his finger on the table. "Aren't you angry, Scott? You threw away your future for what? A few thousand dollars? A thrill? Sex with an older woman?"

Scott didn't have anything to say to that. He finally leaned back in the chair and said, "I want a lawyer."

Luke slowly got up from his chair. There wasn't much more he was going to get from Scott anyway. "If you have anything else you want to tell me, you know how to reach me."

"Am I free to go?" Scott said, standing.

"No. I'll bring a phone in so you can call a lawyer. I read you your rights when we picked you up at the diner. You're under arrest. You'll have a preliminary hearing in the morning."

"My father will get me out of this," Scott said, that defiant cocky tone returning.

"We'll see about that," Luke said as he closed the door behind him. He walked a few feet down the hall and saw Tyler sitting at his desk. He had never returned with the soda. Luke walked over and realized he was on the phone. He went to his desk and sat.

Scott could stew in the interrogation room for a few minutes. He leaned back in his chair and stretched his hands overhead. The message icon was lit up on his desk phone so he grabbed the receiver and typed in a few buttons. There was a message from a man who claimed to be on a call with Chance the morning Holly had been killed. He said there was no way that Chance could have done it because they were on a video chat. They had already established that the video chat was at eight and Holly had been murdered well before that. Chance would have had time. Luke scribbled the man's name and phone number and then hung up just as Tyler spun around to face him.

"Captain Meadows is breaking the bad news to Sawyer right now. He's been screaming and hollering and demanding to see his son. I gave him the recording to listen to." Tyler leaned back and grinned at Luke.

"What?"

"We got more news from the crime scene investigators. We took that hammer out of Jason's toolbox and it was a match for Holly's blood. There were small specks on there. The rest had recently been cleaned with bleach, but he must have missed a few spots."

That was an interesting development. "Where did you find his toolbox?"

"In the back of his truck."

"Anyone could have had access to it."

"Sure," Tyler said skeptically. "I thought you'd be happy about this."

"I am," Luke reassured. "I was thinking about what Jason would say. If that toolbox was in the back of his truck, then anyone could have had access to it. Even if he kept it in his office in the trailer, someone else could have had access."

"True, but it's not like we found a random hammer at a worksite. This was Jason's personal property."

Luke wasn't sure why his gut wasn't happier about the discovery.

Did he want the killer to be Chance so badly he wasn't even happy that they identified the murder weapon? "Could the hammer have been switched with another? Don't most hammers look alike?"

Tyler narrowed his eyes. "What's with you? You're the one who wanted us to bring in all the hammers we could find for testing. It sounds like you're defending Jason."

Luke shook his head even though he did feel like he was defending Jason. "I'm glad we have it. I don't know what I'm talking about. It doesn't feel like the win I thought it would."

"So you want to bring Jason back from the jail and interview him again?"

Luke suddenly didn't want to be there anymore. He wanted to get the perspective of the one person they hadn't interviewed yet. For some reason, it felt important for him to do that right now.

As he gathered his things to leave, Luke said, "You can bring Jason in. I got someplace I need to be."

"I don't understand, Luke," Tyler said with confusion in his voice. "You got Scott in interrogation on ice. Sawyer is in with Captain Meadows and now you want me to interrogate Jason and you're taking off. What gives?"

Luke thumbed over his shoulder. "Scott asked for an attorney. I'm going to pop in and talk to Captain Meadows before I go. You might do better with Jason than I did earlier. You've got this, buddy." Luke slapped him on his back before walking across the room to Captain Meadows' office.

He knocked once and waited for his boss to tell him to come in. Luke smiled down at both him and Det. Sawyer. He stepped into the office and closed the door. "Scott asked for an attorney. Sawyer, listen, that kid of yours is in serious trouble."

By the look on the man's face, Sawyer already knew. He didn't say a word, but Luke wasn't done yet. He gave a fast overview of all the evidence against Scott and then explained to Captain Meadows he had something to take care of and was leaving.

As Luke went to the door, Det. Sawyer finally spoke up. "I can't believe you set up my son. This isn't over, Luke."

Luke turned back around and smiled, the widest smile he could force. "I didn't set up your kid. You set him up to fail when you continuously encouraged his poor behavior and overlooked how he bullied his peers. You set him up when you never provided him a consequence for his actions and showed him that you were willing to bend the rules to get him out of trouble. He's sitting in there right now convinced that you're going to protect him from this. If you do, Sawyer, he'll never learn and he'll be one more idiot in and out of prison for the rest of his life. If anyone set up your son, it's you. The question now is if you'll continue to set him up for failure or let him finally learn the lessons that he should have learned a long time ago." With that, Luke closed the door and left.

CHAPTER 42

It was close to eight when Cooper's cellphone rang on the coffee table. Adele had already gone to bed because she had an early hearing in court and Cooper stayed up to watch the end of a television show he had been regularly missing. Even now, he was so tired that he wasn't watching it. He had been staring off into space convincing himself to get up from the couch and go to bed. The cellphone jolted him to the present.

Cooper picked up his phone and saw a number he didn't recognize. He didn't want to answer but he did anyway. Before he could even say hello, a young man on the other end said six words that stunned him into silence and made him sit up straight on the couch.

"Did you hear me?" the man asked again. "I know who killed Holly Bell. I heard you were working on the investigation and thought you might want to know."

"Of course. Thank you for calling. Who am I speaking to?" Cooper sat on the edge of the couch.

"I saw someone go into Holly Bell's shop the morning she was killed. It was early, around six-forty-five." The man paused, shuffled what sounded like papers, and then cleared his throat. "I live right across the street. My backyard is right up against Kavanaugh. I got up and happened to look out a back window and I saw her standing outside of Holly's shop. She glanced around and then went in."

"Do you know who she is?" Cooper asked.

"No. I thought it was odd because it was a Sunday morning, but there were a couple of cars parked on the road in front of the shop and the shop's lights were on so I figured they were working. I don't know why I stood there but I did and not even ten minutes later, this young woman came running out of the shop. I mean running. She dashed to her car and then took off. I didn't know what to make of it. My wife told me to mind my own business."

Cooper could understand that. The man didn't know what he was looking at that early in the morning. "Can you tell me what she looked like?"

"I was at a weird vantage point," the man admitted. "But she had short dark hair, probably average height. She kind of looked like she had an athletic build like she played sports. I'd say she was no more than twenty." Cooper started to speak but the man interrupted him.

"Listen, the reason I'm calling so late is I saw her a few minutes ago. She's at Prospect Bar & Grill on Kavanaugh. If you want to speak to her, you should probably go there now. Otherwise, I don't know how you are going to find her again."

Cooper asked him a few more questions and then asked the man his name. He hesitated but then Cooper explained that if it came down to it, a prosecutor might need him to testify that he saw her coming out of the shop. He might be the only witness who could place her there.

"Robert Preston," the man said. "Try to keep me out of this if you can. My wife doesn't know I'm calling and I can't listen to her tell me I should have minded my own business."

"If this woman turns out to be the killer, Robert, you'll be the hero. I think your wife will be able to forgive you," Cooper assured him before hanging up.

Cooper held the phone in his hand and debated calling Luke, but it was late and he wasn't sure the woman would even be there. He didn't want to send Luke on a wild goose chase without knowing more. He pushed himself off the couch and went to the bedroom and pulled jeans from the back of the chair and grabbed a clean shirt from the closet. He left the room and closed the door behind him, hoping not to wake Adele who was sleeping soundly.

Cooper went to the kitchen and wrote a note on a decorative chalkboard that hung on the kitchen wall near the fridge. He and Adele had such hectic schedules that they'd leave sweet messages there for one another. Sometimes it ended up being where the grocery list was kept, too.

Cooper grabbed his keys and his wallet and headed out the door. It took him less than fifteen minutes to drive to the Heights from the downtown loft and enter the bar. There was more of a crowd than Cooper would have thought for a weeknight. He scanned the crowd of people until he spotted a woman who fit Robert's description. The young woman stood with a group of people who all looked college-aged. She had a beer in her hand.

Cooper made his way to the bar and asked for a Coke and then asked the bartender if he knew the woman in question.

"I think she's got a boyfriend," the bartender said, giving Cooper a "nice try, bro" glance.

"Not what I asked," Cooper said, taking a sip of his drink when the bartender returned. He threw a ten down on the bar and told him to keep the change. "She might have some information I need."

The bartender raised his eyebrows and Cooper casually flipped his private investigator badge. "I'm trying to do this as discreetly as possible. I don't even know that she is involved."

"Kendall," he said. Then he yelled to the girl and waved her over to Cooper. When she bounced up to the bar all smiles, he pointed. "This is my friend. He wants to talk to you." He pointed to a section of the dining room that had been closed off.

Cooper shook the guy's hand. He didn't have to go out of the way for him and Cooper appreciated it. He walked with Kendall over to the closed section that had small round tables and chairs set up in front of a massive flatscreen television.

"What's up?" Kendall asked as she sat. She took a sip of her beer and looked at Cooper from across the table. She pursed her lips together and then bit her lip with her teeth. It was a flirtatious move that Cooper wasn't into.

Cooper explained who he was and why he was there. "Did you know Holly Bell?" he asked, not wanting to waste time.

Kendall set her beer down and dropped the flirtatious act. She didn't say a word but looked over to her friends. Cooper didn't want to play games.

"Kendall, listen closely to me. We've had a witness come forward and say he saw you going into Holly's shop the morning that she was murdered. He also said you came running out a few minutes later. You had more than enough time to kill her." He watched as fear came over her face. "If there is a reasonable explanation for why you were there, tell me. This will go a lot easier if you tell me what happened."

Cooper knew he was taking a risk putting his cards on the table like that. He didn't know if she'd get up and leave him sitting there with nothing. Kendall appeared scared, but he could tell she was hedging. He gently pressed her one more time for information.

"I didn't kill Holly," she said finally relenting. "I went to her shop to confront her, but she was already dead."

Cooper leaned into the table to make sure he had heard her right. "What do you mean she was already dead?"

"Dead as in not living," Kendall said with force. She had a callous and detached tone that surprised Cooper. "There was blood everywhere. I didn't see her when I first walked into the shop. I called her name and thought I heard someone so I walked through the maze of clothing racks calling for her. No one answered me. I walked to the back of the shop and that's when I saw her on the floor. I didn't get close enough to see what happened to her. There was too much blood. I got the heck out of there."

"How did you know she was dead? She could have still been alive at that point," Cooper admonished her. "Did you call for help?"

Kendall shook her head. "No. It's not my problem. I didn't want to get involved."

Cooper felt his anger rising. He didn't know how someone could be so cold and unfeeling. "Why were you there that early in the morning?"

Kendall sat back and folded her hands on the table. "I had stuff to say to her."

Cooper was starting to wonder who Holly hadn't angered. It sounded like every woman in Little Rock had some beef with her. "About what?"

"She got my boyfriend caught up in a lot of stuff he shouldn't have been involved in."

Cooper ran through a few names but Kendall shook her head to each one. He looked at her with skepticism on his face. "Is your boyfriend still in high school?"

"I'm a freshman in college. I don't see how that would be a big deal."

Cooper pointed to her beer. "I don't care that you're dating someone a year younger than you, but the bar might care that you're in here drinking. They could lose their license for that." Her eyes darted to her beer and she looked on the verge of saying something but didn't. Instead, she took a defiant sip.

Cooper sighed and ignored it otherwise. "You go into Holly's shop to confront her about your boyfriend. Why'd you choose a Sunday morning?"

"I heard that Holly went into the shop early on Sundays and figured she'd be alone."

Cooper nodded. "You get there and hear someone and then see that Holly is dead. You take off and don't tell anyone. Is that accurate?"

"That sums it up. Can I go?" Kendall pushed her chair back and then caught the look on Cooper's face. He was visibly disappointed that she was being so difficult. "There was someone in that shop other than me. I'm sure of it. That's why I took off. I was scared, okay?"

"I would have been afraid, too," Cooper admitted. "Is that why you didn't call the cops?"

Kendall looked away but nodded. "Holly was dead, and I didn't want to give the killer a reason to come after me. I figured if I kept my mouth shut no one would know anything. I'd be safer that way. I didn't even tell my boyfriend that I had gone there."

"When you said he got caught up with Holly. What does that mean?"

"You saw the news tonight. He's been arrested for burglarizing those stores."

"Scott Sawyer or Jimmy Ragone?"

She looked pained to admit it but she did. "I've been seeing Scott for the last two years. We've been on and off since I left for college though."

Cooper asked a few questions about her relationship with Scott, but she didn't provide any more information than they already knew. The longer they spoke, the more Kendall seemed tired of talking. He didn't want to push too hard. "You didn't see who else was in the shop. What did you hear that made you think someone else was there?"

Kendall thought for a moment. "Before I went into the shop, I paused at the door, trying to get my courage up to confront her. I thought I heard a woman talking. I figured Holly was on the phone, but when I went in, there was no one there. When I got into the shop, it was more a feeling that someone else was in there. Have you ever felt like someone was behind you but you couldn't see them? Like you're being watched?" Cooper confirmed he knew what she meant.

"That's what it felt like. That's when I realized Holly hadn't been on the phone – she was already dead."

CHAPTER 43

Luke strummed his fingers on his desk. He was waiting for a call back from the prison permitting him to interview Davis Smith. He had gotten to his SUV only to realize he should call the prison. He did only to be told the interview would have to wait.

Instead, Luke drove to Chance's house to confront the man about what Scott had told him.

He hoped to have caught Chance in the act of something incriminating. There was no one at Chance's place. His truck wasn't in the driveway and the house was closed up tight. Luke waited for more than an hour and even got out of his SUV and walked around the property. The search warrant they had was still good.

The only part of the property that had been accessible was the barn, and Luke gave it another thorough search. The only thing that caught Luke's eye was a shovel that had fresh dirt on it. It was a farm though so that wasn't all that suspicious. He closed the barn door and left for the night.

Cooper had left him a message earlier that morning letting him know he'd be by his office to give him an update on a witness who had come forward with pertinent information. Luke told him to come by around ten.

"Luke!" Captain Meadows called from his office door. "Meet Tyler and me in the conference room. We need to wrap up the Holly Bell case."

Luke sent off a quick text to Cooper letting him know where he would be. As he hit send and stood from his desk, he saw the top of Cooper's head as he ascended the stairs. Luke called out to him. "I was texting you to tell you Captain Meadows wants me in the conference room."

Cooper followed Luke down the hall and they joined Tyler and Captain Meadows. "Cooper called and said he has some relevant information to the case. We were meeting at ten," Luke explained Cooper's presence in the meeting. He assumed they wouldn't mind.

"Pull up a chair." Captain Meadows slid a file folder across the table to Luke. "Case closed on the Kavanaugh shop burglaries. Jimmy gave us everything we needed. We have Scott dead in the water and we brought in the two other guys and they were eager to point the finger at Scott."

"What about Sawyer?" Luke asked, skimming through the statements that were in the folder.

"I gave Sawyer some paid time off," Captain Meadows said with a tone that indicated no one better argue with him. "I have no evidence that he knew Scott was involved. He made a rush to judgment in a case, which I think I can safely say we have all been guilty of from time to time. He told me he'd convince Scott to plea it out. Jimmy has immunity for his testimony." He pointed to Tyler to carry it forward.

Tyler flipped open a case file in front of him. "I spoke to Jason Manning yesterday afternoon and no dice. He won't confess to killing Holly. We have the murder weapon tied to him, but as you said yesterday, Luke, anyone could have taken it from his toolbox and returned it. There were too many prints on there to decipher much of anything. Jason's are on there as we expected and a few of the guys who worked directly with him."

Luke interrupted, "We also can't rule out that someone took it, used it to kill Holly, and then wiped it clean knowing Jason and others would handle it later."

"Correct," Captain Meadows said with disappointment in his voice. "It's not the solid evidence we need in this case. I spoke to the prosecutor's office and he said he'd need more to charge Jason with murder given he's got an alibi. What's the motive?"

"The money," Tyler said.

Captain Meadows shook his head. "No one seems to know where that is. Crime scene investigators searched Jason's worksites and his office, vehicles, and home and turned up nothing. MaryBeth was not pleased with the home search especially because she is his alibi and assured us he was at home. She was open with the crime scene techs though and didn't put up a fight. She answered their questions, too."

Tyler added, "Jason will be transferred out and charged in each of the jurisdictions for the bank robberies and charged for his role with the burglaries and planting bugs, but that's all we have him on right now. Without a direct eyewitness or evidence, we aren't going to get him for murder."

Luke turned to Cooper. "What's your evidence?"

"If the witness I spoke to last night is accurate, I don't think it was Jason. I think we are looking at a woman for Holly's murder." Cooper detailed the call he received and the eyewitness in the Heights who led him to Kendall.

"The kid has a thing for older women." Cooper went on to explain what Kendall told him. When Cooper finished, he angled his head to look at Luke. "I believe her story. I can't imagine that in less than ten minutes she could have confronted and killed Holly. The witness didn't see any hammer in her hands. Didn't see any blood on her clothes when she left. He said it was less than ten minutes. Unless we are assuming this young college girl went to confront an older woman about her boyfriend and immediately flew into a homicidal rage, she's not the killer."

"How would she have gotten access to Jason's hammer?" Tyler asked what Luke had been thinking.

"She wouldn't have." Luke didn't think Kendall was the killer. He wished she had come forward sooner though. "She didn't see anyone in the shop?"

"As I said, Kendall thought she heard a woman talking before she went in. She initially thought it was Holly speaking on the phone but didn't see anyone there. When Kendall went in, she didn't see or hear anyone again. She told me she felt like there was someone else there, watching her. You've been in the shop. There's not anywhere to hide except behind the counter where the register is. Kendall said she didn't look behind the counter, she went straight through the shop to the back. That's when she saw Holly on the floor and got out of there. Someone else could have been behind that counter."

They discussed the viability of Kendall as a suspect but there was no link between her and Jason other than Scott. Given the other factors, not one of them thought Kendall was the killer.

Captain Meadows pointed to Luke "Any other women as viable suspects?"

"MaryBeth is the only one who comes to mind with motive and access to Jason's toolbox. But she is Jason's alibi and he is hers. They'd both have to be lying."

"What do you think, Tyler? You're the one who interviewed him. Is he lying to protect his wife?"

"I don't know," Tyler said with enough uncertainty that Luke felt vindicated for believing the man was innocent. "There's no love lost between them. If Jason wanted to steal the money to get a divorce and if MaryBeth used his hammer to set him up, he'd have every reason to implicate her and be rid of her for good."

Luke agreed. Jason had no reason to protect her. "There's one main sticking point for me about Jason and MaryBeth. In the video of the bank robberies, Jason was visibly shaking. He kept turning to Davis Smith for direction. He didn't even break into the shops. They sent kids in first. He has no criminal record. We broke him easily in that first interview. I have trouble believing he pulled off this murder, and he has every reason to implicate MaryBeth if it was her."

Captain Meadows, Tyler, and Cooper considered it and agreed that it might be a stretch.

Tyler asked, "What's the plan?"

Luke considered his options. After a moment, he knew what he needed to do. "I'm going to follow the money. It's time we interviewed Davis Smith in prison. I tried last night and I'll try again today. We know he didn't kill Holly because he was locked up, but it doesn't mean he didn't have a hand in it or know something."

They agreed that was the next logical step.

Nearly two hours later, Luke sat at a metal table in a prison interrogation space frequented by cops and inmates. The stark cinderblock walls complemented the drab of the prison. Davis Smith was brought in and sat down roughly in the chair. The guard asked Luke if he wanted the prisoner shackled to the table and Luke waved him off.

When they were alone, Luke asked, "Do you know why I'm here?"

Davis shrugged his muscled shoulders. "I assume you're here about the bank robberies. I got notice that we've been found out."

Luke watched him carefully. "You're not denying it?"

"No point. I knew this day would come. Who turned me in – Jason or Holly?"

Luke didn't respond. It was clear he had no idea Holly was dead or that Jason had been arrested.

"How'd you know to move the money?"

Davis sat back and a smile spread across his face. "I knew it was only a matter of time before one of them double-crossed me. I figured I'd move the money, send them on a wild goose chase, and then enjoy my spoils when my time was up. How'd you connect me?"

Luke told him that Holly had been murdered and Jason had been arrested. The man didn't hide his shock. Luke asked, "Do you have any idea who killed Holly?"

"I'm surprised Holly ended up dead. I figured she'd have bumped him off." He shook his head. "I have no idea who killed her. This is the first I'm hearing she's dead."

Luke asked a few follow-up questions, but Davis didn't know anything. He didn't get much news inside the prison and wasn't in touch with anyone on the outside or so he claimed. He wouldn't talk about the bank robberies in any detail, but Luke got the sense that what Jason had told him had been the truth – Holly had been the ringleader. It was her plan from the get-go.

Before he left, Luke only had one question. "Where's the money? Holly and Jason went to a lot of trouble searching all the shops on Kavanaugh where you said you hid it. They never found it. I don't understand how you were able to take it from them."

"Holly had been stashing the money in her shop. When I got word they were going to get me sent back inside, I made my move. Then I threw them a few false clues where it could be found."

"So, the money isn't in one of the shops on Kavanaugh?"

"Do I look that stupid?"

"You had Holly fooled."

Davis chuckled and gave Luke a knowing look. "Never try to con a con. Holly's biggest problem was that she was arrogant. She thought no one could get one over on her. Because of that, she was blind to her shortcomings."

That didn't surprise Luke. That's usually what tripped up people like Holly. Luke leaned on the table and locked his gaze on Davis. "Well, where's the money?"

Davis laughed a loud cackle that lasted far too long. "I'm not giving up my bargaining chip. If you came here to get that from me, you might as well send me back to my cell. I have it safeguarded. That's all you need to know."

Luke didn't even bother trying again. He got up from the table, knocked once on the door, and yelled for the guard.

"Detective," Davis called to Luke's back. "Holly had a lot of people around her that she shouldn't have trusted."

Luke started to ask a question but Davis cut him off, saying he had nothing else to add. The guard came and opened the door for him. Before turning to leave, Luke took one last look at Davis who sat at the table pleased with himself.

Holly had sought the help of a criminal and in the end was murdered and had the money stolen. It seemed a fitting end, even though he hated that he had no empathy for her. From screwing around on her husband to dating a high school student and robbing banks, Holly made the choices that ultimately ended her life.

Luke didn't like not solving a case though. He made his way through the prison and at the desk before exiting, he asked to speak to someone who could show him the visitor's log. Luke wanted to know who had visited Davis in prison recently.

It was a hunch that paid off.

Minutes later when he stood in the warden's office staring down at the log, which went back more than a year, Luke couldn't believe what he was seeing – two names that were all too familiar to him. One came as no surprise. It was the other that explained what he had been missing.

Luke counted twenty-two visits in all including the afternoon before and the day after Holly's murder. Holly's death suddenly started making a lot more sense.

Hours later, Luke's tires kicked up dust as he sped toward Chance's farm. He gunned it and flew down the road faster than he should have been going. He took the hard left into the driveway and squealed the brakes in enough time to miss hitting the front of Chance's truck. Luke had his gun unholstered and in his hand in seconds flat. The driver's side door to the truck was open but Chance was nowhere in sight.

Luke got out and took a few steps and finally spotted Chance sauntering out of the barn with suitcases in each hand. Luke planted his feet wide in the dirt and aimed his gun. "Drop the bags, Chance, and put your hands up."

Chance stopped cold in his tracks and wavered for only a moment before doing what Luke asked. He raised his hands and snickered. "What's going on now, Det. Morgan?"

"Go sit over there on the ground, Chance, and don't move."

When Chance plopped on the ground in the dirt, Luke advanced. He yanked a suitcase away from the man and opened it. There staring back at him was exactly what Luke assumed he'd find.

CHAPTER 44

Emma and I decided to try a different shop for coffee and treats. She wanted to check out Hattie's shop and I agreed. We sat at a table at the far wall and chatted about her kids, my work, Luke, and a range of topics. We refilled our tea twice while we sat there and finished off all the treats Emma had purchased.

Hattie came and went. She waved when she saw me and then disappeared behind a red velvet curtain with a young woman who looked on the verge of tears. The young woman emerged about an hour later all smiles. Hattie then went back behind the curtain with yet another distraught-looking woman.

A few minutes later, a tap on my shoulder drew me out of my conversation with Emma.

"You are the last person I ever expected to see in here," Harper said with a smile.

"Right?" I giggled and then introduced Emma to Harper. "Emma wanted to check it out. Pull up a chair and join us."

Harper grabbed a chair from another table and sat down. "I've been coming to this shop since I was a little girl visiting from New York." Harper told us about her summers visiting Hattie and how much she'd enjoyed Little Rock since she moved. "There's a lot more to Little Rock than meets the eye. I figured it would be a quiet sleepy town."

"So did I but trouble seems to follow me."

"Me too!" Harper described some of the mysterious happenings she'd encountered since she moved to Little Rock. It sounded like we lived similar lives only she wasn't inviting trouble by being a private investigator. She had the skills if she wanted to give it a go.

"Cooper might be hiring," I teased.

"I have my hands full with Dan, who is more than I can handle most days." She laughed. Harper got up and got herself some tea and then joined us a few minutes later. "I saw on the news that the burglaries were solved. It's hard to think high school kids were responsible."

"They were taken advantage of by Jason Manning and Holly Bell, but they were arrogant and thought they'd never get caught. It's probably a good lesson for them to learn early on."

Emma popped a brownie bit into her mouth. "Is Luke any closer to solving the murder?"

"Not that he's told me. I've been trying not to step on his toes. I couldn't venture a guess on this one. It seems obvious but then there's a lack of any real evidence except the evidence pointing to Jason Manning and he has an alibi and insists he didn't do it."

"That does make it difficult," Emma and Harper said at the same time and then laughed.

I mentioned to Harper about the witness who spoke to Cooper. I described Kendall, but Harper didn't think that matched the description of the person she saw.

We sat there talking for close to a half-hour longer, and right before we were about to get up from the table, Harper grabbed my arm. "That's her," she said, shifting her eyes to a table in the back of the shop.

"Her who?" I leaned to the side to look around Emma. It was Courtney sitting at a back table reading a book. She didn't have her kids with her. Her hair was down and flowing and she had enough makeup on for a night on the town. As I studied her, I realized she wasn't reading. She was pretending to read while her eyes darted around the shop.

My voice lowered, I asked, "Is that who you saw leaving Holly's shop that morning?"

"I'm sure of it," Harper said, turning to look at Courtney and then back at me. "She had her hair the same way as she does right now, except then she had a big coat over her so she looked heavier."

As I watched Courtney trying to decide what to do, she caught my eye. I smiled and waved casually but she spotted Harper and her expression shifted to something more menacing.

I kept a smile on my face and talked to Harper like we were chatting about the weather while I reached for my phone. I called Luke but it went right to voicemail. I tried Cooper too but it also went to voicemail. I didn't know what Courtney was up to, but the feeling spreading in my gut wasn't good. I had to get Emma out of harm's way. Her husband would kill me if I allowed her to be mixed up in one of our cases again.

I leaned forward on the table and gestured for Emma to lean in. "I want you to go home now. Don't ask me any questions. Just get up, say a friendly goodbye like you need to run home to the kids, and get out of here."

Emma's eyes got big as she caught the seriousness of my tone. She nodded once and said goodbye to Harper. As Emma pushed back her chair to stand, Courtney shoved her table forward, making a dragging sound on the tile. She leaped up with a gun in her hand and pointed it in our direction.

"Everyone shut up!" she yelled, drawing everyone's attention to her. The shop quieted quickly and all eyes turned to her. A few women gasped and Emma slowly sat back down, a panicked expression on her face. It was exactly what I was trying to avoid.

I kept my hands up and stood. "Courtney, what are you doing?" I

301

asked more calmly than I felt inside.

"I want that money and I want it now!" She waved the gun around in a haphazard way that made it seem like she didn't handle weapons often. "Davis Smith promised me that money, and I want it."

"I don't know where it is." I looked around at the people in the shop. "No one here knows where it is either, Courtney. Let them go."

"Not until I get my money!"

I moved to the middle of the room. Courtney aimed the gun right at me. "We can figure this out together, but you have to let all these people go. I can't help you if you're scaring everyone."

Courtney didn't move. My mind raced at what she was doing. *How did she know Davis Smith?*

"Do you think the money is here in Hattie's shop? Holly already searched here."

"I know it's here!" Courtney started to shake and tears of frustration formed in her eyes. "Holly had everything and she wanted more and more. She doesn't deserve that money. I do!"

I moved closer to her and gestured behind my back for Harper and Emma to move people toward the door. Out of the corner of my eye, I caught movement near the red velvet curtain. Hattie peered out. I looked at her with an expression I hoped she caught, and she retreated.

"We can figure it out," I reassured Courtney. "Put the gun down and we can talk about this reasonably."

"No! I'm tired of getting jerked around. It's been months and I'm being jerked around by everyone like I'm some idiot!" She screamed at the top of her lungs, "I want that money!"

"Who told you the money was here?" I asked, remaining calm in the face of her explosion.

"Davis," she screeched. "That was the plan. If I watched Holly for him, he'd give me the money. I did my part! I told him Holly would double-cross him. I told him he had to hide the money better. Once he got sent back to prison, I was going to take it from his hiding spot and get out of town with it until he was released." Courtney wiped a tear from her cheek with the back of her hand. "It wasn't where he said it would be! I assumed Holly already found it so I went to get it back."

"Did Holly say she found it?"

"No, and she called me an idiot and stupid and told me that I shouldn't have gotten involved. She said that I couldn't trust Davis because he screwed us all over. I didn't believe her. Holly always lied!" Courtney began to cry in earnest now. I worried she might accidentally shoot me. Her hand wasn't steady on the gun.

"What about your family?"

"I don't care about them! I hate my husband and my stupid snot-nosed kids."

Courtney seemed even angrier while talking about her family so I changed gears. "How did you know Davis Smith?"

"He was my high school boyfriend!" Her face grew red, and she started ranting. It was hard to even understand her. "He wasn't good enough for my daddy. He broke us up and found me the most boring man on the planet. I'm supposed to be a good little housewife. Pop out a few kids, bake a few pies. It's not enough for me!"

She screamed, "I want that money!"

As Courtney huffed and calmed herself, she saw Emma and Harper moving the others toward the door. She pointed the gun at them. "Get back here!" She fired off a shot toward the ceiling.

I knew if I tried that I could overpower her, but she was so wild with the gun, I was afraid someone would get shot in the process.

"Let them go and I'll help you find the money."

"I will too," Harper said. "Let's all calm down and we can search, Courtney."

Defiantly Harper turned and shoved the shop door open and

everyone cleared out of the shop before Courtney could respond. She seemed thrown off that people would defy her. It was clear though she wasn't going to shoot them.

My stress lowered a notch as I watched Emma leave the building. Harper closed the door and turned back to Courtney. It was the three of us in the room now.

Harper took a couple of steps toward her. "Where is the money supposed to be hidden?"

"Here in this shop. It was this big joke with Davis. He said he'd see how psychic y'all were. He bet you wouldn't find the money."

Harper laughed. "Well, he was right. We didn't find the money."

"I don't understand, Courtney," I said. "How did you get involved? Maybe if I know more, I can figure out where it's hidden." I needed to keep her talking.

Courtney didn't lower the gun, but she did explain herself. "Holly told me about her stupid bank robbery plan and how she was going to run away with Jason. She knew Davis through me and wanted his help. I told her not to involve him. He was finally out of prison and we were going to make a life together. I had already asked my husband for a divorce."

Courtney closed her eyes. "Holly wouldn't listen to me. She took what she wanted. She never cared who she hurt. I begged Davis not to get involved."

I could tell how much this was hurting her.

Courtney took a breath and then continued. "He said he'd help Holly but told me he was doing it for us. He was going to use Holly and Jason and then hide the money from them but before he knew it Holly called his parole officer. I told him she'd do that."

"What happened then?"

"Holly didn't know that Davis and I were still involved. She confided in me that she was going to get him busted on a parole violation. I told him right away. Davis told me he hid the money here in a place no one would ever find it. He told Holly and Jason it was in one of the shops and he found it funny that they'd drive themselves crazy trying to find it."

"I don't think they ever found it. Did you search here for it?"

"No. There are always people here! I figured Holly had found it already. She swore she never found it, but I figured she was lying like usual." Given the tone in her voice, I knew there was more.

"What happened when you confronted her?"

"Holly told me I was stupid to trust Davis and started calling me names. I snapped. I killed her."

I knew that wasn't true. She didn't snap. It had to be planned because she killed her with Jason's hammer. "Holly was killed with Jason's hammer. You planned to kill Holly."

Courtney let go a string of curses. "You think you're so smart just like Holly. I could kill you right now."

She could but I didn't think she would. "Why set up Jason? Why blame it on MaryBeth?"

"Why do you think, dummy?" Courtney asked, rolling her eyes at me. "With Jason in prison and Holly dead – the money would be mine. I figured someone might have seen a woman at Holly's shop that morning and MaryBeth was an obvious suspect. Plus, with MaryBeth out of the way, too, I'd be set."

"You went to his job site and took his hammer and then returned it after you killed Holly."

"Where is the money?" Courtney advanced, and Harper and I took a step back.

"Yoo-hoo, sweetie," Hattie sing-songed from the velvet curtain.

I had hoped she'd leave the back way and call the cops. I had no idea what she was doing.

She gestured for Courtney to follow her. "I found the money in the freezer earlier this morning. There's a spot way in the back. There's a note for you. Davis knew you'd find it. Come on, follow me."

Courtney hesitated. Harper took a step toward her aunt and I followed right behind, playing along. Courtney didn't have a choice if she wanted the money.

As we followed Hattie through the curtain and down a long narrow hallway, Hattie explained, "It was the darndest thing. I was in there moving things around and there it was stashed in the back. I hope you'll take it and go. We can forget you were ever here."

I wasn't sure that Courtney was even registering what Hattie was saying. She seemed so focused on getting her hands on the money. We walked to the back of the shop and Hattie pulled open the big freezer door.

"Sweetie, look there at the bottom in the back. See the cash on the floor. It's all in a big pile."

Sure enough, there were a few twenties and a one-hundred-dollar bill tossed on the floor in the back of the freezer.

Courtney hesitated at the threshold seeming unsure if she could trust Hattie.

Hattie urged her. "Do you want the money or not? I can't go in there again. My arthritis is acting up from being in there this morning."

Courtney turned the gun on us. "Don't move from this spot or I will kill you."

We assured her we wouldn't move. She turned back and had her eyes fixed on the spot on the floor, but she didn't move.

"Come on, sweetie. Get in there. I don't want my food to go bad."

Courtney took a tentative step inside the freezer and then a few more steps. Hattie turned to me and winked. She slammed the freezer door shut, pulled the bar down tight, and clapped her hands like she was brushing off the dust.

"Looks like our criminal is on ice." She giggled. "She can sit there till the cops come."

Courtney pounded on the inside of the metal door to be freed and threatened to kill us all. She had no way out though. I couldn't believe Hattie had pulled it off so flawlessly. For a moment, she even had me questioning if she had found the money.

Hattie shooed us back down the hall. "I already called the cops. Let's go get a snack and give her some time to cool off."

Hattie had rendered me speechless. We had solved a murder and captured the killer all without additional bloodshed. This time when Luke arrived instead of being a hostage, I'd be snacking on a brownie. He definitely couldn't complain. Hattie was absolutely the aunt everyone needed.

Epilogue

A few evenings later, Cooper, Adele, Luke and I sat around our dining room table finishing dinner. This was the first time since Luke and I were back from our honeymoon that we all had a chance to get together.

We only had one rule for the night – no work talk through dinner. We forced ourselves to find topics other than murder and crime to discuss. It was more of a challenge than we realized. We managed to make it until the last bite before finally giving in to discuss the Holly Bell murder case. I checked my watch – we had lasted nearly ninety minutes without discussing crime.

I had been surprised when it wasn't Luke who showed up at Hattie's shop to arrest Courtney. Det. Tyler and two other detectives had come to our rescue. For a few hours, no one could reach Luke. Hattie, Harper, and I had gone to the police station to give our statements as to what Courtney had admitted to us. It turned out that while Harper and I were trying to get Courtney to talk, Hattie had been hatching a plan.

Even though she could have escaped out the back door of the shop, which is where she had sent her client, Hattie stayed behind and cooked up the freezer idea. She had thrown some cash from her safe on the floor and faked the whole story. I had been impressed with Hattie's acting skills and her willingness to put her life at risk to save ours.

Hattie and Harper had left the police station making me promise I'd stop in to see them sometime soon. I finished my statement and then heard Luke's booming voice from the detective's bullpen. It seemed he had found not only Courtney's name on the visitor's log but Chance's as well.

He made the calculated decision to visit Chance's farm again and found the man packing his car to leave town. Luke had his weapon drawn and instructed Chance to sit on the ground. Then he searched Chance's suitcase and found stacks of cash in that suitcase and several others already in the truck. Chance was making a run for it.

"How'd you know, Luke?" Adele asked, standing to help me clear off the table.

"I know Chance and there's no way he didn't know what was going on with his wife. He's a sociopath and I figured with that much money at stake, he'd be manipulative enough to find it."

Luke reached for his beer and took a sip. "I thought at first he had killed Holly and then framed Jason, but Courtney visiting Davis in prison confused me. Before I left the prison, I asked to speak to Davis again. All I had to do was mention Courtney's name and he knew he'd been figured out."

"Had he made a deal with Chance?"

"No," Luke said. "Davis didn't tell me about Chance because he still hadn't realized he'd been manipulated. Chance visited him in prison and asked enough questions to figure out where Davis had hidden the money – in a hole in the ground behind his rental house. I saw the shovel with fresh dirt in Chance's barn and he's not a man to do any kind of manual labor. It clicked for me all at once."

"Was Davis ever going to run away with Courtney?" I asked, leaning against the kitchen counter.

"No. Davis used Courtney like he used Holly and Jason."

"Do you think Davis asked Courtney to kill Holly?" Adele asked. I had been wondering the same thing.

"Not directly," Luke said evenly. "I believe he led her on with promises of being together and made it seem like he needed Holly out of the way to ensure that happened. Courtney was desperate and jealous of Holly so she did what she probably wanted to do all along." Luke raised his eyes to me and saw the expression on my face. "Don't tell me you feel bad for her?"

"I'm not sure what I feel." I was being honest. It annoyed me that I had any emotion for Courtney. She had premeditated the murder of a woman she claimed was her best friend. Then she carried it off and framed someone else. There was something about her though that tugged at my empathy. She had a husband and children and threw it all away. I explained that but no one else shared my feelings.

"You'd feel differently if you had to tell her husband. He travels for work and was away the weekend of Holly's murder. The kids were with Courtney's mother while she was killing Holly. It was her husband's gun that she had at Hattie's shop." Luke shook his head and sighed. "Those poor kids."

Cooper sipped his beer. "I don't think we've ever had a case with so many people involved."

Luke agreed. "The only way they pulled it off was because no one knew the whole story. I heard the prosecutor is giving the boys probation, which is fair enough. Scott is getting a longer probation sentence and some community service for being the ringleader and framing Izzy. They didn't steal from the stores and were caught up in something much bigger than they could have imagined, so they got off fairly light for their actions. Courtney is looking at a life sentence. Jason is facing at least twenty years. I think MaryBeth knew about the bank robberies, but we have no evidence to prove it. She'll be happily divorced soon. Davis might never see the light of day."

Adele finished drying a dish I had washed. "What about Chance?"

"He's looking at some time, but I'm not sure how much. He didn't

310

kill anyone and he wasn't involved in the bank robberies or the burglaries. All he did was steal from a thief. I knew Chance was guilty of something." Luke laughed.

"I don't even understand how Chance pulled it off," Adele said with disbelief in her voice.

"Chance knew Holly and Jason were being led on a fool's errand. There was no way Davis was going to tell them where it was hidden. Chance went to the prison and congratulated Davis on fooling everyone. He never asked about the money and didn't even seem interested in it. He let Davis think he had won and then they talked about their time inside prison and Chance did what he does best – draw people out and manipulate."

Luke looked pleased with himself as he should be. It was a complicated case, but in the end, it was simple enough – greed and lust took one life and destroyed many others.

Jordan Collins had been right at the start – Holly didn't care who she hurt to get what she wanted. The irony was she spent so much time judging other people, she didn't bother cleaning up her own life. That's usually the way it went with people like Holly. In the end, she paid the ultimate price. I didn't know anyone truly mourning her.

After a break in the conversation, Cooper cleared his throat. "We'd like to ask you both something." He waited until we were all seated around the table and then he reached for Adele's hand.

"Adele and I would like you both to come with us to St. Thomas when we get married. We want you to be our witnesses and share in our day with us. We are going to stay at one of those all-inclusive resorts. It will be a few months from now."

"We are still planning, but we don't want to do this without you both there," Adele added.

"Absolutely," Luke said, smiling at them. "It sounds like the perfect wedding."

I echoed his enthusiasm. I wondered if Adele was okay with forgoing a big wedding, but she seemed perfectly happy with the decision so I was happy for her.

I raised my glass in a toast. "To the perfect beach wedding!"

About the Author

Stacy M. Jones was born and raised in Troy, New York, and currently lives in Little Rock, Arkansas. She is a full-time writer and holds masters' degrees in journalism and in forensic psychology. She currently has three series available for readers: paranormal women's fiction/cozy Harper & Hattie Magical Mystery Series, the hard-boiled PI Riley Sullivan Mystery Series and the FBI Agent Kate Walsh Thriller Series. To access Stacy's Mystery Readers Club with three free novellas, one for each series, visit StacyMJones.com.

You can connect with me on:

- http://www.stacymjones.com
- https://www.facebook.com/StacyMJonesWriter
- https://twitter.com/SMJonesWriter
- https://www.bookbub.com/profile/stacy-m-jones
- https://www.goodreads.com/StacyMJonesWriter

Subscribe to my newsletter:

✉ http://www.stacymjones.com

Also by Stacy M. Jones

READ PI Riley Sullivan Mystery Book #7
Harbor Cove Murders

Access the Free Mystery Readers' Club Starter Library
PI Riley Sullivan Mystery Series novella "The 1922 Club Murder"
FBI Agent Kate Walsh Thriller Series novella "The Curators"
Harper & Hattie Mystery Series novella "Harper's Folly"

Sign up for the starter library along with launch-day pricing, special behind-the-scenes access, and extra content not available anywhere else. Hit subscribe at http://www.stacymjones.com/

Please leave a review for The Night Game. Reviews help more readers find my books. Thank you!

Other books by Stacy M. Jones by series and order to date

FBI Agent Kate Walsh Thriller Series
The Curators
The Founders
Miami Ripper
Mad Jack

PI Riley Sullivan Mystery Series
The 1922 Club Murder
Deadly Sins
The Bone Harvest
Missing Time Murders

We Last Saw Jane
Boston Underground
The Night Game

Harper & Hattie Magical Mystery Series
Harper's Folly
Saints & Sinners Ball
Secrets to Tell
Rule of Three
The Forever Curse
The Witches Code
The Sinister Sisters

Harbor Cove Murders

Five young tourists have gone missing on the island of St. Thomas. The most recent only a few days before PI Riley Sullivan travels there with her husband. Vowing not to get involved, fate had other plans. Faced with obstacles and push-back from local cops, Riley must race to stop a killer. But the clock is ticking…can she stop them in time?